GRACE

First published in Great Britain in 2023 by
Archetype Books.

A CIP record of this book is available from the British
Library.

ISBN 978-1-7395593-0-4

Set in Adobe Garamond, 10/13pt

Archetype Books
Frome, Somerset, UK

archetypebooks.net
info@archetypebooks.net
x: @books_archetype
f: @ArchetypeBooksLtd
I: archetypebooks

For Martha, Laura, Jess, Jack

ONE

Chelsea
Midsummer 1920

WAVES FROM PASSING BARGES are sloshing up against the granite wall. Grace – with her mother's help – has climbed up to watch the military parade: two black horses tossing their heads; soldiers keeping in step with the booming bass drum; sunlight glinting on rows of golden trumpets.

Balancing along the top, she tries to march to the beat. Her mother is holding her hand so it's perfectly safe. She's laughing, looking down at her favourite shoes peeping from under the lace hem of her white dress.

A cloud drifts in front of the sun. There's a sudden coolness in the air.

Her mother sneezes, releasing Grace's hand for a moment to retrieve a handkerchief from her triple-buttoned cuff, the silk as dark as thunderous sky.

A splash on top of the wall and Grace's white shoe slips. In panic she reaches out, but no one catches her as she tilts towards the water.

A screeching seagull takes flight.

Sounds are suddenly muffled. She holds onto a bubble of air inside her chest. Her mother will reach down and pull her out; bring her back into the light and sound.

Her feet stretch for the riverbed but it's not there.

She stares up at the murky light above.

She holds on … holds on …

Her heart beats frantically: *Mo-ther! Mo-ther! Mo-ther!*

A flurry of bubbles heading for the sun.

A giddy, sparkling light bursts in her head.

Five Acre Wood, Epsom
The same day

EPSOM ROAD RUNS east-west and is crossed by Arbuthnot Lane, an old drovers' track. At this crossroads, according to rumour, a huge oak stood with strong horizontal boughs over which a noose was sometimes thrown, used to punish those who had fallen foul of the magistrate. The tree has since been cut down; just a stump remaining, a convenient resting place for weary travellers. Some say the tree's timbers were absorbed into the fabric of the Bell Inn.

The landlady, Mrs Fielding – previously a teacher in South London – grips the edge of the bar. It wasn't meant to happen this way. They'd prepared the bedroom with new candles: Mr Fielding had insisted on the purchase in spite of funds being low. Panting hard, she comes around the bar holding her wet skirts rucked up between her legs, beneath a large belly. She falls to her knees. A customer shouts: *Get Marcus*.

Mr Fielding hears the call, runs in, kneels beside his wife.

Mr Jones, the barman – recently demobbed from the King's Shropshire Light Infantry – ushers everyone out with a commanding wave of his deformed left hand.

The men carry their tankards and gather around the tree stump. For hours they listen to Mrs Fielding's cries, slowly sipping their ales and ciders.

Inside, a baby girl is delivered onto the sawdust floor. Her first cry is met by a raucous cheer from the men outside. New life feels more precious than ever since the war. Mother and baby are helped to the bedroom.

A proud Mr Marcus Fielding offers free drinks, but most shake his hand and pay anyway.

TWO

Croydon
2000

GRACE DIPS THE POWDER PUFF into the dusting box, dabs it under her arms, and stares at the old face in the mottled mirror. 'What shall we have today?' She chooses a lipstick and twists the gold cylinder, smears a line of crimson, presses her lips together.

She wriggles her feet into her lambswool slippers. Today, she'll use the stairlift: it's there so she might as well, and Hariti never uses it in spite of being nearly fifteen years older than Grace. She raises the chair arm, rotates her body, using her bottom to lower the seat. It hums all the way down, wobbling on the bend, then halts obediently for her to step out as if she's genteelly disembarking from a carriage.

The dog watches from the top of the stairs.

'Caesar! *There* you are.'

He humps his sausage body down each step and races ahead on his little legs. She unlocks the back door and laughs as he races, yapping, into the yard.

She waddles back through the hall to the front door, unlocks the Yale, the Chubb and undoes the chain to collect her bottle of milk from the step, the gold foil top – as so often – pecked, probably by her favourite robin.

Caesar races around the house and dives in past her.

'Orlando will be here soon, then we can all go out, that'll be lovely.'

She kneels in front of the gas fire and turns the knob. It always takes three clicks before the gas ignites with a *boff*. All those years ago – during the war – it was her job to make up the fire in the blackened grate, first rolling up newspaper, then laying the chopped-up bits of furniture, then sparkling lumps of coal – when they had it – brought up from the sooty basement.

The gas fire's three bone-white bars slowly turn a glowing red.

What will she start her day with? Purity or passion? She peers at the narrow spines of the LPs, pulls one out: a pastoral scene that she recognises as Constable. She slips the record from its sleeve; an iridescent rainbow shimmers on the black vinyl surface. The new record player – 'hi-fi' or whatever it's called – has too many buttons. How to get the damned turntable to start? It doesn't even have a 78. It was a present from the younger one. She hardly ever sees him. Buying Grace such an expensive present was probably driven by guilt. The boys were always fighting. Ironic that it should be Orlando who's the most loyal to her, as if he's trying to atone. But it wasn't his fault. *She* abandoned *him*.

She presses a button: the whole thing lights up. Her hand shakes as she lifts the needle; a scuffle and a scratch as it finds the groove. What a stroke of genius by Schubert, turning a quartet into a quintet by scoring for two cellos.

Caesar whines.

'Orlando will be wiping up your mess if he doesn't get here soon.'

The dog watches as she picks up one of the statuettes from the mantelpiece – an ivory Shiva with a hard stare – and polishes it with a yellow duster. Hariti hasn't cleaned them for a while, they need to be taken care of. Where is she this morning?

She replaces Shiva. Vishnu is warmer, made from red stone. The small Buddha smiles at her. And the other one? She forgets its name. She polishes the elephant head then slumps back into her armchair.

Where the hell is he? She needs a pee. Such a bother going all the way upstairs.

Caesar watches Grace holding onto the furniture as she makes her way into the kitchen, his ears cocked forward. She locks the back door, reaches under the sink for the big saucepan reserved especially for this task. She'd never cook in it, heaven forbid; she does have standards.

The dog sniffs the pan placed in the middle of the floor. Grace lifts her skirt and balances over it; she doesn't bother with knickers these days, they're just a lot of fuss.

She pees to the strains of Schubert's adagio: poignant upper register; but most sublime are the cellos, pizzicato, a fragile pulse, a certain sadness. She's not surprised this was his final work. She empties the pan into the sink, rinses it, unlocks the back door and goes back to the sitting room. She must get ready, no use sitting around all day.

Epsom
Midsummer 1927

SUSPENDED IN DAZZLING BLUE – high, high above – a dark shape, a thing with feathers, circling slowly.

The girl blinks. Tall grasses bend towards her; a faint breeze carries the sweet, acrid perfume of tar.

A young woman's dark face leans over her, lays her head on the girl's chest; her long black hair smells of coconut. 'Her heart is beating, Mrs Fisher.'

Behind her, a thin woman: glitter on the shoulders of her black dress. 'Oh my good lord.'

A man's voice. 'Sorry ladies, stand back, there'll be a train any minute.' He slips his arms under the girl's knees and shoulders. She's raised up. Cowslips wave to her as she's carried up steps.

The young woman is excited. 'Mrs Fisher, it's Grace.'

The thin woman sharpens her voice. 'Do mind the steps, the gardener has left the wheelbarrow … careful … through here.'

'She's come back!'

'Hariti, go and make tea.'

Through a door. Dark green walls in a narrow hall. Now a brighter room, a white ceiling rose flowering on pale blue.

The girl is lowered; the man's face is near, dark brown eyes. It's like she's known him forever. He straightens, breaking the spell: a fleeting smile. 'Her feet are ripped to shreds, she must have walked miles.'

'It's fortunate that you were passing, Mr …'

His hand stretches out. 'Leyland Cornell.'

'My husband would know what to do, but he's away.'

'I was on the footpath when I saw her.' Mr Cornell looks down at the girl. 'May I ask, what is your name?'

A lump in her throat, her face burning with shame. Everything has a name. Every tree, every bird …

The girl with the long black hair is carrying a silver tray. 'You've come back, Grace. It's seven years to the day. Seven is an auspicious—'

'For goodness sake, Hariti.' Mrs Fisher looks pale. 'You and your ridiculous superstitions. Bring Mr Cornell some cake.'

Mr Cornell holds up a hand. 'I'm sorry, Mrs Fisher, I can't stay for tea. Thank you.'

Hariti opens the front door for him. 'You are Grace's guardian angel now.'

Mrs Fisher clamps her hands together in front of her black dress.

THE GIRL CREEPS DOWN the stairs on freshly bandaged feet.

Mrs Fisher's raised voice behind the closed sitting room door: 'You must stop this talk, Hariti.'

'But it's the summer solstice.'

'She's *not* Grace. A mother would know.'

Footsteps. The door opens. Hariti is scowling. Through the open doorway, the girl can see Mrs Fisher sitting at a polished bureau, head bent to her writing.

Mrs Fisher looks up. 'Hariti, do something with the girl's hair. It's a crow's nest.'

Hariti puts her arm around the girl's shoulders and turns her towards the stairs.

In her bedroom, Hariti chats happily as she takes out clothes interleaved with tissue paper from a chest and holds them up. 'You hated this suit ... scratchy wool ... your favourite dress, you loved the lace around the hem.'

She picks up the ivory-handled hairbrush. 'Come on, let's get the crows out.'

July 1927

FROM HER POSITION sitting halfway up the stairs, the girl watches as Hariti opens the front door. Mr Cornell removes his cap and unbuttons his tweed jacket. Hariti leads him to the sitting room, closes the door behind him. She smiles at the girl. 'I said he'd come back. Your guardian angel!' She strides off down the corridor to the kitchen.

Voices murmur behind the dark, wood-grained door.

She sits in silence. The brass weight in the grandfather clock's tall case hangs still. A rolled umbrella is slotted in the rack of the hall stand; two of the three S-shaped hooks bear coats.

The girl's feet are placed in perfect alignment on the diamond-patterned stair carpet. Brass animal claws glint on the ends on the wooden stair rods. Rainbow colours from the stained-glass fanlight dapple the tiled floor.

The sitting room door opens. Mrs Fisher holds onto the ivory handle. 'My husband never met Grace. I was sent back from India. You understand.'

His voice is soft, familiar. 'No place to have a baby.'

'I expect we'll move back to London when Mr Fisher returns.'

'Then I'd better come again soon.'

'This isn't our house, you see …'

'I'd assumed—'

'It belongs to a dear friend of the family. Mr Smith is in Germany at the moment. Government business.'

'I'd better be going.'

Mrs Fisher offers her hand. 'I'm sure we'll find her parents soon.'

Hardly noticed, Hariti slips past them.

Mr Cornell glances up, positions his cap and smiles at the girl. Hariti opens the front door.

August 1927

IT'S THE FIRST TIME she's been alone with Mrs Fisher and the girl doesn't know what to say. The sun – warm on her back – is casting her shadow over the book in her lap. It's a story about a Swiss family shipwrecked on an island. Her yellow dress is too tight – she's worried the buttons will pop.

Mrs Fisher is snapping off pea pods, laying them in a wicker basket. She rubs her fingers and thumb together. 'The whitefly get absolutely everywhere …'

The girl loves the little white shoes, they fit perfectly, and she swings her legs, tapping her heels against the white iron chair.

'… the only solution is to squish them, but it makes one's fingers so greasy.'

Mrs Fisher is so tall and thin that her apron strings wrap right around her waist and make a bow at the front. She takes a pair of scissors from her apron pocket, snips at some crinkly leaves. 'I must say, the pumpkins are starting to grow well, it would be so lovely to have them for All Souls' Night. Do you know what a Jack-o'-lantern is?'

'Yes, Mrs Fisher.'

A brown hen waddles into the garden, pecks at the earth by the beanpoles.

Mrs Fisher places the basket on the table and looks at the girl's book. 'I do wonder how old you are. You must be at least six, maybe seven, look at you, thin as a rake. You can read well; you are clearly well bred, which makes it even more surprising …' She gathers her long fair hair into a bunch behind her head and ties a green ribbon around it, then lifts a pea pod from the basket and squeezes the tip: pop! 'I received a letter last week …' She slides her fingernail along and scoops

the little green peas out into a brass bowl. 'It was from my husband.'
Pop. Peas tinkle into the bowl. 'He's been slightly injured. It's nothing
to worry about, but it does mean he'll be home to convalesce. Maybe
we won't have to carve out a lantern to guide him.' She hesitates. 'He's
recovering very well. Really, it's not serious.'

Pop. Tinkle.

'The world's going mad.'

The girl is not sure what to say. Mrs Fisher doesn't feel like her
mother – as Hariti insists she is – and the old woman doesn't believe it
either, so that's an end to it. But where *is* her mother? And why is Mrs
Fisher dressing her up in these clothes?

'What with all the strikes … I don't for a minute believe all they say
about roving gangs. Mind you, there are gypsies, I've seen *them*. We'll
be safer when Mr Fisher is back.'

The girl can't keep track of what Mrs Fisher is saying, and peas are
popping out all over the table.

'But don't you worry, we'll be fine. Two things a country always
needs, and that's soldiers and civil servants.'

The peas look amazingly green. The girl plucks up courage and
picks one up, place it on her tongue, then bites: it tastes of sunshine.

'You *really* don't remember where you came from?'

The question is like a slap. The words in her book are blurring
through her tears. She quickly wipes her eyes with the back of her hand.
She turns a page: a boa constrictor is threatening to wrap itself around
one of the Robinson children.

Mrs Fisher is looking down at the bowl. 'I must say, the police
sergeant is flummoxed …'

Pop.

'I know Mr Fisher is sympathetic to native ideas, but this is a step
too far, even for him.'

Pop.

'News of your real family is bound to emerge.'

One of the hens waddles over, scratches the grass, steps back and pecks at the earth.

'When he returns we'll review everything. And we'll move back to London. I couldn't stay there ... before. But now, perhaps.'

She makes a cradle with her apron and gathers the empty pea pods into it. 'It wouldn't be right for you to ever call me Mother, you understand? It'll be confusing when we meet people.'

She looks around the garden, takes a deep breath. 'I can't say I approve of Hariti calling you Grace, but I have to address you somehow.'

The hen jerks its head up.

'You *really* don't remember who you are?'

The girl stares at a perfectly round pea sitting on the table, a slight crease in its skin, a tiny creamy tip.

Mrs Fisher looks up to the blue sky, as if she's trying to see through to heaven. 'So for now I'll agree to call you Grace, but it's best you don't grow too accustomed to it.'

The hen squawks, ambles away.

'Would you like to pick some sweet peas, they are so pretty?'

The girl closes her book. 'Yes please, Mrs Fisher.'

'Grace loved their perfume. They make me feel hopeful.'

… running, running towards the moon … now it's gone … she falls into black … something rustles. She shudders. He's close. Wait, wait. Nothing. She sits up, hugs her knees, holds her breath, shivers …

HARITI'S COOL FINGERTIPS stroke her forehead. 'It's all right.'

She lifts the girl, carries her over to her own bed. 'It was just a bad dream.'

'There were flames everywhere.'

'It's just one of your past lives.' Hariti squeezes her hand. 'It's healing to remember.'

'A man was chasing me.'

'You're safe now.'

Hariti's body glows with warmth. Slowly the nightmare fades. 'Mrs Fisher called me Grace yesterday.'

Hariti laughs. 'I told you. She just needed time.'

'Can *you* be my mother?'

'I shall have to go back to India one day.'

'Then I'm coming with you.'

'You wouldn't like it, it's hot and insects bite you …' she tickles the girl, '… all over.'

'Indian elephants have smaller ears than African ones.'

'How do you know that?'

'I saw it in a picture book.'

'Yes. That was your favourite, Mrs Fisher put it away after—'

'I don't remember.'

'It's in a trunk, I'll see if I can find it.'

'How did she … Mrs Fisher's little girl …?'

'You slipped into the river.'

'I don't—'

'It will all come back when you are ready.'

'Did I know *you*?'

'I loved you very much. Mrs Fisher was always very busy. *Mr* Fisher never actually met you.'

'Does that make him sad?'

'Mrs Fisher and I were sent from India when she was going to have you.'

'Didn't he want to be a father?'

'He has his duty. He's a very honourable man. He saved my life ... but that was a long time ago.'

'Really? How?'

'I was going to be burned.'

A shiver runs down the girl's spine. 'He saved *you* ... from a fire!'

'I'll tell you another time. And Mrs Fisher is always very busy. Before the war she campaigned for women to have rights like men. I looked after you all the time. We played and played. I wish you could remember. It was like you were my own little sister. And now you are back.'

The girl is worried. If she *has* come back, why doesn't anything feel familiar? And where had she been *before* she woke up on the railway line? 'I don't want you to go back to India with the silly elephants.'

Hariti curls around the girl, kisses the back of her neck. 'Sleep now my little *Ranee*.'

The girl wants to keep Hariti talking to stop the nightmare from coming back. 'What's a—'

'A princess.'

THE GIRL HAS NO IDEA why Hariti has woken her so early, it's not even dawn.

A large enamel bowl filled with water sits on a towel in the middle of the kitchen floor. She has to stand in it, shivering.

Hariti dips a little brass bowl into the water, lifts it above the girl's head and pours. 'It's an auspicious day; we have to be cleansed for Rahu.'

From a dark chest, Hariti has picked out a cotton dress with a big square pattern and a pair of canvas summer shoes.

The girl shivers. 'Doesn't Mrs Fisher mind?'

'They were yours, remember? See how perfectly they fit.'

'Mrs Fisher doesn't think—'

'You'll start to remember, don't worry.'

The girl has seen the photographs in silver frames on the mantel-piece; in one, a little girl stands in front of a much younger Hariti; Mrs Fisher's long hair is in a bun. The little girl has a gentle smile and is wearing the same patterned dress. Peering into the photograph is like looking into a mirror. If Hariti is so sure ... the clothes fit ... it must be true. She must be Grace.

*

She can't keep up.

Hariti turns, runs backwards, waving her arms and laughing. 'Hurry, Grace.'

Birds are making a racket in the hedges. The earth on the other side of the graveyard wall is much higher and there are hundreds of crosses, and some of them are falling over. Grace is worried: the wall is leaning outwards and it looks like it will collapse at any minute and all the dead bodies will spill onto the road.

She runs to catch up. 'Where are we going?'

'Hurry, it's coming.' Hariti lifts her onto the stone parapet of the railway bridge.

The rising sun warms Grace's back.

Hariti stands in front of her, dark eyes shining with excitement. 'It's no coincidence … your return at this moment; the gods are sending a message.'

A strange tingling ripples up Grace's back.

'It's starting, can you feel it?'

'Something. I don't like it.'

Hariti takes the girl's hand. 'I'm here. Do you trust me?'

Grace nods.

'What do you feel?'

Strangely, the birds have stopped singing. A slight breeze, and she shivers. This is too big. 'I don't understand—'

'Rahu is going to gobble up the sun.'

Grace's eyes widen and Hariti laughs. 'Everything is as it should be. Life and death in perfect balance.'

'Am I going to die?'

Hariti looks up. 'It's happening.' Her face is turning to ash. 'Look!'

Grace turns around. The sun is still low but nearly half of it has gone. The blue of the sky, the greens of the hedges and trees – all are turning grey.

In the dark, Grace desperately holds on to Hariti's voice; the strange words tumbling out, a prayer. Grace finds a crescent of light in Hariti's eyes.

Hariti whispers. 'And now. We are reborn.'

Relief in the chatter of the birds. Warmth returning to her back.

Hariti pulls Grace into her arms.

A church bell's sombre chime floats across the field.

'You see, Grace? You understand?'

'What just happened?'

A panting sound from far away. Over Hariti's shoulders she can see white smoke puffing above the curve of the hill.

'I cried so many nights, Grace, even though I knew we'd be reunited one day.'

A dark shape appears in the distance, panting towards them.

Grace wraps her legs around Hariti's waist and squeezes her neck. The train growls towards them and thunders under the bridge. Grace screams, buries her face into Hariti's long black hair, tries not to breathe, tears rolling down her cheeks. A familiar bitter taste on her tongue. The engine blasts from the other side, a huge sooty cloud in their faces.

Hariti bounces her up and down. 'My poor little Grace.'

Slowly the air clears. Hariti puts Grace down and they set off along the lane. Brambles reach out, trying to hook on to Grace's dress and her skin beneath.

'Have *you* died before, Hariti?'

'I've been born many times.'

'So you are really *very* old?'

Hariti laughs. 'I'm only twenty, I'll have you know, little miss.'

'Can you have babies?'

'I'd need to find a good husband first!' She offers Grace an apple from her canvas bag. 'Do you remember *anything* from before you drowned?'

'The day you found me. You stroking my hair and the nice man lifting me up.'

'We are bound together for eternity. You, me, Mr Cornell.'

'I've never met him before.'

'But you have. You'll remember in time … it's your fate.'

'Why is Mrs Fisher always snapping at me?'

Hariti crunches into her apple. 'She was very, very sad when you died, but you could make it better now by calling her Mother.'

Upside-down U-shapes in the dry mud. Grace is worried that horses might gallop past any minute and run them down. 'But she's not my mother.'

'You could just pretend. It would make her very happy.'

'But that wouldn't be the truth.'

'It's hard for Mrs Fisher too, you know. It will all be better when we return to London. You will be back in your favourite room in the attic. And Mr Fisher will be back, and we'll all be happy again.'

'Will *you* be my—?'

'No, but I will always look after you.'

'Promise?'

Hariti starts to sing strange words, her voice beautiful and sad. With her fingertips she wipes the tears from Grace's cheek, then she picks her up and spins her around in a bubble of magical sound.

September 1927

THE WHITE FLOWERS of the hedgerow's honeysuckle look to Grace like tiny swans dancing on thin white stalks with dusty yellow ballerina shoes. Mist is steaming off the fields. Hariti and Grace are walking a few paces behind Mrs Fisher, who is holding her black woollen shawl tight around her shoulders, the hem of her black skirt skimming the tall grasses growing in the centre of the track.

Grace is worried. The lane seems to be heading towards a wood. She's not looking where she's going and steps into a shallow puddle.

Mrs Fisher turns. 'For goodness sake, Hariti, don't let her ruin the shoes.'

'I'll clean them when we get home, Mrs Fisher.'

Mrs Fisher turns and walks off, the word 'God' clearly audible.

They stop at a wooden gate. Hariti climbs onto the top bar. 'Come on Grace, you can see right across to the woods.'

Grace holds a post for support and pulls herself up. 'Do you believe in God?'

'There are many gods.'

'I've tried praying but I never get an answer.'

Hariti laughs. 'And I *do* believe in miracles.'

'What's Mr Fisher like?'

'He's the best man in the world. I can't wait for you to meet him.'

'Mrs Fisher says he'll find my real parents.'

Hariti taps her heels against a bar of the gate. 'He understands India.'

'But what will he do. About me?'

'Well …' She rocks slightly. 'If he were here, he'd lean against the gate, bring out his curvy pipe from his jacket pocket, open his tobacco tin and press flakes into the bowl. Then he'd grip the end of the pipe with his teeth, flick his silver lighter and suck the flame down onto the tobacco.'

'But what would he be *thinking*?'

'He'd tell you all about India, how beautiful it is in the Himalayan mountains. He probably wouldn't say anything about how he fought the bad thuggees, and the King giving him a medal.'

'Would he tell me about how he saved you?'

'He'll never talk about that.' Hariti reaches up and pulls at the branch above their heads, breaking off a twig. 'See these little cup shapes, that's where the acorns used to live. You can make little boats out of them and float them in the bath.'

'*Quercus robur.*'

'How do you know that?'

'An alphabet game. Q for *Quercus* – leaves crisp and soft; R for *Rowan* – poisonous berries never to be picked; S for *Salix* – the fluffy tails of squirrels.'

Hariti takes her hand. 'You loved looking at Mr Fisher's books.'

Mrs Fisher emerges from the wood.

'It's just a game.' Grace jumps down, her shoes splash in the mud, her fists are clenched, her voice tight. 'You don't know. You don't know *anything.*'

'But you learned all the Latin names of our native trees.'

October 1927

GRACE HOVERS on the landing. Mrs Fisher is in the hall below speaking on the telephone to her friend Mr Smith; she's asking if he's coming in his wonderful Austin. She replaces the receiver and calls to the kitchen. 'Hariti. Come quickly. We have a lot to organise.'

*

The soup is thin, brown, with tiny speckles of red in it. Mrs Fisher is chatting about India. Grace hasn't yet picked up her spoon. Her hands are clasped together in her lap. If she moves she'll cry.

Hariti glances across the table, looking worried.

A spot of soup on Mrs Fisher's chin; she dabs it with her napkin. 'Grace, you need to buck your ideas up. London will be good for you. A young girl shouldn't be stuck in the back of beyond.'

PILED UP IN THE HALL: two leather suitcases, a travelling trunk with labels pasted on its sides, a hat box, an umbrella, a tin trunk with much of its red paint scuffed and scratched, and two tea chests.

Mrs Fisher has spent days fussing over clothes, pinning and padding and layering with tissue paper to protect things, especially clothes that would fit a six-year old girl which are now all neatly compressed into a leather suitcase with straps. Grace had watched as Mrs Fisher – kneeling by the case – had carefully placed in a wooden spinning top from India. Grace remembers the feeling of winding the string carefully around the top's fat body and giving it a flick of the wrist to send the top buzzing across the floor.

*

The hollowed-out pumpkin on the front porch has started to rot: slit eyes and jagged mouth slowly sagging.

Grace knows what Hariti is doing: keeping her busy, distracting her from their impending departure. Another tear in her life, a wrench. Hariti offers a bristle broom. 'Here, brush the leaves, I'll get the shovel.'

A black car crunches the gravel path, the word 'Austin' emblazoned on the silver grill. The engine splutters to a stop. The air is tinged with tangy, smoky oil.

Mrs Fisher runs down the steps. '*Dear* Oliver, how good to see you, and coming to the rescue again!'

Mr Smith steps out of the car. 'My dear Kitty.'

'Girls! Where are your manners?'

Mr Smith holds out his briefcase. 'Good evening Hariti. And I presume you are the girl to be known as Grace.'

Grace feels her face reddening. She dislikes the way he stares.

*

The last night in the Epsom house. Hariti has allowed Grace into her bed before blowing out the candle. Grace cuddles against her in the dark. 'I don't like how he looks at me.'

'Mr Smith?'

'He's creepy.'

'I've never liked him either.'

'I don't want to go to London.'

'It's no wonder you're worried. It's the place where you died, but returning will help you remember.'

'That not it.'

'I'll tell you what, from now on let's call him *Smith*. But just between you and me. Mrs Fisher would be appalled. She adores him.'

*

Smith holds the steering wheel with one hand, his leather glove stretched over the knuckles.

Grace is red-faced with shame. She'd lost control that morning, made such a spectacle of herself in front of Smith. The van had arrived for the bulky items, and the suitcases had been strapped to the car. She just knew in her bones that it was wrong to be leaving. She'd grabbed the gatepost. Gripped it for dear life. Mrs Fisher had handed over the house keys to Smith and threatened to leave Grace there. Grace had screamed and sobbed. Hariti had promised that one day – no matter how long it took – she would bring her back. Smith prised her fingers off the post and told her to behave.

She's feeling sick – she'd hardly touched the kippers at breakfast – and it's not helped by the reckless way Smith takes the bends. Hariti leans forward and points at the instruments. Smith is happy to explain their function. 'The big round one on the left is the revolutions counter, see, when I press my foot down, the needle goes up …'

Mrs Fisher is staring out of the passenger window, both hands resting protectively on the Gladstone bag on her lap, the gold initials 'R' and 'D' turned towards her.

'… and this little one in the middle is the oil indicator, and this is the amperes. Do you see: Discharge and Charge?'

Mrs Fisher – in a rare moment of sensing Grace's mood – turns her head. 'Don't worry Grace; I've given our address to the police sergeant and I've also given it to your Mr Cornell, it seems he feels obliged.' She turns to face the road ahead. 'If there's any news of your family, we'll be the first to hear.'

THREE

Croydon
2000

CAESAR YAPS AT THE squeaking back door. A rough voice. 'Mother?'

He's playing his usual game, he knows Grace hates to be called Mother. She never asked to be one; it was just a huge distraction from her life's real purpose: her music. She'd been trapped by men, often felt she'd be better off dead, but then – as Hariti would remind her – she'd only be reborn, and knowing her bad karma as something really dreadful, maybe even a spider!

Orlando chases Caesar into the sitting room. 'Fucking hell dog, come here!'

'There's no need to swear, it's so uncouth.' She leans forward and grabs Caesar by the scruff of the neck. 'It's all right, it's only the chauffeur come to take us shopping.'

Orlando's hair has been clipped close to his bony head. He grunts, attaches a lead onto Caesar's collar, then drops Grace's shoes near her feet. 'Hurry up, Mother.'

Grace slips her feet into them and leans forward to reach the laces. Orlando kneels, ties the laces too tight. She's learned it's better not to complain, he has a vicious tongue in his head.

She heaves herself – unaided, thank you very much – out of the armchair, and brushes short black dog hairs off her corduroy skirt. Orlando holds her coat open. She slips her arms into the silk-lined sleeves and searches in the pockets for the car keys.

Orlando presses buttons on the hi-fi without lifting the needle; the allegretto grinds to a halt.

'You can damage the record doing that.'

'Bloody racket.'

'You should try listening to serious music, it would improve you.'

'I'm fine as I am.'

'You need to broaden your horizons. I listen to your music, you know: Elvis, the Kinks, but they leave nothing in your soul.'

'You're living in the past, Mother.'

'There's something about Marianne Faithful, though, she's rather beautiful, don't you think?' Grace hands him the keys with the silver Jaguar on the leather fob. 'Although I must admit there is a primitive attraction to Mick Jagger.'

'Pretentious wanker!'

*

Shoppers glide dreamily around the supermarket. Orlando leans on the trolley's handle, nodding slightly as if he has music in his head. Poor boy, tone deaf in spite of having Grace as a mother.

'Orlando, can you get me three Spanish onions.'

'I thought you were making Indian curry.'

'Don't try to be clever, it doesn't suit you.'

'Do you need sprouts from Brussels?'

'Very funny.'

As it happens, she *is* planning to make a vegetable curry. Hariti's favourite. All those years Hariti had done the cooking but she never ate the meat herself. No wonder that she was so thin. Mind you, there wasn't much in the war for anyone; it was amazing what Hariti could rustle up with just a few scraps.

A young man behind the fish counter is spreading ice cubes around a display of beady-eyed, silvery bodies. He looks fragile. A bit like her son. The second one, not this lout.

'Hello. May I be served?'

He wipes his hands on a smeared apron, approaches the meat section.

'I need two pounds of your best liver, cut into strips, if you'd be so kind.'

The man slaps liver on the marble slab. His thin knife – curved as if it's been sharpened many times – cuts into claret-red flesh.

'My dog refuses to eat that dreadful mess you sell in tins, I'm sure it's horse meat, and lord knows what else.'

The youth looks over the counter, points his knife. 'Dogs aren't allowed.'

Orlando uncrosses his arms. 'For fuck's sake.'

Grace senses trouble. 'Could you pick up Caesar, and take him out for some fresh air, please? He's looking tired.'

Orlando takes the dog's lead. Dear little claws click on the hard floor as he's led out.

The man wraps the liver in butcher's paper and a paper bag, then hands it over. Grace gives him her best smile in spite of knowing he hates her: all he can see is a fussy old lady. He has no idea what she's endured, the lives she's lived; how many times she's been reborn.

'Men have been my downfall.'

He looks anxious and hurries away: she must have said that out loud.

She feels faint, leans on the trolley, pushes it slowly to the fruit and vegetable aisle. Courgettes, she needs three. And, oh bloody hell what are they called, the purple shiny things, a name like artichoke? Aubergines! Her poor brain. She does all she can to keep alert: the crossword every day, reading, and constantly testing her general knowledge. The Prime Minister? Was it still that dreadful man Harold Wilson? No, silly Grace, that was years ago. It's that nice young man, now. The Norman Kings? William, William, Henry, Stephen. And then there's her beloved Shakespeare.

Through the glass doors she can see Orlando leaning against a wall looking bored. Caesar's little head is jerking nervously, watching every passer-by, anxious for Grace to return.

No human has ever loved her so unconditionally, except of course Hariti, but then, it's more than earthly love. It's divine connection.

Chelsea
March 1928

TALL WINDOWS, red velvet curtains tied back with silk sashes. Sunlight angling across the oriental carpet dazzles on the open lid of the piano. Mrs Fisher sits on the stool, reflected in the piano's mirror-black surfaces. She lifts her hands slowly, then presses the keys with amazing speed. Grace shivers: she can't understand the words but she's sure the song is about love.

'*Liebst du um Liebe, o ja – mich liebe!*
Liebe mich immer, dich lieb, ich immerdar'

Mrs Fisher holds the last notes for a moment, lifts her foot off a pedal, rests her hands in her lap, and smiles. 'Wonderful Clara. Robert's – Mr Fisher's – favourite. I have so missed her.' She stands and brushes imaginary crumbs off her black-and-white-striped dress.

It's the first time Grace has seen Mrs Fisher wearing something that isn't all black. 'Who is Clara?'

'Clara Schumann, she was the wife of—'

Hariti pulls at Grace's arm. 'Come and look, they've come home.' She leads Grace to the mantelpiece above a crackling fire. 'This one is Brahma, he's the creator of everything.'

'What, even this house?'

'Yes.'

'And everything in it?'

'Yes.'

'And all the houses, and the river?'

'*Everything.*'

'And Mr and Mrs Fisher?'

'Even you!'

Mrs Fisher has come up behind them. 'There is only *one* God, Grace.'

Hariti is too excited to stop. 'This one is Vishnu who keeps everything going, and this dark one is Shiva, the destroyer.'

Mrs Fisher's voice tightens. 'You people have some strange ideas … gods with elephant heads, a goddess with six arms, or is it eight?'

Hariti lowers her voice. 'I believe in *your* God, too, Mrs Fisher.'

'Come now, both of you, this is all rather confusing, we still have a lot of unpacking to do, why don't you show Grace to her room.'

'Yes, Mrs Fisher.'

'And …'

Grace and Hariti stop at the door.

'… I think if Mr Fisher were here he'd say it was time, Grace, that you were allowed to use our Christian names, Kitty and Robert.' She pauses, looks down at her black-strapped shoes, straightens and clears her throat. 'We're not stuffy old Victorians, after all, and we're in London now.'

Their footsteps are muffled by the wide stair carpet. Hariti opens doors. 'This is my room, and this is Mr and Mrs Fisher's, and the bathroom. And up here … I'm sure you'll remember.'

At the top of a curving staircase, Hariti lifts a latch, climbs the last step and holds the door open. 'You always loved it up here.' Hariti sits on the bed, pats the eiderdown.

Grace sits next to her.

'I remember the day you were born: I was twelve. We'd just got home from India. Pretty and pink, you were, with an angry scowl – which you still have!'

'Did Mrs Fisher like me then?'

'You're to call her Kitty from now on, remember. She loved you so much that she went a bit mad when you died.' Hariti stands. 'Come over here.'

By the window, Hariti points. 'I told you, didn't I, we're right next to the Embankment and the Thames.'

'It looks scary.'

'That's because some part of you is remembering … how you—'

'I want to go home.'

'But that was Smith's house. This is your home.'

Hariti's voice is droning; Grace's head swims with a strange roaring sound; she closes her eyes, tries to calm her breathing.

Hariti strokes her forehead '… the river is a reflection of the cosmos, you see. Energy flowing through us all. Mr Fisher understood. He's so, so clever, I can't wait for you to meet him. He studied the Hindu teachers, he understands …' she lays her hand flat on Grace's chest. '… *Anahata*. Where the masculine unites with the feminine.'

Waterloo
September 1928

KITTY PUSHES THROUGH the crowd, glances up at the four-faced clock suspended above the concourse and strides towards platform eight, where the Portsmouth train is due. 'For goodness sake, hurry along you two.'

Grace is feeling strange. The nightmare is still in her head: she was running through a black wood. She'd tried to share it with Kitty but she was too busy fussing with the long row of tiny buttons on her black dress. She'd been in a really bad mood ever since the telegram had arrived.

A chaotic chorus: shouting porters, shrill whistles. Grace presses her palms to her ears and stares across platforms. From three black engines, columns of steamy smoke rise into the cavernous iron and glass space above. Hariti holds Grace's hand. 'Don't worry. I'm looking after you.'

A fearful panting grows louder as a train approaches the station, rattling over points and aligning itself with the platform. Grace steps back, sees the driver's coal-smeared face, his head turning, watching her as the engine rumbles past. A whistle. The carriages creak. A voice shouts, 'London Waterloo, all change.'

Emerging from a fog of steam, a tall man, leaning on a stick. He takes his hat off, removes his round glasses and waves.

Kitty catches her breath. 'Oh, Robert.'

He taps his stick towards them, puts his free arm around her, holding her against the brass buttons on his grey jacket.

'My darling Kitty.'

He releases her. 'Hello Hariti, you've grown, you're quite the woman now.'

'Welcome home, Mr Fisher.'

'And the girl holding your hand so tightly, is that the lost soul?'

'Yes, it's Grace, she's come back to us Mr Fisher.'

'Well, we'll talk about that later.'

He bends down stiffly. 'I am pleased to meet you.' He pats Grace's shoulder. 'Don't worry, we'll get you home in no time.'

Kitty pulls a handkerchief from her sleeve and takes his arm as they walk towards three suitcases.

'I'm really not sure it was wise to call her Grace.'

'Let's go home. The girls have made cake.'

*

Teacups rattle on saucers as Hariti puts the silver tea tray down on a table carved with elephants. Wisps of steam curl up from the teapot's spout.

Mr Fisher smiles. 'It's good to see you again, Hariti. We'll have to think about your future too.'

Grace has a horrible twisting feeling in her tummy. The words just jump out. 'You can't send her away.'

Kitty puts her hands together in her lap. 'Hariti, don't forget the cake and bring some of that marvellous blackberry jam, would you?'

'Yes, Mrs Fisher.'

Grace can't help staring at Mr Fisher's leg.

He notices. 'I'll tell you how this happened if you like.'

Kitty straightens. 'Robert, I hardly think it appropriate.'

He heaves himself up on his walking stick, hobbles over to the bureau, strokes the red leather surface. 'My old desk.' He turns to Grace. 'This is a precious heirloom, I never feel better than when I am sitting here attending to my correspondence, as my father did, and his father before him.'

Kitty lifts the teapot lid and stirs carefully with a silver spoon.

'You must forgive me, Kitty, I'm all at sea.'

Kitty pours the tea, notices Grace rolling and unrolling the hem of her dress. 'Robert, darling, your tea is getting cold.'

'I've waited so long to be here: now it feels like a dream, as if I'm living someone else's life.'

'And I've told Grace she can use our Christian names.'

'Of course, dear, we're not stuffy old Victorians.'

An awkward laugh. 'That's exactly what I said!'

Chelsea
October 1928

WIND RATTLES THE TOP OF THE sash window. Sitting at her desk, Grace pulls the blanket tighter around her. The sailor suit is the warmest clothing she has, plus her itchy one-piece underwear and thick knee socks but she's still shivering. She checks the latch on the window. On the pavement below she spots poor Mr Fisher – Robert – struggling to clear wet leaves off the steps and from the pavement in front of the black railings. From the way he's limping, it's evident that pushing the bristle broom must be painful.

She follows the smell of fish down the stairs, perhaps she'll be able to help him, but he's already inside, easing his feet out of his boots. He heaves his coat onto the hall stand and reaches for his stick.

Kitty is laying out three plates on the dining room sideboard. The fire crackles behind the brass guard. Robert sits down in front of his newspaper.

Kitty lifts kippers onto two plates and places one in front of him. 'How is the world today, darling?'

Grace sits opposite them and opens her book, she's re-reading *Swiss Family Robinson*. She loves the part where one of the boys rescues a girl called Jenny and they soon fall in love.

'There's an editorial on that international peace agreement that Germany signed last month.' He turns a page. 'And more freezing weather is on the way, I'm afraid.'

He folds the newspaper, picks up an envelope and eases the sharp blade of his letter opener under the flap.

Kitty sits down facing him. 'I was thinking of going up to Regent Street before the weather gets worse.'

He pulls a letter from the envelope. 'That sounds nice, dear. I have my interview this afternoon in Whitehall, I could travel in with you.'

'And I might go to my old hairdresser, have a bob cut.'

'That's a bit daring, I like your hair long.'

With her fork, Kitty pushes food around her plate. 'Are you worried about the new position?'

'With my service record, I'll be fine. And Oliver Smith is on the interview panel so he'll make sure they see me as an asset.'

'Dear Oliver. How would we have managed without him?'

Robert unfolds a sheet of ivory letter paper, examines a newspaper cutting folded within it.

'Anything interesting, darling?'

'Just old regimental gossip, dear.'

Grace spreads butter on her toast, the knife rasping on the crispy, burnt surface.

Kitty carries her plate to the sideboard. While her back is turned, Robert unscrews his pen, shields the envelope and writes something. He grunts as he stands, and just for a second Grace sees the word, written in black ink: *Grace?*

A knife slips from Grace's hand, clattering on the floor. Her heart is beating in her ears. Mrs Fisher turns in slow motion. 'Grace, you look pale, you must eat more than a slice of toast; you'll fade away.'

At the bureau, Robert slides the envelope into a little drawer, turns a key, tips the key into his waistcoat pocket and returns to the table. 'I see you have a new skirt.'

'You men really are blind: they're baggy trousers, I don't know why we bother!'

'You deserve something new. Colourful.'

Hariti enters with a silver dish piled high with scrambled eggs.

Kitty pours coffee. 'What should we do about Grace's education?'

Robert leans back, his chair creaking. 'Well … while we wait for any news from the police, I suppose she will need tutoring. I know a Professor Lockhart – he has a daughter the same age as Grace, she'd have company of her own age.'

'And could she have piano lessons with your old teacher Mrs Blumen if she's still in town?'

'She must be a hundred by now.'

'Well not quite, darling! She was in her seventies when …' Kitty dabs her mouth with her napkin. 'She thought very highly of Grace. A pity you never heard her play.' She spoons scrambled egg onto her plate. 'I think she inherited your talent, Robert.'

'I'll give you the Professor's address.'

'With God's blessing, we'll all have a new start.'

November 1928

'FOR GOD'S SAKE, GRACE, put that book down and go and change into a smarter dress. Mrs Blumen will be here any minute.'

Grace can't understand why she has to look smart for an old piano teacher. Since they've moved to London, Kitty has become stricter about everything. Robert was supposed to be finding out where she came from but he always has his head stuck in the newspaper or writing letters at his precious bureau.

Kitty raises her voice. 'Grace!'

Robert looks over the top of his newspaper, places his pipe in the ashtray, gives her a little nod and the secret smile he saves especially for her.

She drops her book on the sofa, makes her footsteps as heavy as she dares, climbs the wide curving staircase, mumbling under her breath: 'Blooming bloomers.' She knocks on Hariti's door, opens it a few inches.

'What do you want, Grace?' The room is dark, the curtains closed.

'Can you help me choose a dress?'

'You're not a baby.'

Even Hariti hates her now. She doesn't know what she's done wrong. Maybe Hariti has worked out that she's not her precious Grace from before.

In her room, at the window, a dirty white bird perches on the sill; Grace bangs on the glass and it flies off with a squawk.

*

Mrs Blumen takes her place on the wide piano stool beside Grace. 'Now Miss Fisher, let us see how you are getting on with *Für Elise*.'

Grace puts her fingers on the white keys.

Mrs Blumen stops her. 'Oh my dear, when did you last cut your fingernails?'

Grace looks up at the kindly old face that is trying to appear strict. Mrs Blumen opens her bag – it looks like it's been made out of a square of carpet – and brings out a tiny pair of scissors. She holds each of Grace's fingers in her cool wrinkly hands and snips, catching the tiny crescent curls in her cupped hand. 'Off you go dear, Ludwig is waiting.'

Grace places her fingertips back on the cool white keys. She doesn't know who she is, she has no idea where she belongs, but she knows this one thing: there's a logic to the notes. A certainty. They are in her head and her fingers know where to go.

After the lesson, Mrs Blumen makes a triangle of her scarf, places it over her grey hair, knots it under her chin. Grace has been told by Kitty that she must show Mrs Blumen to the front door after her lessons and shake her hand and say, 'Thank you for the lesson, Mrs Blumen.'

Kitty passes them in the hall. 'How is Grace doing?'

Mrs Blumen holds her bag in front of her with both hands. 'I just can't believe she hasn't played the piano before. It's only her fifth lesson but she can already play *Für Elise* beautifully, just as well as Grace could.'

Nobody moves for a moment.

'I am s-*so* sorry, Mrs Fisher, I didn't mean …'

Kitty makes herself even taller and looks hard at Grace. 'What Mrs Blumen is saying, is that *my* Grace used to play the same piece, rather well as it happens.'

Mrs Blumen fiddles with the clasp on her handbag. 'Although Grace *did* play it in the wrong key today.'

Kitty smiles softly. 'Oh dear, I'm *so* sorry, I heard it from the kitchen, it sounded nice.'

Mrs Blumen looks relieved. 'For Grace to be able to transpose to a different key without even realising it shows she has an acute musical ear.'

'Of course, down to good teaching, no doubt.'

Robert's cane taps across the hall floor. 'What about the other ear?' He lets his hand rest on Grace's shoulder as he passes. 'Well done, little angel.'

'WHERE ARE WE going?'

Kitty is in one of those moods where she seems to resent Grace for existing; she's taking ages in front of the hall stand mirror, buttoning up her blue cotton coat, winding her hair into a bunch at the back, stabbing in pins.

A brass rectangle on grey stone, and etched in capital letters: 'Professor Lockhart'.

The concierge waves a white-gloved hand towards the staircase without looking up from his *Daily Herald*. Kitty takes Grace's hand, and as they climb the polished marble staircase says aloud, 'Uncouth lout.'

The Professor opens the door. He's not at all like Grace had imagined, he's even taller than Robert, with a red bushy beard. He takes off his glasses and offers his hand. He sounds just like the American President Grace has heard on the wireless: 'Mrs Fisher. How do you do.'

'How do you do. This is … Grace.'

To prove she is well bred, Grace holds out her hand. 'How do you do, Professor Lockhart.'

'Come in, come in. May I take your coat, Mrs Fisher?'

Bookcases along a wall and books piled on the carpet as if the Professor has been playing at building castles. He pulls out one of the two small chairs from under a little table for Grace. The table top is made from a big square of green leather and has lovely golden squiggles all around the edges.

The Professor uses words that Grace has not heard before: 'Algebra', 'Plato' and 'Renaissance'. Kitty tries to explain the situation with Grace: Mr Fisher has it all in hand, no stone will remain unturned, he has an 'influential position' in government.

Running footsteps, the door flies opens and a girl in a white leotard with a mass of red hair bounds into the room.

'*Désolée, Papa, j'arrive.*' She gives Grace a great big smile. 'Hi, I'm Nancy! I'm ten, how old are you?'

'I think I might be seven. Or maybe eight.'

'You think! You're funny. Have you come to share my suffering?'

Professor Lockhart leads Kitty to the door, apologising for his daughter's brash behaviour.

December 1928

Most days, Grace is allowed to stay and play with Nancy after lessons. They usually go up to Nancy's bedroom and bounce on the bed and leaf through the pile of old *Vogue* and *Lady's Companion* magazines, devouring stories of motor shows, theatre gossip and the makers of music, and giggling at illustrations of nightdresses and cami-bockers. But today, they're going out together into the rare December sunshine.

'Nancy, you have bees in your bonnet!'

Nancy is skipping ahead. 'I'm taking my best friend to meet La Signora.'

'I'd never be good enough to be a dancer.'

Nancy's shadow spins on the pavement. Grace runs to step on it but the shadow darts away.

The changing room smells of talcum powder and sweat. Three girls sit on a bench, winding silk laces up over their ankles. Nancy chats to them as she ties her hair back into a flaming red ponytail. The girls glance furtively at Grace.

The teacher enters; her own ponytail is so tight it's stopping her face from smiling. 'I am La Signora Carluccia, you may sit for the first lesson. If you decide to come to my class, I talk to your parents.' She claps three times and leads her students into a room of mirrors. The girls take positions holding a rail.

'Good. First position … and … demi-plié … good …'

Grace sits against a wall and watches the girls responding to Signora Carluccia's clapping hands and barking instructions as if they were puppets on strings. Grace can't stop looking at Nancy, the white fabric of her leotard stretching over her flowing arms, twisting shoulders, and undulating belly. She can feel her heartbeat pulsing in her neck.

Signora Carluccia claps again. 'Our pianist is still not well today so we go through grand battement to my clapping … ready …'

Nancy puts up her hand. 'Signora, my friend plays the piano.'

Everyone turns to look at Grace. She wants to shrink but she knows she has to prove herself. She stands.

The teacher shows her the sheet music. It doesn't look too hard, 3/4. Grace deliberately takes time adjusting the height of the stool. She can hear Mrs Blumen saying, 'Head up, dear'. Her fingertips touch the dirty keys; she turns to Signora Carluccia and, on her signal, music echoes around the room. This is no Steinway – some of the notes are really out of tune and the action is heavy – but, magically, the sounds animate the white bodies.

At the end of the lesson, Signora Carluccia nods to Grace. 'Girls, please show your appreciation to our new pianist, I'm sure she'll come again if we are nice to her.'

Grace gives a stiff little nod to the clapping.

'Signorina, would you mind staying for ten more minutes while I take the boys through their warm-ups? The music keeps them disciplined. Your friend will wait for you, I am sure.'

The room starts to fill with boys also wearing leotards. Grace has to look away, the little bumpy shapes between their legs are embarrassingly obvious.

*

'Gracie, I must get out of all this, I'm *so* hot.' Nancy flings her coat on a pink chair, pulls her jumper over her head. Grace sits on her bed watching Nancy slide off her skirt, then pirouette before flopping next to her, pulling her down to lie in her arms.

'I was so proud of you, Gracie, they were all talking about you afterwards, wanting to know where I'd found you.'

'You can tell them I was rescued by a prince.'

'You're funny.' She kisses Grace's cheek. 'You are *my* Gracie and no smelly Prince Charming is going to take you away from *me*.'

June 1929

THERE IS A CERTAIN SPOT, just near the top of the stairs, where Grace often sits. She's close enough to the landing to run to her room if the sitting room door is flung open.

Kitty is in a rage. It's the same subject: the *other* Grace: '…it's not as if there were no ships between England and India!'

'But darling, it would have taken half a year.'

'*I* had to make the journey, and every day being ill. You could have, Robert, you *could* have.'

'I had my duty … there were troubles—'

'And your duty to your family?'

'Oh, Kitty. You know we needed some time apart.'

'It would never have happened if you'd been here.'

Since Robert's return, Hariti has been different. More distant. Maybe she's jealous of Nancy. Maybe she can't stand the arguments between the Fishers.

Grace notices the way Robert gives Hariti secret smiles, but not so secret that Kitty doesn't see. Sometimes Grace can hear Hariti crying in her bedroom. It's hard to bear. If Hariti turns against Grace, then she is *really* lost. And she doesn't even have Nancy now, because *she's* gone off to her stupid school in Switzerland. It'll be ages until she comes home.

Hariti appears in the hall holding the family's old recipe book. She hesitates by the sitting room door, then knocks. Kitty's voice, curt. 'What is it?'

Hariti enters, closes the door. Muffled voices. The door opens.

Kitty is adamant. 'There will be no more said about that.'

Robert's voice is soft. 'It's only natural that Grace should have a birthday, and Hariti's suggestion is logical.'

Barging past Hariti, Kitty grabs her coat. The front door slams.

NINE CANDLES FLICKERING on a fruit cake.

Grace is not comfortable with everyone looking at her as she takes her place at the table. A brown paper package with an Indian symbol drawn on it sits in the middle of her plate. She looks at Hariti for explanation. Hariti looks down, strands of black hair falling over her face. 'It's just something small.'

Robert has delayed leaving for the office. He takes a key from his waistcoat pocket and goes to his bureau, opens the little drawer. For a moment, Grace imagines he's going to get the envelope with *Grace?* written on it. He brings out a little parcel. 'Happy birthday, Grace, we thought you were old enough to be introduced to Shakespeare.'

She pulls on the ribbon and parts the tissue paper.

Kitty lifts a forkful of kedgeree. '*Romeo and Juliet,* just what young ladies of your age need to learn about the silly antics of men.'

'Thank you.' Grace wants to cry; there's something familiar about the way the gold letters are pressed down into the book cover.

The door knocker makes Kitty jump. 'I wish people would use the bell.'

Hariti leaves the table and moments later leads in Nancy and the Professor.

'Gracie!' Nancy throws her arms around her. 'Happy birthday.'

'How did you get here? How long—'

'Daddy's just picked me up from Waterloo Station.'

Robert offers his hand to the Professor. 'Do join us, please.'

'I, er, yes, for a moment, thank you.'

Hariti heads for the kitchen.

Kitty forces a smile. 'Oh Grace, darling, do blow the candles out before they melt all over the cake.'

Taking a deep breath, Grace blows. All the candles go out except one. Nancy leans over and puffs it out. They both laugh. Everyone claps, and nine thin spirals of smoke rise from the cake.

Hariti carries in the teapot, puts it down carelessly on the brass trivet.

Nancy gives Grace a pink parcel. They all watch as she unwraps it to reveal a narrow box. 'Oh! A fountain pen. It's beautiful, thank you, Nancy.'

'Now you can write to me when I go back to school.'

'I will, I will, I promise.'

Kitty starts to slice the cake. 'That is *so* kind of you Nancy. Grace, don't forget your other present.'

'What does the writing mean, Hariti?'

'It's Sanskrit – it means "new life".'

Grace carefully tears around the writing. Inside is a tiny statuette.

'It's only a small thing, it's the Buddha.'

'Thank you, Hariti. I shall treasure it all my life.'

'All your lives!'

Kitty lays a knife carefully on her side plate. 'Grace, why don't you play *Für Elise* for our guests?'

'I can't, it's not—'

'Nonsense, Mrs Blumen is very proud of you.'

Grace is surprised by the compliment, and in public too, so she gets up and crosses to the piano, feeling more nervous than she can ever remember. Her fingers have completely forgotten where to go. Her face and neck are burning. She must not fail Nancy now. The timing is 3/8, *poco moto*, she remembers that. She hears the music, but from somewhere else. The first note is E. Then she remembers the second: D sharp. She presses a key and suddenly her fingers obey. Thank god she's got a good memory.

FOUR

Croydon
2000

THE CAR IN FRONT TURNS RIGHT without signalling. Orlando brakes hard and shouts his usual vulgarity: 'Wanker.'

The cigar lighter pops out. Grace keeps a pack of Senior Service in the glove compartment for emergencies. She holds the glowing coil to the tip of her cigarette.

Orlando pushes a button on the radio: a disc jockey with a fake American drawl, the Queen's English dying by a thousand cuts, the Americans invading … again.

Caesar whines. Orlando reverses the car too fast – although, Grace must admit, expertly – onto the paving slabs in front of the house. He's out of the car in a flash and holding Grace's door open. She releases Caesar and he rushes off to balance on three legs under the *Magnolia grandiflora*. At least Grace still remembers her Latin. 'Don't let him pee on the lead.'

Orlando unlocks the front door, holds her elbow, helps her to take off her coat. She hands him her paisley-patterned silk scarf. 'Use a coat hanger. It always goes out of shape when you throw it over the hook.'

'So you keep saying.'

Grace calls upstairs. 'Hariti?'

'Tea, Mother?'

'Thank you. I'll get the lunch going in a minute.'

She opens the record cabinet and flicks through the LPs. Maybe Yehudi Menuhin and Ravi Shankar. Hariti loves the precision of the violin, whereas Grace has always adored the fluid complexity of the sitar. Where is Hariti?

She decides to open the box set of Cassals.

Her rescuer, the man who lifted her from the railway tracks all those years ago: Leyland Cornell. Where is he now? He loved hearing her play the cello, especially Bach. He'd said, oddly, that it reminded him of his Irish roots.

She slips a record from its sleeve, places it on the turntable, blows dust off the needle. She remembers the feeling of her cello vibrating against her body. Of course the piano is a joy, but each note is fixed; the cello bends and slides in the same way as Hariti's voice used to float up to her open attic window on hot summer days.

Grace wanders into the kitchen, but she's forgotten why she's there. Orlando is unpacking the bags, putting tins in cupboards, letting the doors bang shut.

'Pass me the frying pan would you?' She lights a burner, half fills a frying pan with water and lays in the slippery strips of liver. 'Be a good boy and sharpen this, please.'

Orlando takes the old knife, opens the back door and kneels at the concrete step, scraping the blade in a see-saw motion.

She carefully peels the foil top off the milk bottle. 'I drowned, you know.'

'Here we go again, bloody mumbo-jumbo.'

'It's the truth, I've died many times. So have you.' Water simmers. Liver scum bubbles up the sides of the pan. 'I died in a fire, too, I remember the feeling. Or did I escape that one?'

He approaches with the knife. 'That smells fucking disgusting.'

'Hariti saw it all. I slipped off a wall, fell into the Thames, plop, as simple as that. Ask her. Nothing wrong with *my* memory.'

Caesar whines.

'Had to wait seven years before I came back. Some sort of purgatory I suppose, or maybe another life in-between.'

Orlando places the teapot on a tarnished silver tray and pours cream from the top of the Channel Island milk into Grace's chipped bone china cup.

'*Tabula rasa.*'

'You what, Mother?'

'My debts are paid. I'm ready to start again.'

'Let's get you back to your armchair.' He follows her in with the tray.

She lowers herself carefully. 'You're not a bad boy, Orlando.'

He places the tray on a nearby stool and slumps into the other armchair.

'Have you seen your brother recently?'

'*That* wanker?'

She sips; tiny fat globules glisten on the surface of the tea. 'This is nice.'

… running, stitch in her side … a dark wood … scrambling into a thorn bush … a woman's voice … 'A' for …

She wakes but keeps her eyes closed. The racing commentary is from Newmarket. She's walking through a woodland glade, Hariti's hand in hers. Now she's on a railway bridge, the tinge of acrid smoke in the air, an apple brought out from a satchel, sparkling light as Hariti spins her magic songs.

She'd better get on with the curry, it needs time to sit after cooking. 'Can you turn the volume down a bit?'

Orlando makes a drama of crawling across the carpet to the television set. He's fed up: he wasted five shillings on a nag. Why does he do it? Money down the drain. A tune comes to her: 'Camptown Races'. She lays her head back on the lace coverlet, just for a moment. 'I'll bet my money on a bob-tail nag …' and closes her eyes, 'Somebody bet on the bay.'

The commentator's voice is rising to a crescendo. She remembers. Leyland holding her through a long night in the tunnel while the earth shook; Messerschmitts, Junkers, Heinkels, their bellies filled with hate. Later, the swirling fog and the bitter tang of cordite.

Chelsea
April 1936

… B is for Buzzard. C is for Carrion Crow with black eye and dreadful beak …

The nightmare has left a feeling of dread in Grace's chest. She can't focus on the lesson. Mrs Blumen has guided her through the Trinity exams and is now preparing her for Grade Seven. The old woman seems to have shrunk, but that's because Grace has become tall and thin, and her fair hair has grown so long that she has to hold it to the side to avoid sitting on it when she takes her place on the piano stool.

Mrs Blumen still occasionally inspects Grace's fingernails before lessons, although she's not had to reach for her scissors for years. Grace likes the feeling of having someone watching over her. The sense of 'Mother' rises in her and her throat constricts. Mrs Blumen puts her cold hand over Grace's to calm an erratic arpeggio.

In the bathroom mirror Grace stares at a thin, unsmiling face framed by long, lanky hair parted in the middle. Horrible hair that has appeared under her arms and, frighteningly, between her legs. Somehow, she's always known that men had it. She didn't realise women have it too.

The cramps are getting worse and worrying her. Yesterday, Grace plucked up the courage to tell Kitty, who just looked embarrassed and said, 'I'm surprised it hasn't happened already. You need more fresh air. I suppose I should take you out, get you away from your stuffy attic.'

What did she mean? Pain was a sign of something wrong, surely. She'd asked, 'Can we go to a bookshop in Charing Cross Road so I can get a present for Mrs Blumen?' She could tell Kitty wasn't keen, but she did agree.

*

Kitty calls from the landing below, 'Grace? Something has come up, darling. We'll have to put off the shopping. I have to pop out in a few minutes. There's food on the sideboard when you're ready.'

'I'm not hungry.'

'Darling, you must eat.'

'I'm not feeling too good.'

'Just as well we didn't go out then.'

In stockinged feet, Grace descends the long curving stairway onto the hall's cold tiles. She can smell boiled cabbage.

In the sitting room, millions of dust particles dance in slanting sunlight, seemingly immune to gravity. She crosses to Robert's bureau. All she has to do is slide up the roll top and there will be the drawer with the little ivory handle. What's stopping her?

She'd once asked Robert about the envelope with *Grace?* written on it, but he'd said she must be mistaken. She'd let out a sigh of relief.

Hariti is at the door. 'Come on, Grace, I've got the hairbrush.'

Grace positions herself on the end of the piano stool. Hariti places one hand flat on Grace's head and starts with short strokes, from the bottom up.

'When you were in India—'

'A *lifetime* ago!'

'You said once that Robert rescued you.'

'He was very brave.'

'But how, what happened?'

The strokes of the hairbrush are gradually becoming longer. 'Well, I was married to an old man.'

'What! How old were you?'

'Younger than you are now. But then he died.'

'So you were free again?'

'Not exactly.'

'That's terrible. I mean about you being so young. How did Robert—'

'They were going to burn me.'

'Oh my god, is that true?'

'Robert stood up against the whole village, against their customs. He pulled me up onto his horse and we rode into the mountains. Fortunately while he was still alive my husband wasn't very capable, if you know what I mean.' She starts to laugh.

Grace feels awkward, naive, but she nods, although she doesn't understand.

'Have you heard from your Nancy recently?'

Hariti has changed the subject, maybe her memories are too painful.

'She sent me a hand-tinted postcard of a Swiss mountain and gossip about the other girls in her school. She promised she'd be back for the holidays next week. I'll believe it when it happens.'

HARITI CALLS UP. 'Telegram for you, Grace. I'll leave it by the telephone. I'm going to the shops.'

*

By the time she knocks on the Professor's front door she's out of breath. He's still in his dressing gown. 'Oh! Grace, how nice—'

'Good morning Professor, Nancy sent me a telegram, is it all right if I come in?'

He opens the door wider. 'Of course, she's up in the, er—'

'Thank you.'

Grace is not sure if she should knock on the bedroom door so she peeps around it. 'Is it all right? I couldn't wait.'

Nancy tosses the *Daily Mail* onto the floor and lifts the bedclothes. 'Come on, get into bed.'

'I don't know, I—'

'It's freezing, I won't bite.'

Grace slips off her coat and lays it over the back of a chair, undoes her shoelaces. 'Why didn't you write, tell me you were coming back?'

Nancy puffs up the pillows. 'Come, sit here, Gracie.'

'How long are you here?'

'Take that off, you don't want to crease it.'

Grace's fingers shake as she undoes a long row of tiny buttons down the front of her dress. 'What about your father?'

'I could dance a *Scheherazade* in front of him and he wouldn't notice.'

'I've got to get back before Kitty gets home.' Grace sits against the pillows. Nancy pulls her onto her arm. 'She's got you well trained!'

Goosebumps tingle on Grace's arms. She's not sure what Nancy feels for her. The same as Kitty feels for Robert? Or like sisters?

'I have to go to Paris via Rye tomorrow—'

'*Paris?*'

'You should come and visit me in Rye – not now, obviously, but when I get back.'

'It's not safe, Nancy, I listen to the news.'

'I can look after myself, silly.'

'The Nazis are goose-stepping all over—'

'Anyway, you have your lovely Hariti to look after you.'

Breath catches in her chest. A worry that Hariti might not always be there, in the background, her dark eyes watching. And there's something else, a sudden anxiety at knowing that Nancy sees Hariti as 'lovely'.

'I'll not be anywhere near Germany, or the Rhineland or wherever. They'll never invade France, they just want the Germanic territories.'

'Robert says—'

'Anyway, who knows what's in store, all I know is that I have you here, now.'

'But … what are we? You and me?'

'You worry too much, this is all perfectly natural – in a deviant sort of way.' She laughs. 'You remember at Signora Carluccia's? I could feel you watching me all the time.'

'What's going to become of us? If the Germans invade, people like us—'

'You'll find a dishy Hun, make baby Nazis.'

'Nancy, that's treason!'

'They're all just boys, half of them, following orders. Like we all do.'

'It's very different, we're a democracy.'

Grace is soothed by the gentle waves of Nancy's breathing, while outside the world reverberates with the noise of men's affairs: a distant drone of an aeroplane, a car engine, horses' hooves clopping on cobbles. 'I want to come with you. I know it's impossible, but I must get away.'

Nancy stares up at the ceiling, her fingertips idly stroking Grace's arm. 'Men are driven. You need to be careful, Grace.'

'What do you mean?'

'Now I'm being silly. Ignore me. I'm tired from the journey.'

'I should go, Kitty will be back soon. You'd better write to me.'

*

Grace spots Hariti on the front step, looking for keys in her bag. 'Hariti … wait.'

Hariti senses Grace is upset, picks up the wicker shopping basket. 'Come on in and you can tell me all about it.'

The front door bangs behind them. Hariti takes Grace's hand, leads her to the sitting room. Dying embers in the grate. Grace's statuette of the Buddha on the mantelpiece next to Hariti's. She cries. She can't say why exactly. Self pity? Frustration? For fate cruelly taking Nancy away again so soon? Or for her life stuck in this house with the world going mad? She needs to escape, but where to?

'Where is my home … I mean, if I *was* reborn …'

Hariti places her hands on Grace's burning cheeks. 'My little Grace.'

'I must be two inches taller than you!'

They laugh.

Hariti places her index finger on Grace's forehead. 'Love is a spiritual path, not limited to a man and a woman.'

'Nancy is going away.'

'I know. And I understand you are trying to create your future, but you need to accept your past in order to be free.'

'I'm not creating—'

'Your death …', she moves her hand flat on Grace's chest, '… is part of a deeper journey. Universal energy, *prana*, flows through the physical manifestation of your body …'

A shiver.

She moves her hand further down over her belly. Grace holds her breath.

'This is our destiny, Grace, we are bound, our energies united.'

A fearful pounding in Grace's chest, as Hariti touches gently between her legs. 'This is *yoni*.' Hariti's dark eyes. 'Now I will tell you about *lingam*.'

EVEN IN THE FAILING LIGHT of dusk, seagulls cry relentlessly over the chugging engines of the coal barges on the black river. In her window, a ghostly reflection, a Grace from another world.

She turns the pages of an old newspaper, picks up her scissors – silver, with a little extension that makes the grip more effective – and cuts around a picture of a dog being hugged by a sailor. Hariti's words reverberate. Somehow, she'd always known about men ... a dark understanding too heavy to bring into the light. Hariti said Grace will remember when she's ready, that they are united at the centre of a turning cycle. They will be joined beyond the physicality of body. Beyond male and female. Yin and yang.

She pins the cutting to the wall. Her skin is hot. The ache in her belly bends her forward. Hariti's ideas are so strange. What of God? If he'd been watching her in Nancy's arms – reading her heart – then surely judgement would follow. But what if God *doesn't* exist: how freeing that would be! Hariti says love and desire are natural, although confusingly one mustn't be attached to the idea of them. Maybe the black statuette with all those arms and twisting fingers would be more forgiving than a thin man nailed to a cross.

Wet on her legs. She stands, quickly, pulls up her dress. A dark red patch is seeping over her combinations. She holds her hands between her legs, for an instant hears the cry: *Mo-ther!* in her head.

So this is it, her punishment.

Kitty will kill her.

May 1936

SITTING IN HER USUAL SPOT near the top of the stairs, Grace feels comforted: something about being in-between, not fully in this house, in this family, in this life. Grace can see Kitty through a half-open bedroom door, standing in front of the wardrobe mirror, wrapping a flesh-coloured corset around her waist.

'Grace, darling, you couldn't help me could you? This darned thing is a devil to do up.'

Kitty must have eyes in the back of her head. Grace has never actually been into Kitty and Robert's bedroom; it feels strange, as if she's trespassing into the other Grace's life. She stands behind Kitty and guides the corset's tiny silver hooks into their metal loops.

Kitty strokes her flat tummy. 'You have such nimble fingers, I'm quite envious.'

Grace shudders, imagining for a moment being a baby inside that taut body. Maybe Kitty was nicer, a kinder Mummy, before her little girl …

'And your hair is lovely in a long ponytail, Hariti is so clever.'

The church bells start ringing: a tumbling chromatic scale.

Robert calls upstairs. 'Darling, we need to leave soon, the Major needs to parley before the service.'

'Five minutes.' She smiles at Grace in the mirror. 'You're a good girl, Grace.'

A tightness in Grace's throat; she must fight it.

'I wonder what that silly old Major is huffing and puffing about now. Robert is at his beck and call. They go back aeons, you know. India—'

'You don't really believe, do you?'

Kitty turns. 'What, Grace?'

'You don't believe I'm *your* Grace, do you?' She wants to hear certainty, wants desperately to be taken in, lifted up, accepted by Kitty.

Kitty opens the wardrobe door and slides a blouse off a coat hanger. 'I know it's hard for you to understand at your age ... how it feels ... I'm doing my best for you.' She slips a silk scarf around Grace's neck. A faint perfume of violets. 'She used to love the flowers on this one ...'

The door closes, catching in its sweeping reflection Kitty's over-smiling face, and behind her Grace, ghostly, gaunt, sullen.

'And besides, it's good to have young people around, it helps to keep one on one's toes.'

Robert tucks his scarf into his coat, straightens Kitty's fur collar, and lifts his hat from the hook. He gently taps the face of the grandfather clock. Every morning he opens it, inserts the key and turns nine times, bringing a comforting heartbeat to the hall.

Hariti passes a pair of kid gloves to Grace and they all step carefully out onto the wet pavement.

Robert's stick taps out a measured tempo.

Kitty slides her arm through his. 'We must invite Oliver to supper soon. I don't know what I'd have done without him while you were away.'

'I see him at the club occasionally. He's working on something hush-hush.'

'And what is the Major so concerned about that can't wait until Monday?'

'Behaviour unbecoming.'

Hariti puts her arm through Grace's, forcing her to mimic the Fishers' steps.

Kitty laughs. 'You mean homosexuality?'

Grace is surprised to hear the word spoken so brazenly.

'Apparently it is of great concern.'

'You've read Mr Freud; he says it is nothing to be ashamed of, although, admittedly, it doesn't offer the advantages normal people enjoy.'

'Children, you mean?'

They walk in silence. As they near the church, Robert rattles his cane along the railings. 'I used to do this with a stick when I was your age, Grace.'

They reach the corner. 'Robert, dear, you can tell the Major from me that it is not an illness – far less so than making war.'

August 1936

GRACE LOVES THE CHALKY smell of the ink. She screws the top back on her pen, the precious gift from Nancy, turns the letter over, presses it against the blotting paper, transferring a few more marks to the spidery web of blue-black.

August 1936
Cheyne Walk, Chelsea

My dearest Nancy,

I insist you to come back from your beastly school immediately. Switzerland is far too far away. Whenever the Professor mentions your name, I'm sure my heart literally misses a beat. This week he tried to teach me quadratic equations – did he ever torture you with them? What on God's earth is the point? He said it's about finding the solution to various unknown quantities. To me, the world is already full enough with unknowns and no ready formula to shed light on the truth of things.

Did you hear the news about that incredible Jesse Owens? Put that in your pipe and smoke it Mr Hitler.

The other evening I overheard Robert telling Kitty about that horrible little man Mussolini. Robert thinks Hitler won't stop until he has conquered all of Europe. I suppose your father must think differently, otherwise surely he wouldn't keep sending you abroad.

Hariti is crying in her room. I really don't understand why. If I ask what's wrong she sometimes gives me such a big hug I can hardly breathe. At other times she turns her back on me and storms away, like she's finally realised I'm not her Grace from before. But when she's in a good mood she tells me about Indian philosophy and what happens between a man and a woman. I know you'll probably be laughing at me right now, but I didn't know. She says it's about becoming 'one'.

What else can I tell you? I had a horrid dream, I'd fallen into the sea, I couldn't float. As I sank, I was surrounded by brilliant bubbles of air. Hariti said what she always says, that I'm remembering the dying moments of my last life. She says I'll soon be remembering more. I don't see how that will ever happen as I can't even remember the time before being found on that railway line. Seven years. It's as if they'd never existed.

Mrs Blumen gave a concert in church the other day. I was amazed. She played a sonata by Beethoven that was wonderful. One brute in the audience shouted 'Germans go home' – he obviously didn't realise she's Austrian. She ended with Chopin Études, which I don't think are meant to be performance pieces but they brought the roof down (as far as Chelsea good manners would allow). And she is so humble.

Are you dancing, Nancy? I wish you were here, dancing for me. No. Even more than that, I wish I was away from here. With you somewhere. We could live in a big house in the countryside. I could play my music. You could dance.

As I read my letter back, I realise I sound so ungrateful, I don't mean to be. What would have happened if that Mr Cornell hadn't rescued me, and Kitty hadn't taken me in?

Sometimes I hear Kitty crying behind her bedroom door.

Sometimes she and Robert are quite loud. The other day I heard them arguing about Hariti. I didn't get many of the words but there's something odd going on. Afterwards, I saw Hariti crying and Robert put his arms around her. Most irregular!

I feel sorry for Kitty, though. Sometimes she is really nice to me, and I wonder if she yearns to believe Hariti's ideas about reincarnation. It's all too fantastical.

I'm getting to the end of this page so I shall stop. I hope you have not given in to any of those boys – they are just smelly. That is my last word on the subject, so don't dare touch one!

Come home soon or I'll die and you'll have to wait all over again for me to be reborn!

Your Grace, for ever and ever.
And ever!

GRACE PUSHES THE DINING room window up a few inches: the rotting smell from the mud banks is carried on the evening breeze, the Thames must be low tonight.

Kitty is hanging up her coat. 'Do hurry up with the table, Grace.'

The sad dog is howling again. A man on a bicycle rides over the cobbles, his bell tinkles, white paper packages shake in his wicker basket.

'Your father won't be pleased if everything is not tip-top. Mr Smith is a very important man, you know.'

'Should I lay the bone handles, Kitty?'

'For goodness sake, Grace, we always have them when we have company, hurry now.'

Why must Kitty always be so prickly? Grace didn't ask to be her daughter. When Robert is around, Kitty tries to be nice and Grace starts to believe that she likes her, then behind his back it's like this. Grace knows she will never be enough.

Circling the oval dining table, she places a knife next to each blue-patterned plate, then takes the heavy silver forks from a drawer in the sideboard and circles the table in the other direction.

A car engine purrs outside. A squeak of brakes. She hurries to the window. Robert, stretching his legs out of the passenger door, heaves himself out and lays his cane over the car bonnet. He reaches into the back and brings out a big black case. Grace wants to call out, but knows he would think it rude. Smith gets out of the driver's door, pauses to drop a cigarette stub on the cobbles and steps on it.

Hariti is already at the front door. Voices in the hall.

Robert's warm hand cups Grace's chin. 'Good evening, Grace, have you been good today?'

She nods.

'Good evening, Kitty dear.' He pecks her on the cheek.

Smith pulls off his gloves. 'Good evening, Kitty. And hello, Grace, so nice to meet you all again, you have grown somewhat.' He passes his coat to Hariti without looking at her, or thanking her.

Robert catches Hariti's eye and she looks down.

Smith turns to Robert. 'Grace is such a … what's the word? Innocent.'

'And tomorrow is her sixteenth birthday.' Robert stands the big case on its end: it's shaped like a fat lady and has a red ribbon tied around its waist. 'I have a present for you, Grace.'

Kitty catches her breath; she clearly doesn't know about this.

'I lent it to a friend who plays in an orchestra. I think it's time it found its way back into our family.'

'But …'

'Pull the ribbon, it won't hurt.'

The red bow unravels and the ribbon slides to the floor. Grace unzips the case. Snuggling in blue velvet is a golden cello. Grace touches one of the strings, senses its potential. 'Is it *really* for me?'

Kitty is wearing her polite smile. 'Robert used to play in an orchestra, didn't you, darling?'

Grace shakes her head. 'Is it really for me?'

Robert laughs. 'Of course! I believe the cello to be the most beautiful of all the instruments in the orchestra.'

'Thank you, father.' She's never called him that before, it just sort of slipped out, but she likes it.

'It's from your mother too!'

'Thank you, Kitty.'

*

Candle flames dance as the conversation around the dinner table inevitably turns to Europe.

Hariti spoons thin brown stew from a tureen. She catches Grace watching, winks as she leaves. It's all a game to her, she isn't at all offended by the way Smith treats her; she might as well be a ghost.

Robert is sounding annoyed. 'You must understand, Oliver, he's in the Rhineland, it's breaking international law.'

Kitty pushes a cigarette into a long holder. 'Grace, you must forgive these two, they've known each other since they were up at Cambridge, they've always been – how can I put it – *direct* with each other.'

Robert laughs. 'It's true, Oliver was the star student.'

Smith shakes his head. 'Robert is exaggerating, without his extra tuition, and keeping me on the straight and narrow, I doubt I'd have got through my final exams.'

'Nonsence. And the way you supported Kitty when she had to return from India, I'll always be grateful.'

'You would do the same for me, dear friend.'

Robert lays his hand on Smith's arm. 'So let's get back to Herr Hitler.'

Kitty taps her cigarette against the rim of a silver ashtray.

Smith leans back in his chair. 'I admit he's embarrassed the League. And you, Robert, know better than anyone that I am not a supporter of the National Socialists, but we must accept it, Hitler is right: the Rhineland is, after all, German territory, in spite of Versailles.'

'Conscription. His support for Franco. Where is this all heading?'

Kitty picks up the ladle. 'Darling, if we had treated the German people better the last time … well, what I am saying is that you can't condemn the ordinary man in the street for looking up to Herr Hitler.'

Smith nods. 'He'll not go further, mark my words, dear Kitty, he just needs security, naturally. As we all do.'

'Oliver, you'll have some more, and Grace? You're as thin as a—'

Grace shakes her head. 'No thank you.'

'You must eat, you've only had a morsel. She's off her food. I despair, I really don't know what is wrong with the girl, I've told her that to be a musician is to be an athlete, one must look after the body for the soul to flourish.'

Smith points his fork at her. 'You mother is right. You have a duty to take care of yourself.'

Hariti is at the door. 'Mrs Fisher, do you want me to start the custard?'

'That would be so kind, Hariti, thank you.' Kitty turns back to the table, 'All this trouble – riots in the streets, that dreadful man in Italy, our own Sir Oswald Mosley – it will all settle down, I have no doubt.' Robert seems about to contradict her but she hasn't finished. 'I read the papers, dear husband, even the *Daily Mail* has turned on the Blackshirts.'

They've retired to the sitting room to – as Kitty calls it – sit soft. The men have cigars and Kitty is pouring blood-red port into four glasses. She offers one to Grace with such a warm smile that for an unguarded moment Grace thinks Kitty might actually *like* her. And what would that feel like? What if Kitty softened, smiled, opened her arms …

'So, Grace, do you like your present?'

'I love it. Can Mrs Blumen teach me?'

Robert reaches to the side table for his glasses, lifts the cello and holds it between his legs. He plucks the strings and turns the little furled nuts at the end to fine tune them.

Grace frowns. 'The bottom string is too low.'

'How do you know?'

'It just sounds wrong.'

Robert plucks the string again, turns the nut a little more, then looks over to her with a raised eyebrow. Grace nods.

'I fear you are cursed with perfect pitch.' He picks up the bow, holds it for a moment then pulls it across the strings.

Her heart feels as though it might burst, the sound is so full, so rich, so tender; she can't stop the tears.

Kitty's chin sticks out proudly. 'Robert was in the choir in Cambridge when he was your age, you know, and when his voice broke, he took up the cello. He won prizes, you know.'

'Let's not bore our guest.'

Grace didn't know a voice could be broken, she wonders if it hurts.

Smith blows out pungent smoke, rolls his cigar between finger and thumb. 'We should drink a toast. To the day when we turn on the wireless and Grace is playing with the BBC Symphony Orchestra.'

Glasses clink.

Outside, the lonely dog howls again.

FIVE

Croydon
2000

Orlando looms over her, holding a glass of water and in the palm of his hand two little pink pills. 'Wake up, Mother, time for your arsenic.'

'I wouldn't blame you.'

She sips the water and swallows the pills. Her doctor says her blood is too thick.

Orlando places a plate of charred black liver on the carpet. Caesar sniffs, looks up at Grace.

'Be a darling and put some milk down for him, he'll starve to death rather than eat that.'

'He'll eat it if he's bloody hungry – he's spoilt, he is.'

'He's just sensitive.'

'You treat him better than you ever did us.'

'Actually, you're right …' She'd done her best. It wasn't very good. 'But ask any general: you feed the horses first, then the men.'

'You always say that.'

'You're a good boy.'

The gas fire hisses. Caesar has given up on the liver and is lying on his side, the pointed pink tip of his little manhood poking out. She laughs. Men puffing themselves up, thinking they are all so important, but they're really just silly little boys playing games. Led by their little cocks. English cocks versus German cocks, invading where they had no right to go.

Rainbow bubbles pop behind her closed eyelids. An irregular beat in her ears. Pounding through a network of tunnels. Leyland. Her head on his shoulder in the dark. Her soulmate, a chivalrous knight, turning up whenever he was needed.

Orlando is deliberately making up ridiculous answers to *University Challenge*. Something about Oedipus.

She opens her eyes, explains – not that he's interested – 'Oedipus unwittingly married his mother and was father to his sisters.'

'Yes, we all know you're clever.' He yawns and scratches his crotch.

'Electra had sexual desire for her father which brought her to heterosexual maturity.'

'Whatever you say, Mother. I'll get you another cup of tea.'

Grace just can't fathom Orlando: why is he here? Probably just wants her money. The other one rarely visits.

She leans forward, preparing to get up. 'What have you done with my cello?'

'You should sell that bloody thing.'

She knows he doesn't mean badly, but his tone stings. She isn't a natural mother, she knows that. She pulls herself out of the armchair.

'Are you okay?'

'For goodness sake don't fuss. I'm perfectly capable …' She bends and lifts the tray.

'*Mother!*'

Cups slide off saucers.

The teapot smashes.

The world tilts as she falls.

A stain creeps towards her head. What's that hissing? Another gas main? Or a V2, no warning: you were here one minute, gone the next. When will the war ever end? Flames licking over the glowing, bone-like fire-bricks; iridescent blue-green, she's never noticed, so beautiful, like the plumage of a fabulous bird.

Her glasses are lying on the carpet a few inches away. An out-of-focus dog waddles into sharper view. Dark brown eyes staring at her, piercing black centres with two golden spots on anxious brows. Such beautiful, black fur. He licks her cheek and sits against her outstretched arm. She reaches out to a broken shard of bone china but the movement is just in her head; her body isn't listening.

Her sense of smell clicks in: burnt liver.

Orlando is swearing.

He's kneeling, holding an arm that she guesses must be hers.

He's in the hallway, talking on the phone.

A bubbling growl gurgles in the dog's throat, then a sharp, snapping bark. A wave of enlightenment. Of course. Her beloved Caesar.

A man she's not been introduced to squats beside her. She wants to tell him he has lovely aftershave. A big ginger beard. Something illogical about that, she can't work it out. She wants to laugh. He's tapping her arms and legs.

She's strapped, trapped, and trundled into the street.

Neighbours pretend not to be looking. Like before, where was it? A dark street in Hastings. A bomb. A baby.

Sirens wail. She's on a rocking boat. Leyland's shadow above her.

Chelsea
March 1939

29th March, 1939
Cheyne Walk, London

My dearest, and most decidedly absent, Nancy.

Such exciting news about your performance. Which ballet are you in? I am sorry to hear that your conductor had to leave, that's horrid.

I had my awful nightmare again … a monster with a deformed hand … coming towards me out of fire … I do wonder what it means. Probably it's the world going up in flames.

Kitty says the Jews are not to be trusted – which I find disturbing, especially as she doesn't know any. The BBC says millions of them are trying to leave Europe but no country will take them. Have you heard the same thing? There was a conference in London and the Jews and Arabs wouldn't even sit in the same room. What hope is there?

Did I tell you before? I have been working on the Ravel. I love it. It's strange: I wonder if he ever went to India, there's something in it that reminds me of Hariti's singing.

The other day she had the window open: it was a lovely spring day, and she was singing so beautifully. I went downstairs and knocked on her door and she went silent, pretending not to be in. I sat on the stairs and waited and waited but then I'm sure I heard Robert's voice coming from her room and I retreated fast.

Perhaps I shouldn't listen to the news. What a mess. Now it's poor Czechoslovakia. Having said that, there have been bombs in London. Robert says it's the Irish Republicans.

Oh Nancy. The more Kitty and Robert reassure me, the more worried I get. What will happen if Mr Hitler takes over Switzerland? Please just get on the next train. *When I started this letter I was determined not to be miserable but it has come out.*

You could always come and live with me. We'd have such fun. Write back or you'll be responsible for me going completely mad.

Your Grace

For ever and ever, and ever and… for eternity!

September 1939

THE PEG CREAKS AS SHE tightens the cello string. It hasn't taken long to get the hang of making the instrument sing. Music is logical and structured; every note has a place. And Grace belongs in music.

Robert turns a page of the Sunday newspaper. Kitty is knitting, a new pastime she's started in order to be prepared for the worst.

Grace hasn't heard from Nancy for so many months she's lost count. She is so stupid, waiting, hoping every day for a telegram or a letter. She's a musician, that will have to be enough. She doesn't need anyone.

She's supposed to be practising the arpeggios but she's impatient to move on. She loves the Bach cello suites, especially the one in G major. The sounds are in her head and she's finding the notes without the sheet music, but her fingertips are beginning to hurt. She drops her arms to her sides, rests the tip of the bow on the carpet, dips her head to relieve the aching in her shoulders.

Kitty looks up from her knitting. 'You still have ten minutes of practising, Grace. You must take it seriously.'

Grace hopes Robert will give her one of his secret smiles, but he tugs the silver chain of his watch. 'Kitty darling, we'd better warm up the wireless. Grace, would you mind calling Hariti, there is about to be an announcement by the Prime Minister.'

The wireless clicks.

Hariti is already at the door. She rarely needs to be called, she seems to know when she is needed. Grace turns the nut on the bow to loosen the tension.

'*This morning the British Ambassador in Berlin handed the German Government a final Note…*'

Chamberlain's voice has a tone of sad finality.

'*… it is evil things that we shall be fighting against, brute force, bad faith, injustice, oppression and persecution. And against them I am certain that the right will prevail.*'

The tobacco remains unlit in Robert's pipe. Over the last few weeks, Grace has overheard enough muffled conversations to know that the world is going to change, and for the worse, although she has no idea how. The wireless broadcast signifies a line has been crossed, but everything is exactly as it was a few moments earlier: a cart trundling by, the seagulls keeping up their shrieking chorus.

Robert leans on his stick, rises from the armchair and heads for the wireless: the exotic names in the orange panel fade, places she has no hope of visiting, at least not while the world is going insane.

Kitty stares into the fire. 'Oh Robert. Nothing will ever be the same again.'

'You mustn't fret, darling.'

Hariti sits down on the sofa, reaches for Grace's hand; it's the first time she's touched her in months. 'Mr Fisher, are the Germans going to take over our country?'

'Don't worry dear, of course not: our navy is the biggest and best in the world. A German rowing boat in the dead of night couldn't get through. You mustn't be concerned.'

Grace has never heard Robert call Hariti 'dear' before. He turns to Grace. 'And there is no need to be concerned for Nancy, she is American and has diplomatic protection. Switzerland is neutral and she can come back via France. The French Army is not about to let the Germans walk into Paris. We must all keep calm. Our nation has been through worse.' He strikes a match, sucks the flame onto the wad of tobacco. 'We'll need you to be very grown up, Grace. Hariti, you've always been a great support to us and we'll need to rely on you even more. We'll all be called upon. You do understand?'

Kitty reaches into her handbag for a cigarette packet. 'Robert, what should I do?'

'I'll make enquiries. We need to have a proper talk. Grace and Hariti—'

'Before you start that again, I have no intention of sending them off to some distant member of your family. One is as likely to die of boredom in London as at German hands. Anyway, I depend on Hariti.'

Robert stares down at the oriental rug. 'I received a telegram today from the Canadian—'

'I was thinking that Grace could help the WVS in hospitals or somesuch, there's likely to be a need.'

Robert turns to the window, a silhouette.

'Robert darling, if you are worried, I'm sure we can find somewhere out of London for Grace to billet. Professor Lockhart is in Rye, Grace could be a godsend to him when his daughter gets home.'

'I don't want them to go away any more than you do. The information clearly indicates that things will only get worse. There are credible threats from the air.'

'Isn't this all rather hysterical?'

'If we have learned anything from Spain—'

'Let's talk about it later. Grace and Hariti, you can go to the kitchen and make us all a nice cup of cocoa.'

Robert takes his round glasses off and rubs his eyes with his knuckles.

October 1939

KITTY TAPS EVENING IN PARIS talc into her tight leather gloves and wriggles her fingers in. Hariti holds out the regulation gas mask box to Grace.

'I'm not taking *that*, I hate it.'

Hariti loops the string over Grace's head, 'Do as Mrs Fisher says, there's a good girl', and pushes her towards the open door.

'It smells horrid, I'll never put it on.'

Kitty slides her gloved hands into the silk-lined sleeves of her coat. 'Your father insists, Grace. If you ask me, there is no way the German people would countenance such a terrible thing as dropping bombs full of gas. You'll see, you'll be reading Goethe and Schiller soon and then you'll understand, the Germans are a highly cultured race. Hurry, darling, we'll be late.'

'Robert said they dropped gas in the last war.'

Kitty pushes three big buttons through their buttonholes. 'You can borrow my bicycle if you hurry.'

'Have I got to be there all day?'

'Oh do come along, Grace, we all have to pull our weight now.' She lifts the bicycle's handlebars clear of the railings. 'Hariti will prepare supper, now hurry darling, there is a war on you know.'

Grace pedals slowly beside Kitty's click-clacking shoes.

Ahead, three men are unloading sandbags from the back of a lorry and piling them up to make a buttress against a building. Grace is sick with nerves; she can't understand how these men can be joking with each other when they might all be dead tomorrow.

At the steps of the hall, Kitty searches her handbag for her cigarette holder. 'Now listen.' She pushes a cigarette into it and snaps her lighter. 'I may be late. Don't worry, I'm sure you can find your own way home.'

Grace picks up the bicycle and they climb the steps. Kitty pulls the long brass handle and holds the door open for Grace to wheel in the bicycle.

As if she'd been lying in ambush, a woman with three pencils sticking out of a bun of silver hair appears from the shadows. 'How do you do, Mrs Fisher.'

Kitty smartens her accent. '*Dear* Mrs Braddock, how very kind of you. I am sure Grace will be a credit.'

'So good of you to offer your daughter's services, don't worry we'll look after her, we have plenty of lemonade and cake.'

Grace is led away into a large room with walls filled with bookcases, rows and rows of red leather spines. The women gathered around a big table are at least as old as Kitty. A few of them look up and smile and make room for Grace: it's all very odd, this happiness in a time of war.

Mrs Braddock explains: 'I've put crayon marks at intervals along the edge of the sheet, you cut here with the scissors, and just pull apart, be confident and it will tear nicely.'

The women chatter while they wind up long strips of white cloth, put elastic bands around them and add them to a pyramid of bandages in the middle of the table. A woman stands and walks quickly out of the room. Another leans over to explain: 'Her family is in Ireland, poor thing. She's not Irish herself, though, so that's a blessing.'

The woman's scissors snip-snip along the edge of a bandage: '… I read in the *Daily Mail*, they burnt an effigy of the Prime Minister and the police did nothing.'

Mrs Braddock's hands are clasped behind her back. 'That's uncalled for Dotty.'

Dotty frowns. 'Some of those police fought for the fascists in Spain.'

'Well, I'm sure some fought on the other side.'

Another woman joins the argument. 'What about those poor people in Coventry bombed by the IRA, as if we don't have enough to worry about with the Germans. They should all be sent back.'

A few women nod in agreement. From the corner of the room a whizzing, rhythmical purr of a sewing machine. The voices rise and fall.

'My rhubarb is doing marvellously.'

'If we go on like this, the country will be swamped with Jews.'

'That Mosley is rather dashing if you ask me.'

'Three bombs in Piccadilly Circus.'

'You can't blame the children for the sins of the parents.'

'We've put our name down to take one of the *Kinder*.'

*

Dotty gives Grace a string bag full of currant buns to take home, saying they'll be stale by tomorrow and that it's obvious she needs building up.

Fog has descended, an acrid taste catching in the back of her throat. Grace switches on the bicycle lamps. A harsh voice: 'Put that bleeding light out.' Grace hangs the string bag from the handlebars and wheels the bicycle along the gutter. She can only just see the kerb but she knows her way home: down to the corner, turn right, right again, and then along the Embankment; count the lamp posts. At the end of the road she can hear the wish-washing of the river. She crosses. Two yellow slits loom towards her. A lorry only just misses the bicycle.

Grace trips on the pavement, and as she regains her balance a hand takes her arm. A young man is standing in front of her, like a genie in a puff of smoke. 'Miss, may I help you? It's a nightmare out here tonight.'

A surge of recognition. Of course, of course. It's inevitable. Fate is toying with her. 'I'm fine, thank you.'

He holds his trilby in one hand and offers the other. Grace shakes it and lets him take the handlebar. 'Is that an Irish accent?'

'You have a good ear, miss. It's dangerous out here. Allow me to take your bicycle, I'll meet you at your home.'

He disappears into the gloom – the clicking of the bicycle's gears diminishing – and she realises she'd not given him the address. If he knows where she lives, it means he must have been spying on her. For how long? She doesn't know anything about him. He could be working for the Germans or, worse, a thief. Kitty will be furious with her if she loses her beloved machine.

Grace runs her hand along the granite wall. That familiar rotting seaweed smell of the low tide.

Eight lamp posts; then she stops, leans against the wall. A child is laughing somewhere; far, far away the eerie strains of a brass band; fog does strange things to sound. She crosses the road: she can tell he's there by the smell of his cigarette. 'That is so kind of you, thank you.'

'I took the liberty of taking one of your buns. Will you forgive me for the theft?'

'Yes, of course. Thank you again.'

He puts out his hand. 'It's been a pleasure to meet you again, Miss Fisher.'

'It was so kind of you, Mr Cornell.'

He laughs. 'Leyland, please. I wondered if you'd remember, you were so young.'

May 1940

A GLINTING LUMP OF COAL gripped in the claws of the tongs. Grace puts it on the dwindling fire, then another. Considering the time of year, the house is still cold in the evenings.

Kitty picks up *The Times* and sits in Robert's armchair. 'Do be careful, Grace, coal doesn't grow on trees you know.'

The Professor has taught Grace enough about the Carboniferous period for her to argue the point, but instead she raises the piano lid and positions her fingertips. Scales: chromatic both hands, chords and sight reading.

'For goodness sake, Grace, I can't concentrate.'

'Mrs Blumen says I'm to practise every day.'

'That's all very well, but there's a—'

'No need to say it.' Grace flops heavily onto the sofa and tucks her knees up. Which book shall she read? She's finished *Don Quixote*, far too rambling and confusing; in truth she didn't really understand it, but she loved the dogged Sancho Panza, the loyal squire. She's also borrowed *A History of England* from Robert's bookshelves; a lovely brown leather cover with a page that opens out to reveal an ancient map of England. What will maps of the future look like? England as part of the greater Third Reich?

She picks up *Lucia in London*. After a few paragraphs, its cast of snobby characters starts to irritate, so she opens *The Complete Shakespeare* to Julius Caesar – another conqueror of England. Cassius has a 'lean and hungry look': a brilliant description that rather reminds her of Smith.

Robert is rarely home these days. War work that can't be discussed.

Kitty is acting as if she is equipped to take his place; Grace is sure she doesn't understand half of what she's reading in the newspaper.

The telephone rings.

Hariti calls from the hall: 'Mrs Fisher?'

Who else would it be for? Nancy never ever, *ever* calls.

Grace eavesdrops by the door, sees Kitty shielding the mouthpiece as if German spies might be hiding in the under-stairs cupboard. 'Hello darling, what's the news … I see. It's what you wanted, isn't it?'

The grandfather clock seems to be ticking louder than ever.

'Try not to be too late home.'

The receiver rattles back onto its holder. Grace steps into the hall.

'In case you are interested, Halifax has withdrawn. The Cabinet believes we need a man of the people at a time like this.'

'But you liked Mr Halifax.'

'Like it or not, the next Prime Minister will be Mr Churchill.'

'The wireless smells of burning dust.

... victory, victory at all costs, victory in spite of all terror, victory, however long and hard the road may be; for without victory, there is no survival.

Robert, standing in front of the fire, reaches over and clicks off the wireless.

Grace is perched on the edge of the piano stool staring at a score open on the stand, imagining how the words might be pronounced: '*Der ganze Fingersatz von Frédéric Chopin.*'

'How is your practice coming along, Grace?'

'How can old Mrs Blumen be a threat to us?'

'She's not, Grace. She's been interviewed and has been classed as Category C, so she's not going to be interned, don't worry.'

'So why can't she carry on giving me lessons?'

Kitty picks up her knitting. 'Feelings are running high in the country.'

'So you're more concerned about what other people think than—'

'Remember your manners, Grace.'

Robert clears his throat. 'You must understand, Grace: there's an increasing threat, more and more Austrians and Germans are being interned. And Kitty's right. It's uncomfortable, but we have our positions to consider.'

Grace finds it harder to argue with Robert than with Kitty, she wants to trust him, but punishing Mrs Blumen is all wrong.

The hall clock chimes the half hour.

Kitty bunches stitches along a needle. 'If you want *my* opinion, Robert darling, I don't see why they are hell-bent on sending the children away. Think of the poor mothers. We're all supposed to sit here calmly waiting for the end. And then nothing happens.'

Robert is holding his hands to the fire. 'At a time like this, the best thing to do is to be a good citizen and follow the rules.'

'A bit like in Germany, you mean? Next thing, we'll be sending *all* foreigners home. What about Hariti? I suppose *she* could be a spy.'

Robert taps his finger on the polished top of the wireless, his voice hardens. 'Hariti is *my* concern.'

Kitty laughs. 'Yes, your little pet.'

Grace flushes.

Robert crosses his arms. 'All I'm saying, Kitty, is that it's my role to protect her. *In loco parentis*. And Grace, too.'

A long silence, a log on the fire cracks, sending a shower of sparks against the copper fireguard. It's never occurred to Grace that a bomb falling through the ceiling isn't the only threat to their family. If Mrs Blumen isn't welcome in the country, then maybe Hariti won't be. Grace couldn't bear life without her, she's the only one who understands.

Kitty peers at a dropped stitch. 'Next we'll be sending the royal family to the Tower, they're of German descent.'

'You need to keep those sort of thoughts under your hat, Kitty. You never know who's listening.

'I am aware of that, *mein lieber.*'

November 1940

AN OMINOUS MURMURING in the distance. She knows it means the aerodromes are being bombed.

Her lights are off. Curtains open. A fine red glow silhouettes the southern skyline in the direction of Biggin Hill.

Eerie fingers of light probe the black sky, swaying as if in some slightly drunken dance. It'll be the women of the ATS manning the searchlights. Doing something meaningful.

And now a throbbing, like a hoard of buzzing motorbikes but deeper, all the same tone, and suddenly there's fear in her throat. Pinpoint flashes on the ground congeal into a fiery glow. Grace can hardly bear to look, but she knows she must: in this very moment, somewhere nearby, life is being suffocated, burnt to a cinder, choked out of existence.

Something changes, the droning is getting louder. Hariti screams up the stairs: 'Grace, Grace, for god's sake, Grace!'

She races downstairs. Kitty doesn't even bother to rise from the sofa.

Hariti is breathless. 'Mrs Fisher, what do we do?'

'Just get under the table. Take a cushion each.'

Grace searches Kitty's face to try to make out what she's feeling. Is this what happens when you've lost your child – nothing can really touch you? 'What about you, Kitty?'

'They're going for the docks; they have no reason to bomb the beautiful parts of London.'

'How can you be so sure?'

'Hitler will need somewhere nice to stay, won't he?'

'You can't mean … you can't believe—'

'Just lie down and try to get some sleep.'

Guarded by the dining table's four sturdy legs, Grace and Hariti lie together holding hands.

Kitty's needles compete with the staccato booms of the anti-aircraft guns. Rhythmic eruptions. The earth quakes. In the grate, ghostly soot sifts down onto a slowly dying fire.

The slanting rectangle of Grace's window is etched on the floor in moonlight. Fear twists her stomach. Rising through her. Night after night.

The relentless bombing has shattered the boredom of the 'phoney war'. There's nothing artificial now about living under the German flight path. No part of London is spared: the National Portrait Gallery, Euston Station, Westminster Abbey, thousands of buildings blown to brick dust. Last night it was Coventry. Tonight?

Earlier in the day Robert told Grace that he has received news. Nancy is in Paris.

Grace stands at the window, facing in the direction of France. During the daytime, it's hard to believe that this isn't just a fantastical nightmare. In the dark, Grace imagines millions of frightened souls. For all she knows, at this very moment, under this cruel full moon, Nancy might be standing at a north-facing window in Paris watching the Luftwaffe flying towards England.

And here it comes.

Eerie bass line.

Wailing chorus.

Throbbing pulse.

The pitch rising a semitone.

London cowering beneath the onslaught.

Grace will never get used to this.

Where will it end?

Winston will never give up, not like France.

Herr Hitler clearly intends to blow them all to pieces.

December 1940

A TELEGRAM: *Arriving tomorrow pm.*

Grace paces from rug to floorboards, back to the rug, straightens the magazines on her desk, stares out of the grimy window across the foggy river.

Hariti calls up: 'Grace … visitor.'

A gloved hand on the curving stair rail, a cloud of red hair. 'Nancy! Oh my god. Come up, come up.'

Nancy drops a small suitcase in the doorway and gives Grace a quick hug, then slips off her navy blue trench coat. 'Darling, your little hovel is divine.'

'It's been so long.'

Nancy sweeps around the room, her light blue cotton dress stirring the air. 'This is so exciting: all these years and I've never seen inside your room.'

Grace is annoyed with herself, standing like an awe-struck, love-sick bird.

'But it's freezing in here … oh look!' She crosses to the bedside table. 'What a pretty lamp, a ballerina with red hair.' She runs her fingers along the ceramic tiers of the dancer's dress and down onto the red dancing shoes. 'She looks just like me!'

Grace's face is burning red. 'When did you get in?'

'Daddy's been recalled, ships passing in the night and all that, hardly time to put my feet up. Took ages to get the car packed then he realised that he hadn't left room for my case. In the end I had to get a taxi some of the way and walk the rest. The roads are closed all over. Madness. Honestly, I have never known a man so absent-minded.'

'So, how long …'

'He'll be in Rye until he can get a flight; the convoys aren't safe. I have to go to Rye in a couple of days. You could come too!'

'Really? Oh god, yes, yes. I'm dying here.'

'That's agreed, then.' Nancy lifts her suitcase onto the bed, clicks open the catches. 'Daddy says it's a lovely little town with the cutest little houses.' She holds up a cardigan. 'Oh my god, why did I bring this old thing?'

'I love the diamond patterns.'

Nancy holds the cardigan up to Grace's chest. 'It's yours.' She gives her another quick hug. Grace can't work out what it signifies, friends don't hug like this, but then if it's a sign of love, it's very restrained, especially from Nancy.

Perfume on the cardigan; Grace pulls it over her shoulders. 'Did I tell you? Robert and Kitty won't let Mrs Blumen come anymore.'

'That's not at all surprising.'

'But she—'

'Hariti was nice to me for once, what incredibly dark eyes she has, I could fall in love with her!'

Grace sits on the bed. 'She'll probably be sent back to India, I'm not sure if her papers are in order.'

Nancy laughs. 'Did I make you jealous?' She grips Grace's wrist, flops onto the bed, pulling Grace down with her, kicks off her shoes and sends them flying recklessly across the room. She strokes Grace's arm. 'Oh, look, your skin has gone all goose-bumpy.' Her fingers trace up the fine hairs on Grace's arm. 'My grim little Gracie, you do the worrying for both of us.' Her fingers reach Grace's underarm hairs.

'That tickles!'

'That's better, you should laugh more often.'

'Hariti's been like a mother to me. I turned to her when I started my … you know… the curse. I didn't know what was happening.'

'I wonder how many children you'll have.'

'I have no intention of having saggy breasts and I've no instinct for cleaning dirty bottoms. I'll leave the mothering to someone else. You can have them. I've got my cello – that will have to come to Rye with us.'

'That's my rebel girl, I love that spirit in you.'

'If it wasn't for Hariti explaining what it was, I would have died.'

'Oh darling, when was all this?'

'Just after I came to your room … you know, before you left on your beastly travels.'

'I'm finished with all that nonsense: from now on I'm going to live! What's the point of Latin and deportment? We could all be dead tomorrow.'

'Did you know that Robert saved Hariti's life?'

'That explains it.'

'Explains—'

'Well surely you've noticed?'

'She looks up to him, like a father. As one would. As I would if—'

Nancy laughs. 'He used to watch her all the time.'

'He's old enough—'

'You really *are* blind, Gracie.' She kisses Grace's bare arm. 'Let's go out.'

Their breath vaporises. The meagre sun – now sinking beneath the horizon – tints the edge of distant herringbone clouds; stars are already visible. Arm in arm, they walk along the Embankment. 'What do you think, Grace? Is the tide coming in or going out?'

'I think going out.'

'It's beautiful. Reminds me of the Seine.'

'Was it awful with the Germans there?'

'The Parisians ran away to the countryside: the Germans just marched in. I think they were surprised how easy it was.'

'That would never happen here, we'd never give up our freedom like that.'

'German being spoken on every street corner. Black boots sticking out from under café tables. All rather surreal.'

'Weren't you worried for your safety?'

'The French did manage one act of sabotage before they left, they disabled the lift up the Eiffel Tower! Some poor clot had to climb to the top with the Nazi flag. The German's were actually quite well behaved.' She lights a cigarette.

'You should have stayed in Paris.' She hears the petulance in her voice, hopes Nancy will ignore it.

'They're really not so different from us.'

'According to what I've heard, it wasn't so good for everyone.'

Nancy blows smoke. 'The moon is up already, it'll be a shiner tonight.'

'The bombers …'

Nancy pulls Grace into her arms. 'What are we to do with you?'

A lorry rumbles past; the driver whistles.

'They can't conquer England, Nancy. It's unthinkable.'

Their footsteps echo on the pavement.

'Let's walk and walk until we leave the city behind, Dick Whittington in reverse. You can be the cat!'

'Where would we go? We'd be caught out in the open.'

'Oh, I don't know. Far from all this. Timbuctoo?'

'Where *is* Timbuctoo? I've always wondered.'

'Deepest, darkest Africa where the men really *are* tall, handsome, and deliciously dark!'

'And don't speak German.'

They stand in the middle of Putney Bridge under the ornate lamp posts looking east. Grace leans over. 'The river is going down, you can see the pier footings.'

Nancy lights a cigarette. 'London must look amazing from the air.'

Grace shivers. 'We'd better be getting back, we're very exposed.'

'My little mouse, running back to her hole in the skirting board.'

Anger rises. 'I've escaped before, I've survived.'

'You've been lost since I met you. I worry for you.'

'I just need to know where I've come from so I know where I'm heading.'

Nancy stares down at the water. 'I'm sorry, I was being insensitive.'

The echo of the front door slamming lingers in the hallway.

'Their coats aren't here, they must still be out.'

'I should telephone Daddy, make sure he's arrived.'

Grace picks up the receiver. 'It's working.' She passes it to Nancy and puts her hands flat on the cold marble stand.

'Hello, I should like to make a trunk call to Rye, Sussex please.'

*

Grace pulls the black curtain across the toilet window, flicks the light switch and runs lukewarm water into the basin. Kitty's favourite French soap sits in the dish. She lathers a flannel, lifts her skirt and pulls down her knickers. She's waited so long for Nancy to come, to be with her properly; now she's nervous. For Nancy it's all probably just a childish infatuation. Grace rinses the flannel, lowers the dark wooden lid over the blue-patterned toilet bowl. If she waits long enough Nancy will have fallen asleep; it will be disappointing, but a relief.

Rows of glass bottles line the wooden shelf along the bath. She reads a label to calm herself: '*Milton: The One Antiseptic That Dissolves Mucus*'. Maybe she's letting her imagination run wild. They'll just sleep, wake in the morning and hug, like little girls. '*Kay Linseed Compound for coughs caused by hard phlegm.*'

Nancy's footsteps pacing the floor above.

In front of the mirror, Grace taps Johnson's talcum powder onto her hands and rubs the perfumed dust into her armpits. She stares at her ghostly face, her fingers gripping the edge of the basin. Tap, tap, tap, an arpeggio, a bass line in her left hand, treble in her right, opposing chromatic scales. Bach playing games in her head.

Two candles throw ghostly shadows from the bedside table.

'Nancy, could you blow them out so I can open the curtains?'

'But I like seeing you floating around, you look divine.'

Grace had found the nightdress in Kitty's wardrobe, silk, a little too lacy around the top, emphasising what isn't there. 'Please, Nancy, I need to see the sky.'

'You think some German pilot is going to see us from miles up, drawn to us like a moth to a flame?'

'If there's a German heading for me, I want to see him coming.'

The room fills with the incense of smoking wicks. Grace pulls back the curtains. The moon is reflected in the black river, ornate street lamps are silhouetted along the Embankment.

'Oh Nancy, I don't like it.'

'Come to bed, it will be all right, you'll see.' She lifts the sheet.

They lie side by side holding hands, watching the faint reflections of moonlight flickering on the ceiling. Grace is relieved, it's simple, like they are still children. 'Tell me more about Paris.'

'Most of the Germans were just young boys far from home.'

'But they are different from us, they want global domination.'

'I'm a foreigner here too, remember.'

'Yes, but you don't want to take over the world.'

'It was like being a news reporter, somehow floating above it all, watching history unfold in front of my eyes, but never feeling I could intervene, touch it, feel it.'

Nancy strokes her thumb gently over the back of Grace's hand. 'Neutral is a strange concept when you think about it.'

'Let's *not* think about it, you're here now, at last.'

'The worst thing was the way everyone kept their heads down so as not to attract attention. Some couldn't hide so easily.'

'Isn't it just a matter of biding one's time?'

'Do you think it would be any different here if Britain loses the war?'

'Don't say that.'

'You have no idea.'

'This is beastly, let's not talk about it.'

'Your precious musicians would suffer too.'

'The British character wouldn't allow it, we'd resist to the bitter end.'

'That's what you've been made to believe. I've seen people just stand by and watch, but then so did I. Them and us. And mark my words, Grace, there are many people in this country who would welcome certain measures.'

'You're wrong, Nancy, that's why we're fighting this war: we have jealously protected our rights since Magna Carta; we are not about to abandon our countrymen, we would never be so barbarous.'

'Unlike the French, you mean?'

'Now you're being deliberately provocative.'

'I need a ciggy, or a drink, or something. Have you got any wine?'

'Not in my bedroom!'

'You need to live a little.' She pulls Grace onto her bare shoulder, takes Grace's hand and lays it on her belly. Warm skin, a particular smell – Grace can't quite place it – like liquorice sherbet but more perfumed. She feels absurdly grateful to Nancy for taking the lead but is so nervous she can't stop talking. 'I read a story in the newspaper the other day: a little dog was injured by shrapnel, and the lights had failed because of a raid. All they had was a candle for the surgeon to operate by.'

'Is there a punch line, darling?'

'The report said, "By candlelight the flame of life was saved". That sort of story gives me hope.'

'Gracie. Being together like this. You're younger, I should be responsible.'

'I've got another newspaper cutting about a small puppy who was found on a piece of floating wreckage far out in the Atlantic: he was rescued by a ship and became their mascot. What are the chances of that happening? Just imagine how the poor little thing must have felt in the middle of a dark ocean.'

Grace knows from the guilty times when she has touched herself where Nancy will want her. Nancy's belly is rising and falling under Grace's hand. A rush of courage … Grace moves her fingers down, touches a nest of hair. In response to Grace's transgression, the sirens wake – the sound she dreads every night. She pulls her hand back.

'Don't stop, Grace.'

Warm air between the sheets, sweet and salty.

A low, steady hum.

Nancy.

Grace will never love anyone more than she does in this moment.

The distant dull thumping of bombs. Clusters.

One … two … three.

One … two … three … four.

Nancy clamps her hands over Grace's. 'Darling …'

'Sorry if I—'

Nancy laughs out loud, her whole body shaking. 'Precious girl.'

... Come out you bloody little minx ... moon hangs above black branches, a fine wispy cloud, a ring of gold ... she closes her eyes ... play the game ... C for Chicken. D for Dove. White wings stretched out. E for Earth, a big blue ball floating in black space. ... twigs crack ... a sudden burst of light shrinks to a pinpoint of flame ... a deformed hand holding a clay pipe ... wait till I bloody get you ...

SHE WAKES, HER FACE wet with snotty tears. Through the window, fluffy white clouds move slowly across pale blue.

Nancy rolls onto her back. 'Oh my darling, bad dream?'

'Being chased. Haven't had it for a while. Horrid.'

'Let's go down to Lyons Corner House. I'll buy you a cup of tea and a cream bun. My treat, I insist.'

'It seemed to go on forever. I was being chased by a beastly man. I wonder what it means.'

'I would say it's ambivalence towards the male of the species.'

'Hariti will say it was a past life.'

'You need a big tickle.' Nancy sits up, throws off the sheet and blanket and shuffles down to grab both of Grace's feet.

'No! I hate my feet.'

'They're lovely, you should have been a dancer.'

'They're hard and knobbly, and very ticklish so please don't.'

'Okay then, let's try this ...' Nancy strokes her legs, then kisses her knees. 'Oh Gracie, sweetheart, you are perfect, I could eat you up ... we'd better go out before I do.'

*

Grace picks up the newspapers from the hall mat and carries them to the dining room. 'Kitty's coat is here, she must be back.'

'No sign of Mr Fisher?'

'He's still away, I have no idea where. All very hush-hush. Kitty had some visitors the other day, both wearing the same dark coats. I could hear their droning voices through the door and Kitty getting annoyed. Nobody tells me anything.'

Nancy crosses to the gramophone. 'Let's dance, Grace.'

'I'm not really—'

Nancy has selected a record. 'Picture Me In Paradise'. 'I love this, it's Jack Harris, let's play it.'

Grace lays the *Daily Mail* out flat: St Paul's Cathedral rising above smoke and ruined buildings under the headline 'War's Greatest Picture'.

SOMETHING IS VERY WRONG. Grace and Nancy hesitate in the kitchen doorway. A mop handle leans against a wall, a puddle of dirty water spread around it. It doesn't make sense, Hariti would never leave a job half done.

Kitty is sitting at the kitchen table, head bowed, arms outstretched, palms up, fingers half curled. 'It really is too much, going off like that, what is she thinking … at a time like this?' She wrings her hands. 'And I don't know why Robert doesn't at least telephone or send a telegram. It's been weeks; he could be in a bomb crater for all I know. I've telephoned Oliver a hundred times.'

Two eggs lie next to half a cup of milk. Hariti must have been out and come back already. Grace has no idea how Hariti finds these treats; they often appear overnight as if by magic.

Grace crosses over to the mop, lifts the handle and flops the dribbling head into the galvanised bucket, releasing the resin perfume of Jeyes Fluid. She lifts the bucket, carries it a few paces and places it on a dry patch of floor, the handle clattering.

Nancy pulls out a chair and sits down opposite Kitty. 'Can we do anything, Mrs Fisher?'

Kitty gets up, straightens a tea towel on the rail of the cold range, crosses to the window.

Grace leans on the mop. 'What did those men say the other day?'

'They asked a lot of questions.'

'What about?'

'If you must know, Robert's associates – as if *he's* a criminal – and the visitors he's had. I'm out of my mind. How dare they question his loyalty. And they were interested in both of you, and that Irish man, what's his name? The one who rescued you.'

'*Us!* What have we done?'

'Emergency Powers give them the right to detain anyone under suspicion.' She sits down. 'Be careful, Grace.'

'*Suspicion*! Of what?'

'There is a war on.'

'We *know* that!'

'Where on hell's earth is that girl?'

'Nancy and I will go and look for her.'

'I'm so tired, when will it ever end? If they carry on like this there will be nothing left of England worth fighting for.'

Nancy reaches over and touches Kitty's arm. 'Mrs Fisher, Grace and I can help.'

Kitty's chair crashes backwards onto the flagstone floor. 'I'm not a child!' The door slams.

*

Jagged walls with blown out windows. The further east they walk, the worse the damage. Wind whips up clouds of dust and ash. Grace holds a handkerchief to her face. Nancy offers a hand. 'Here, this bit's tricky.'

In a building opposite, a floor sags across the gap between two wallpapered walls. They pick their way carefully over scattered bricks, smouldering beams and shattered glass.

A man's voice from somewhere in the distance: an incantation, like a gramophone record stuck in a scratched groove. 'I bloody hate you … I bloody hate you … don't you fucking … I bloody hate you …'

Two boys are laughing; one throws a stone at a sign with a large white letter 'S'. It must all be so much fun for them, the danger so unreal.

'Oh Nancy, look at that.' They cross the road: a little girl is staring at a pile of rubble as two men in white coats and tin helmets carefully remove broken bricks from around the unmoving leg of a dog.

Sobs rise in Grace's chest. She can't understand it … it's just a dog, so many are dying every day. The thought of life without Hariti … she's always been there.

A bus at an odd angle; its front end sunk into a crater; water streaming down a gutter. They turn the corner. A man standing in a doorway, swaying from side to side. 'I bloody hate you …' A ragged fur coat over dirty clothes. 'Don't you fucking … I bloody hate you …'

*

The police station's windows are taped in crossed lines mimicking the Union Jack. Grace imagines that dreadful swastika flying over England and shivers.

Smoke fills the crowded room. The sergeant nods towards the hard metal chairs and tells them to wait their turn.

People standing in groups; one old man in a torn coat leaning on the glossy cream wall by an old poster: *Public Warning* written in big letters.

Nancy follows Grace's gaze. 'The authorities like to keep us worried.'

'But it's war, it's understandable.'

Nancy stands up. 'I'm fed up with this.' She goes up to the counter. 'What is the problem, officer, why are we waiting so long? Officer? *Parlez-vous anglais? Sprechen Sie englisch?*'

The policeman looks up sharply from a pile of papers. 'As I told you, madam, someone will be out to see you soon. Sit down, my dear.'

'And I'm not your dear, I'm an American citizen and my father—'

'And if I was you, I wouldn't be speaking German or I might have to arrest you as a spy.'

The phone rings. The policeman listens, lifts the desk lid. 'He'll see you now.'

The Inspector's office is lit by a single desk lamp. He sits behind manila folders ranged across the red leather desk top. 'I am afraid there is no record of your maid. I have telephoned the other stations nearby.'

Grace's eyes are tearing up. 'Hariti is not a maid. You *do* realise who she is?'

'People are getting lost all over the shop at the moment.'

'She's like a daughter to Mr and Mrs Fisher. He's in the War Office, directly under Mr Churchill.'

The Inspector strokes his greying moustache. 'I am aware of that, which is why I have taken so much trouble. I wouldn't worry, his people will be looking after his … er, interests.'

'My mother is out of her mind with worry.'

'As I say.'

*

Darkening streets, everyone walking with bowed heads.

Nancy whispers: 'Just like Paris. Rats scurrying to their holes.'

Footsteps seem to have been following them for a few streets. 'Nancy, I think—'

Nancy takes her elbow and pulls her into a cinema foyer. 'Let's see who it is.'

A man in a dark coat, his collar up, trilby pulled down, a slight limp, passes by without glancing towards them.

*

They sit up in bed – it's too cold to undress – a blanket and cover pulled up to their chins. Nancy's cigarette glows in the dark.

Sirens rising.

Kitty crying from somewhere downstairs.

Grace closes her eyes. Hariti's soft voice, floating hair as she spins around. 'I can't lose her, I can't.'

'You know all that stuff about reincarnation is dotty, don't you Grace?'

The challenge tightens Grace's chest. 'Maybe there's no one left.'

'What I don't understand is this, why have the Fishers held on to you for so long if *they* don't believe?'

'Maybe I'm better than nothing.'

Nancy reaches out for the saucer on the bedside table, stubs out the cigarette, lies down, turning her back. Grace wriggles down, not touching Nancy, but close enough to feel her warmth.

The bombers are close tonight.

It might seem mad, but reincarnation – surely – *must* be real. Kitty must on some level think Grace *is* her lost child. As Nancy said, why else would she keep her? And Grace would remember. And Hariti has always been so certain. Grace *has* to trust in Hariti.

Nancy reaches back, pulls Grace's arm around her, holds her hand between her breasts. Their bodies curve together under the candlewick bedspread.

Their ongoing search for Hariti has become aimless. They've tramped all the roads in the area but no one has seen her, not the shopkeepers, wardens, policemen. Grace and Nancy wander further east, into a chaotic landscape of broken roads and shattered buildings. The cinema is displaying posters each side of the foyer for *Gone With The Wind*.

'Grace, let's go in, I've been dying to see this picture. I love Scarlett O'Hara.'

'I'm not really in the mood, we should get back. Kitty—'

'We might all be dead tomorrow. My treat.'

Grace's feet are killing her, so she reluctantly follows Nancy to the ticket booth.

Inside the auditorium, thin spirals of smoke rise in the gloom. Nancy lights her cigarette. 'So many old people; don't they have homes to go to?'

'Hariti could be hiding in here for all we know.'

A man with rolled-up shirt sleeves climbs the steps onto the stage and shields his eyes against the spotlight. 'Ladies and gentlemen, we're sorry but we're 'avin' a bit of a problem with old Bertie our organ, he's makin' a lot of panting noises but we can't get him up.'

The crowd laughs, Grace is not sure why. She looks at Nancy who's also laughing.

'So, while we are trying to raise the organ, we'd be glad if anyone wants to get up on the stage and do their favourite party trick. Any of you young ladies down there?'

Hands shoot up. Two young girls climb onto the stage to sparse applause. One starts to sing with a surprisingly beautiful voice, '*I didn't sleep a wink last night*', and her friend begins to slowly take off her coat.

The crowd roars with laughter.

'Nancy, they can't be much older than twelve.'

'It's just a bit of fun.'

The girl's coat falls to the floor and she starts to unbutton her cardigan. '*Who's taking you home tonight?*'

The cardigan slips off the girl's shoulders. '*Who's holding you tight? And whisper, I love you, I do.*'

The girl starts to lift the hem of her skirt and the man rushes onto the stage to usher them off to whistles and clapping.

'Nancy, I have to get home. I'm sorry.'

Nancy grabs her coat. 'I'm coming, I'm coming.'

*

In Hyde Park, a crowd is standing around a man on a small wooden box, his voice hoarse from shouting. 'Make your peace with Jesus and you'll be allowed in to 'eaven.'

A bloated, elephant-grey barrage balloon is straining at a cable. Two men are cranking a winch.

'Nancy, the balloons are going up, it'll be the sirens next, people are already rushing towards the Tube.' Without warning, Grace is crying, covering her face with both hands. Nancy's arms around her. 'There, there, don't take on so. Hariti will return, I'm sure of it.'

'It's monstrous, the thought of her lying somewhere under rubble.' Sobs breaking her words. 'Even if ... she will be ... reborn.'

The sirens. For a moment they seem reluctant, as if exhausted from their nightly duty.

'Come on Grace, let's find shelter.'

They join the bustle at the Underground entrance. A woman carrying a crying baby pushes past them, turns and shouts to a scruffy child to keep up. A man in a bowler hat scowls. Down they all go, tramping like obedient ants on the long unmoving escalator.

At the bottom, a woman hands them each a rough blanket. 'Get yerself a cuppa over there, luvvie.'

They take their mugs and step over people already sitting against the curved tiled wall. Further along the platform there's a space under a poster encouraging people to enjoy their war work.

The wall is cold on Grace's back. Nancy is unusually quiet. This is not where Grace thought she'd die, in a tunnel with a random gathering of Londoners: men in uniforms, women with knotted headscarves, children squeezed between parents – some crying – and an overpowering smell of urine wafting in from the tunnels. Grace wonders who has to clean it all up in the morning.

Nancy stares across the void to the posters on the opposite wall. *Mothers. Send them out of London.* 'We'll be away from here in a day or two, bound for Rye.'

'I don't know. I can't leave with Hariti still missing. Kitty wouldn't manage?'

'You don't owe them anything. It's *your* life.'

'I've waited so long to be with you, Nancy.'

'We could have so much fun.'

'I need to keep looking, Hariti might need me.'

'You've been my best friend since the first day you came and sat at my little table in father's study. I'll look after you.'

'But if we don't find her …'

Grace sees him first, stepping over outstretched legs, heading towards them.

Nancy spots him, too. 'Now, *he's* a dish!'

A surge of confusion. What's he doing here? And what does Nancy mean, is she really interested in men or just pretending to be 'normal'?

The man leans over them, offers his hand. 'Good evening, Miss Fisher.'

She shakes his hand. 'Good evening, Mr Cornell. This is my friend Miss Lockhart.'

He offers his hand. 'How do you do.'

'I'm Nancy.'

'Christian names from the off, I like that. I'm Leyland.'

Nancy winks at Grace. 'So, how do you two know each other?'

It's so ridiculous that Grace has to laugh. 'He literally picked me up. Some time ago.'

The tea lady stands behind him, her voice surprisingly posh. 'May I interest you in tea?' She places the spout of a watering can to each of their mugs; milky brown liquid flows. 'That will be thruppence each please, unless you would like a confection.' Another woman with a basket strapped to her shoulders approaches. Leyland offers some coins. 'Ladies, you must let me buy you a bun.'

A distant thunder rumbles down the tunnel; the nervous babble stops for a moment. A baby screams. Grace moves closer to Nancy so that Leyland can squeeze in against the wall. Nancy pulls her blanket up and leans her head on Grace's shoulder. Grace's belly is cramping, she left the house totally unprepared.

Leyland offers a cigarette. Grace shakes her head. 'What will happen if a bomb hits a water main, or the river or something? Won't we all be flooded?'

'Then the end will be mercifully quick.'

'Drowning isn't quick.' She's imagined it, dreamed it, maybe even remembers it. But she can't tell him that, it would sound deranged. 'Aren't you supposed to be my guardian angel?'

'Seems that I'm fated to be just that.'

*

The dawn mist floats in patches accross the park. Their footsteps echo off broken walls. Nancy slides her arm through Grace's. 'What happened to Leyland?'

All night she'd been haunted by thoughts of water torrents flooding the dark tunnels. Leyland had put his arm around her and stroked her hair. She'd sobbed. It was silly. Why would such gentleness touch her so deeply?

They pass a gang of children pulling at strands of electric cable in the rubble.

'He left before the All Clear.'

Gradually, the districts become less damaged; a segue from disorder to harmony. They reach the house and close the front door carefully. There are no coats on the hall stand.

In the kitchen, Grace puts the kettle on the gas ring, picks up a bowl and starts to mix water into yellow powder, stirring with a large silver fork.

Nancy lifts the hem of her skirt, unclips a stocking from the suspenders, rolls it down to her ankles and scratches her leg.

'Are you itching too?' Grace stirs a grey mass in another pan. 'I bet it was the blankets.'

'What did you and your Leyland talk about?'

Grace adjusts the flame under the cast iron frying pan. 'He's not *my* Leyland. I don't like men, remember?'

'You'd be better off finding a steady one to look after you.'

'I love *you*.' The words had just come out unbidden. 'I'll never love a smelly old man.'

'He's nice, Grace. You'd have a chance to be acceptable.'

Grace has read all about childish infatuations in Kitty's *Woman* magazine, young girls drawn to female friends, but then in the fullness of time falling in love with a man. Nothing to worry about then. Anyway, she has her music. Nancy will leave; Grace has to be prepared. Be strong. She'll stay until Hariti returns. Then she'll be free. 'There's chloroform in the bathroom cupboard in a little blue bottle, dab that on your legs, it'll kill anything crawling up you.'

'Did you feel anything crawling up *your* leg last night?'

Grace waves the fork. 'Naughty Nancy!'

She divides the congealed yellow mixture and the grey mashed potato onto their plates.

Nancy sniffs and sprinkles salt. 'It smells like egg, anyway. Did I tell you I spoke to my father? I must be there before he goes, you know, handing over keys, showing me what's what and so on and so forth.'

'I thought we had a few more days.'

'Please say you'll come with me.'

'As soon as Hariti returns. I'll be there, in a flash.'

Nancy forks some of the egg. 'This is not half bad, you're full of surprises.'

'Anyway, you and me … this is just a childish—'

'Don't say it.'

They finish eating to the sound of forks scraping plates.

Grace refills the kettle. Nancy spoons tea from a caddy into the teapot. Grace puts two teacups onto saucers. 'We make a great team.'

'The perfect couple.'

'Still no sugar though.'

Nancy takes an apron off the hook. 'Whose gas mask box is this, Hariti's?' She ties the apron around her waist and opens the box. 'Powder compact, a small roll of notes in an elastic band, and lipstick – does Hariti use make-up?'

The cramps are tightening. 'It's probably Kitty's.'

'I guess Hariti took her own.'

'Kitty doesn't believe the Germans could ever do anything as uncivilised as gas England.'

'Grace, I'm going to come straight out with it. Don't you think it's a bit of a coincidence, Robert disappearing, then Hariti not long after?'

'Sorry Nancy, watch the kettle would you, I have to go to the bathroom, I'll bring the chloroform back down with me.'

March 1941

THEY SIT IN SILENCE on the top deck of the bus. Grace has no idea what she's done to offend Kitty. This morning a telegram arrived from Smith, apparently with news of Robert but she won't elaborate. Grace asked if there was mention of Hariti. Kitty shouted and slammed the door.

Grace often creeps into Hariti's room at night and sleeps in her bed. There's a lingering perfume on the pillow and the air in the dark room seems to carry the memory of her beautiful voice. It's hard to describe the magic. She loves her Bach and Mozart, and the passion of Beethoven, but Hariti's singing has no edges: it bubbles like a river flowing across time.

Kitty's hands rest on the crocodile handbag in her lap.

The bus stop-starts along the Embankment. Kitty has finally agreed to take her to Charing Cross Road to buy a pair of red ballet shoes for Nancy. Grace has been dreaming of getting them ever since she saw them in the shop window months ago, their red ribbons splayed out, one of the shoes turned over to show the pinched leather at the toe, like the rays of a red setting sun. Nancy will love them.

Kitty's handbag comes to life: a yawning mouth opens as she tucks away her bus ticket. The bombing raids have stopped but destruction is everywhere; at least the buses are getting through. Hitler, it seems, has turned his attention to the east.

Ahead, a rubbish cart is slowing the traffic. As it pulls up to the kerb, three men jump off and run into a yard to pick up bins. One is tall, with skin even darker than his rough brown leather jacket; he heaves a dustbin elegantly onto his shoulder and in a few steps reaches the cart and tips the rubbish out with such a flowing movement that

Grace imagines him on stage with Nancy: her long arms around him, pushing him away, then tempting him back.

The handbag's reptilian jaws open again and Kitty takes out a pink packet of cigarettes which – to Grace's irritation – she opens and shuts repeatedly.

'Grace, I really don't think you should be practising your music at a time like this, it makes us look like we have time to enjoy ourselves while all around people are suffering.'

'Don't worry, I'll be out of your hair as soon as we find—'

'There are better things you could do to help your country.'

Kitty has always seemed ambivalent about Grace's music, sometimes proud as if Grace were her real daughter, at other times irritated. Robert understood, he was a musician after all.

Her throat tightens; she mustn't cry in front of Kitty. 'I'll be going to Rye soon.'

'Now is not the time to go gallivanting. You could learn to knit, and anyway, while Hariti is away—'

'You make it sound like she's on holiday.'

'I know you miss her, but it really is nothing compared to the worry a wife feels for the safety of her absent husband.'

'You just want me to be your skivvy.'

'Well, that's gratitude. It's for your own good, Grace. Your papers—'

'Robert must have sorted all that out years ago.'

'You need to keep your head down.'

'This is our stop.' Grace leads the way down the winding stairs and jumps off the platform.

'It doesn't really make sense for you to be spending—'

'I don't need your money, I've saved enough playing for La Carluccia.' And, Grace thinks, for a train ticket.

The air is heavy with the odour of burnt dust; on the pavements, footprints in grey ash; and all around the sounds of scraping shovels, the brittle rhythm of hard brooms swishing, and the clatter of bricks falling into galvanised metal buckets.

They turn the corner.

'Kitty! The shop. It's gone.'

'It's probably just as well. Nancy has plenty of money, you don't need to spend yours on her.'

Grace can't stop the tears welling up.

'Please don't make a spectacle of yourself. It's just a pair of dancing shoes, for heaven's sake. People are putting up with far greater losses. You should be thankful you have a roof over your head.'

April 1941

'WHERE ARE YOU GOING, Grace? It's not safe.'

'For a walk.'

Kitty crosses her arms. 'It's getting late. I must say, you do look a little peaky, you might have the flu, there's a lot going around.'

'I'll be fine, you don't need to worry about me.'

'I don't approve of you standing around on street corners.'

'I was thinking of getting a job at the Windmill Theatre, from what I hear it's just a lot of standing around doing nothing.'

'*Grace.*'

'If you're interested, I'm going to listen to Mrs Hess at the National Gallery.'

'You'll need a shilling, and anyway it's Sunday.'

'Oh yes. There's a free art exhibition that'll be open. Don't worry about me.'

'But I do, Grace, you know I do.'

Grace gives up waiting for a bus and starts walking, it's only half an hour to Regent Street. Her head is aching, her throat is starting to tickle; perhaps Kitty is right but she just couldn't stay in the house a minute longer.

She pushes through the store's heavy doors. All the windows are boarded up, large ghostly sheets cover the counters and the smell of charred wood hangs in the air. A sign points to an exhibition in the basement. Halfway down the stairs she feels giddy and has to sit down. She picks up a lump of grey metal, it's smoothness is comforting in her palm.

Footsteps. 'How nice to meet you again, Miss Fisher.'

'Are you following me?'

'Don't you believe in fate?' Leyland Cornell sits down next to her.

She opens her hand. 'What do you think this is, it's like a tiny sculpture?'

'That's shrapnel: it can burn a hole clean through glass.'

She drops it.

'Do you remember the first time we met?'

'Of course. Blue sky, the smell of the grass on the embankment.' And Hariti's dark hair tickling her face. Thinking of her brings a surge of sadness; her peppery smell, her laugh.

'You've come to see the exhibition?'

'I felt a little faint, I don't usually drape myself on public steps.'

'Let me show you my work.'

'I didn't realise you were an artist.'

He stands. 'There's a lot about me—'

'I'm not sure I want to know.'

They go down. Rectangles of brilliant colour float away from the walls.

'This is my degenerate work: I won't last long when the Nazis arrive.'

Crudely painted marks, stabbed and slashed across a large canvas: gradually she starts to discern a human face, pained and distorted. She has no idea what to say. Sweat on her face, she has to concentrate to stop the room swaying.

'Grace? You look peaky.'

'Why did you say, *when the Nazis arrive*? We are winning the war.'

'That's what they want you to believe, but the Luftwaffe will soon control the sky. The sea and land will follow as sure as day follows night.'

'But the Navy—'

'The Americans believe democracy in Britain is in its last throes, Grace.'

'That's so defeatist, I'm surprised at you.'

'It's not the first time we've had a dictator. Read your history.'

'I *do* read history if you must know, you're so patronising.'

'Cromwell – that nice man who has a statue outside the Houses of Parliament – you celebrate him for overthrowing a useless king, but nothing that's happening in Europe compares to what he did to the Catholics in Ireland.'

'Well, I don't think that is actually true, but you can enlighten me more about that another time.'

'Let's get some air.' He leads her up into the darkening street. She shivers. Pale slits of light float by. Purring engines. Crunching gears.

The sirens stir.

She hears her own disembodied voice. 'No, no, not again.'

His arms around her. She pulls away. His voice gentle. 'You're safe with me.'

They go down into the Underground, stepping carefully around the battery of bodies. He lays out the blanket, pulls her down into the crook of his arm. She's never let a man come so close. His smell – sharp, gritty – makes her nervous.

*

They climb the steps into a fine morning mist tinged with a bitter taint of gas. He lights a cigarette. 'I have to go.'

'I don't know anything about you.'

'I am a lowly artist, a layabout, a dilettante.'

She laughs.

'That's more like it.'

'Why do our paths keep crossing?'

'I often come up to London to visit galleries, and friends. I have digs in Charing Cross but I work in my studio in an old cottage in Brede, that's in Sussex. That's all there is to know about me. And I'm thirty-one years old. And you?'

'And you are not a gentleman to be asking questions like that.'

'I'd guess you'd be eighteen.'

'Brede can't be all that far from Rye.'

'About twenty minutes on my motorbike, why do you ask?'

'I'd like to go to Rye one day soon.'

'Miss Lockhart?'

'You are very well informed.'

A dark green lorry speeds by, a red cross in a white circle flapping on its canvas side. In spite of war, birds are singing. The mist is slowly dispersing. Grace stares at the pavement, a memory is trying to break through. Sunlight sharpens their shadows.

'I'm sorry, I really must go. Mrs Fisher will be—'

'Grace, wait.' He puts his hands each side of her face and kisses her forehead. 'Be ready, won't you.'

She's not sure if she's being kissed as a child or a woman. 'I'm fine, I can find my own way home.'

'I didn't mean that. Things are going to be very different.'

Across the street, three men are rolling up a hose along the gutter.

'I can look after myself.'

He walks away quickly, as if he can't wait to be rid of the responsibility of her.

'And I'm nearly twenty-one if you must know!'

He raises his hand but doesn't turn around.

She leans against a brick wall. Strangely, heat radiates from it.

It's difficult to work out which way to go, the street names were removed years ago. Forlorn traffic lights go through their sequence but there are no vehicles to obey them. Laughter behind her: two dirty children pushing a pram with scrap metal piled in it. She asks the way to the river and they point, calling her 'Miss'.

May 1941

A TELEGRAM FROM RYE. *Coming?*

Grace yearns to go to Nancy, but she's trapped. More than once, Kitty has hinted at the validity of Grace's identity papers.

She picks up the telephone receiver but the line is dead, again.

*

Spring has arrived at last; the Earth is tilting towards the sun, hinting at warmer days, but Grace doesn't feel hopeful. She lies awake at night worrying about Nancy: her terse telegram could be a cry for help. And there's been no news of Hariti. Smith has informed Kitty that Robert is on a secret mission. It's been over four months. Smith drops in now and then. Whispered conversations are always conducted behind closed doors.

There's no sign of an end to war. The wireless is constantly calling for women to volunteer for the Wrens, the WAAFs or the ATS. Grace is left behind, washed up on a shore. Able-bodied women are engaged in meaningful work, others are at home, living in fear of the postman delivering the dreaded telegram, a few typed characters on thin strips of paper glued to a form.

The tin opener has become the most precious tool in the house. Rationing is getting tighter. For months before the war, Robert had laid in stores in the basement: tins of spam and fruit as well as toilet rolls and hundreds of packets of cigarettes and pipe tobacco. At first, Grace hadn't understood why he had put crates filled with sand down there, until one day she'd dug her fingers into the cold grit and found wrinkly carrots and beetroots. Tears had rolled down her cheeks.

*

As usual, Kitty is in Robert's chair, the ball of wool on the rug rolling further away with each tug of her clicking needles. She makes a mistake. 'Oh bloody hell.' Click-click, click-click.

Grace pulls out a dining chair, feeling woozy with her monthly pains. She closes her eyes for a moment. When she opens them, the room is silent but for the ticking of the grandfather clock from the hall. Kitty's head has slumped onto the wing of the armchair.

She loves the ritual: sliding out the cello's spike, tightening the nut, taking up the weight and resting the body between her legs. She hasn't tuned it for months. She gently plucks the strings, adjusts the furled nuts to bring them into perfect fifths. Mathematical. Reassuring. She takes up the bow, pauses, ready to bring Bach into the room.

Kitty wakes, grimaces. 'I told you, Grace, about playing music.'

Grace draws the bow with force over the thick C string.

'*GRACE.*'

Grace controls her shaking, lays the cello on its side, stands, a volcano of anger inside – daren't let it go, must hold the line, if she breaks, her world will fall apart.

*

Most days she walks the streets – usually early in the morning – going into shops, forlornly hoping to hear some gossip about Hariti. Some shops are boarded up and dark inside, some are open to the street, glass swept against piles of bricks. London hasn't been bombed for a while now: Göring has turned his attention to Liverpool, Belfast, Hull and Nottingham.

*

Grace's fingernails are always well trimmed. Every day, she conjures up an imaginary keyboard on her desk or the kitchen table, and her fingers make a ghostly tapping sound as they move to an imaginary score. When the war finally ends, her arpeggios will be as fluid as they were before the world went mad. And if the Germans win – which looks increasingly likely – she can entertain them with their fellow countrymen: Bach, Mozart, Beethoven.

Kitty has abandoned the elegance of the cigarette holder. In the morning, Grace often finds her curled up on the sofa, awake, staring ahead, smoke rising lazily from the ashtray.

Although it's late spring, the house is freezing cold. Grace searches everywhere for things to burn: she manages to tear down wooden panels from a partition wall in the basement, and in a dusty corner a rickety chair that she reduces to sticks with the hatchet. She makes the fire with layers of old newspapers, wood, and a few precious lumps of coal.

Kitty watches silently.

'There's a cot in the basement, I could chop that up next.'

'Touch that on peril of your life.'

… inky black … thorns gripping her tight … she touches her head where it hurts … wet on fingers … rustling … wait, wait … nothing. Hooting. O for Owl …

TAP-TAP. HAD IT BEEN in her dream? Then she hears it again: tap-tap. She creeps down stairs. The fire is out. For once, Kitty has gone to bed. Tap-tap coming from the back door. Grace crosses the kitchen, the flagstones freezing to her bare feet, and hesitates. She must answer, it might be Hariti, home from some terrible ordeal. She slides back the bolts as quietly as possible.

She can't repress the disappointed 'Oh, it's you.'

Leyland steps inside. 'I'm sorry, I need to see you.'

She leads him upstairs, shivers and gets back into bed.

He lies on top of the bedspread. 'You're safe with me, Grace.'

'I doubt that!'

'I've been looking for your Indian.'

'What! You didn't tell me.'

'I didn't want to raise your hopes.'

'Have you—'

'I'm sorry, no. But I don't believe she's dead. I think your Mr Smith knows something. Ask him next time you see him. He has a reputation for poking his nose in where it's not welcome.'

'Does he know you?'

'I shouldn't be here.'

'What have you been up to, Leyland?'

'I don't want to get you into trouble. If he ever asks—'

'I'm not about to admit I've had a strange Irishman in my bedroom, now am I?'

'I'll be gone before dawn.'

A TERRIBLE DUST SEEPS into the house: under the doors, around the draughty sash windows, through the keyhole. The dust of dereliction.

Beneath a blanket of boredom, Grace is constantly tense. Every second of the day she's waiting, trying not to think of the terror that will bring an end to existence. Staring into the pitch black of night, she imagines German tanks smashing through the front door, crushing the walls to rubble, caterpillar tracks trundling across the Victorian terracotta floor tiles.

Kitty still believes the Germans to be a civilised race; that when they arrive, they will respect good breeding.

The sirens have been quiet for a while, but now and then their howl reawakens to haunt the London streets, soon to be followed by the dreaded drone in the dark skies.

Kitty's knitting needles click relentlessly.

The hatchet is Grace's nightly companion, resting on the little table by the ballerina lamp in case of emergency. She has no idea if she'll have the courage to fight hand to hand if, or when, the time comes.

*

Tonight she's with Kitty in the sitting room, staring into the dwindling fire. A low hum punctuated by a rumbling bass, the boom of anti-aircraft guns, but still they come: the Luftwaffe is determined tonight.

She looks across at the bureau, passed down through generations of Fishers, its roll top closed, the little drawer inside locked. The truth of her past, perhaps, contained within an envelope marked *Grace?*. But does she really want to know? Maybe a bomb will solve all her problems: piercing the attic roof, descending through the layers of the house, smashing the bureau on its way to the basement, before detonating and sending her into her next life where a new story can begin.

Near dawn, the distant throbbing recedes, lowering a quarter-tone.

Grace gets up, leans on the piano and writes in the dust on the lid: 'B A C H'.

Another drone, broken away from the chorus, intensifying. It must be right overhead.

Kitty stops knitting.

Grace holds her breath.

The blackout curtain explodes.

All the atoms of her body shift sideways.

Shattered glass flies across the room.

Muffled sound.

A fog of choking dust.

Slowly, slowly, the room clears.

Kitty is sitting rigid in the armchair. Is she dead?

'Oh my god, Kitty, are you …' Tiny cuts bleed through the macabre grey dust covering her face and arms. Kitty slowly raises her hand, points to the sofa. Harpooned into the back – where Grace had been sitting a few moments before – is a wooden stake, a short piece of sash cord dangling from it.

Grace runs to the kitchen, finds the tweezers and iodine, rushes back to kneel in front of Kitty and gently picks shards of glass from flesh. She dabs the cuts with iodine. Kitty looks so old: she must be in shock, not flinching at what must be a painful operation. She mumbles sometimes about her beloved Clara and then whispers: 'Oliver'. The poor woman is covered in bleeding yellow patches that look like blood spots in egg yolk.

In the faint light of dawn, Leyland steps through the tattered curtains with a claw hammer. He brings wooden planks from the basement, straightens nails, and hammers boards across the window. All the time he's humming. She can't place the song.

Kitty comes out of her stupor. 'Young man, we are not afraid of the Germans.'

'You should be.'

He accepts a mug of tea in the kitchen.

'What's that song you were humming? It's familiar.'

He puts both hands around the mug and to Grace's surprise, starts to sing, *She walks through the fair* …

Then, before Grace can thank him, he wipes tears off her dusty face, kisses her forehead and leaves through the back door.

Kitty asks, 'Who was that man?'

'That was Leyland Cornell.'

'I'm sure I've heard that name before.'

SIX

Croydon
2000

A WHITE CLOCK FACE: a thin black finger hiccupping the seconds. People gathered at the bottom of her bed. Someone holds a chart: 'Your mother has a strong will to survive.'

They are all fools. She's happy to die, start again. She's not afraid.

A nurse leans over, acrid sweat. 'Hello sweetie, how are you doing?'

Grace seems unable to move.

'You're going to dance out of here, don't you worry.'

Grace isn't worried.

'Well, I can't stand around chatting.' The nurse tugs at the sheet, pulling it timpani-tight.

*

A nurse enters backwards, pushing the door open with her bottom and carrying a jug of flowers. Grace watches her easy, flowing movements as she leans over a table, making wide sweeps with a yellow cloth.

*

How is anyone meant to sleep? So much noise. She grunts.

*

A nurse in a blue uniform loooking over the shoulder of a woman in a white coat. They're studying that chart again; what's so interesting? White coat woman leaves without once glancing at Grace. The nurse fiddles with something at the side of the bed. Grace's sense of smell is sharp and she doesn't like what she's detecting: sweet, pungent pee. It can't be her. She's always so careful.

It's time.
To be released.

*

A warm flannel on her face. Relief on the right side and tingling on the left. It seems her tired brain has decided not to die after all. The nurse looks like Nancy: a great mop of red hair tied back. She speaks to the man. It's Orlando.

He paces like a caged animal, from door to window, back to door. He looks over to her then slumps into an empty wheelchair, rocks forward and back, the front wheels spinning anxiously.

*

All Things Bright and Beautiful.

*

Hariti helped her understand. A bit jumbled again now. So, so long ago, but it still comes into her dreams. Fire. Water.

*

… she's being lifted … opens her eyes, it's him, of course it is … a girl's black hair tickling her face … sweet perfume of coconut … voice nutmeg brown …

Orlando is sitting on the side of the bed, holding a bowl under her chin. 'Mother, drink this.' He spoons liquid between her lips. 'It's your favourite. Mulligatawny.'

For all she knows, he could be poisoning her. She'll just have to trust and swallow. He wipes the spoon across her mouth, like good mothers do with their toddlers; not that Grace ever did that for him.

He walks over to his duffle bag, brings out a tape player-recorder thing, places it on the window sill, take a cassette from a plastic case and rattles it into the recorder. He snaps it shut and presses a button.

Oh bliss! Her cello … she would recognise its tone anywhere. Bach. But who's playing? There was a time … Nancy threading tape from one reel to another and pressing white and red ivory buttons. Of course, it's her. She's overwhelmed with pity for the poor woman who had no idea of the beauty she was creating.

Chelsea
June 1943

SHE LEANS ON THE GRANITE WALL. Somewhere around here is where she's supposed to have fallen. It's hard to imagine, the river is so low.

It's the longest day: her birthday, according to Hariti. Kitty didn't mention it this morning; if Robert had been here, he would have remembered. It's been two years since he left on a secret mission, and Hariti disappeared. Smith – so it seems to Grace – knows more than he admits behind his pretence of sympathy. Her hopes of ever leaving for Rye have evaporated. And still the war drags on.

She turns from the river. Three young women in blue overalls, laughing, probably just finishing a shift. Grace can smell engine oil as they pass. A queue snakes around a corner. She joins it, her wicker basket empty. On the wall opposite, between two sandbag buttresses, a poster: an injured soldier on his knees. *Your Blood Can Save Him.* She stares down at her tight leather shoes.

*

Kitty's cheery voice calls from the dining room. 'Grace, could you come and help me please?'

Grace puts the basket on the marble top next to the telephone.

The dining table is covered in an old blanket, and an assortment of jam jars is spread out on it. With one hand, Kitty is holding one of the lids on the bread board, with the other, her scissors.

'Robert showed me how to make these lamps in India. Sit down, Grace, and I'll show you.' She stabs the lid, making a slit. 'Just thread the bandages through the holes like this.'

Grace mimics her, glad of a moment of calm between them.

Kitty pours paraffin from a bottle into each jar, then pushes the tails of the bandages into the purple fluid. 'Oliver will approve, I'm sure.' She screws on the tops.

'Smith is coming?'

'*Mr* Smith. No need to be so common.'

'I know you look up to him.'

'It's for your birthday—'

'No need to make a fuss.'

'It's not a big one, is it? You've had your twenty-first?'

Strange question for a mother to ask. 'I'm twenty-three.'

'Marvellous. I'm afraid Oliver has meetings so he'll be late. I thought you'd like it, he's a good friend of your father's. And do make make an effort and put on a nice dress.'

*

Weak sunlight angles through the high basement window. The air is tainted with coal dust in spite of their not having had a delivery for months. Military music from the sitting room above – Kitty must be feeling patriotic today. Grace takes up the hatchet and hacks at an old broken rosewood dining chair. She gathers the pieces, goes back to the sitting room, kneels on the rug and starts making up the fire. From the firewood basket she picks out an old *Picture Post* – a smiling 'clippie' with a ticket machine – and rips at the pages, scrunching them to make a bed for the sticks.

Click-click, click-click. Kitty tugs at the ball of wool, her mouth tight.

'I was thinking, I should get a job.'

'You know you can't do that, Grace.'

'I must be the only one in London doing nothing.'

'Don't make me spell out the legal complications.'

In truth, Grace doesn't really understand. She has a ration book so she must be in the records. She strikes a match. 'Must we listen to this dirge?'

'Please don't be so uncouth in my house.'

The doorbell rings. Kitty pokes her needles into the knitting and gets up. 'Come and welcome Oliver.'

Smith takes Kitty's hand in both of his. 'My dear, how *are* you?'

'I'm afraid we are not equipped to give you a proper welcome, Grace says the butcher was clean out today.'

Smith offers Grace a bunch of white flowers. 'They are called edelweiss, it means noble white.'

'Thank you, Mr Smith.'

'How you have grown. Look at your hair, it's so long. The colour of honey, you must be so proud of her Kitty.' He eases his coat off, holds it out to Grace.

Kitty turns to the kitchen. 'Oh dear, the cabbage is burning. Grace, see if you can find Oliver some of our elderberry wine from last year while I rescue the supper.'

'No need, Kitty dear, I have liberated a bottle.'

Grace hangs his coat on the hall stand, leads him into the sitting room. The lights go out. Firelight flickers. The walls close in.

Kitty calls from the kitchen. 'Light the lamps, Grace, there's a good girl.'

Snapping Kitty's lighter, Grace holds the flame to each of the hungry, paraffin-soaked ears.

Kitty carries in the bone china gravy boat. 'Oliver, I am so sorry about the electricity, it's been on and off for weeks.'

'You always were very resourceful, Kitty.'

Smith assumes Robert's position at the head of the table. There's an awkward silence and Grace wonders if Kitty is about to say a prayer.

Smith reaches for the serving spoon. 'Allow me.' He dollops

mashed potato, carrot and cabbage onto Kitty's plate, then Grace's, then his own.

Kitty pours thin brown liquid from a gravy boat that's not seen the light of day for years. 'At least this should be nutritious, it's made with bone marrow.'

Grace clears her throat. 'Mr Smith, you work for the government, don't you?'

Smith lifts the salt shaker. 'Yes, Grace. But I can't talk—'

'I'm surprised that someone in your position can't find out anything about—'

'Grace!' Kitty looks flushed. 'Don't forget your manners.'

Smith laughs. 'She has spirit, Kitty. I like that.'

'It must be the people she's mixing with.'

'Don't you think she should know?'

Kitty stares down at the congealed mess on her plate.

Smith reaches over the table to rest his hand on Grace's arm. 'Robert has returned to India.'

'*What?*'

'Kitty has known for a while. It's all rather hush—'

Grace stands up, throws her napkin onto the table. 'Don't you dare tell me there's a war on.'

Smith slides his fork into the grey mash on his plate. 'While he's away, Robert asked me to look after you. Think of me as a substitute father, Grace. It's what he wanted.'

Kitty draws a handkerchief from her sleeve, her voice gentle. 'Grace. Do sit back down with us, please. Oliver has been putting in a lot of effort to find Hariti, you should be grateful.'

Smith chews, swallows. His voice soft and friendly. 'These are complicated times. I strongly advise you to stay here, stop asking questions and stop drawing attention to yourself. You could bring trouble down on us all.'

October 1943

GRACE PULLS A JUMPER on over her nightdress: she knows it's slovenly but her fresh clothes are too cold to put against her skin. She sits at her little desk. It's morbid letting her life slip away in this room, looking back through old newspapers, searching for clues, but to what? Hariti, of course, but it's more. Young women across the land have been conscripted but she's never received call-up papers. No doubt Smith's doing. She'd considered joining the Land Army but Kitty was angry, said she must stay in London, and anyway, the work would hurt her hands and she might never play music again. If she were a more accomplished musician Grace could give concerts, but she'll never improve without practice.

Words float up from the cuttings: Sarajoglu, Kiosseivanov, Dobrudja. Pictures seems to layer upon each other. A Nazi bomber crew. An old fisherman with a huge white beard.

The doorbell dances in the hall. Grace quickly goes downstairs. For a mad moment she feels a tingling excitement, remembering the way Hariti talked about *kundalini*: spirit energy, rising up through her body.

'Good morning, Grace. I have brought you a present.'

'Oh. Mr Smith.'

'You must call me Oliver.' He steps forward, forcing her to step back. 'Kitty isn't—'

And now she sees it, on the end of a long piece of string, a puppy the colour of pale caramel. She crouches down and it wags its tail furiously, a thin stream of pee flowing over the tiles.

'He needs someone to look after him, and I believe you have time on your hands.'

'I couldn't Mr Smith, I'll be leaving—'

'My dear,' he undoes his coat, 'the poor creature will have to be put down if you refuse to take him.'

'I'm volunteering for the Land Army. I'll be posted away. There will be no one at home to look after—'

'I know that is not true, Grace.' He holds out the end of the string.

She senses the threat in his voice. 'I have every intention—'

'I told you not to draw attention to yourself. To any of us.'

'Mr Smith, you may have sway over other members of my family—'

'Ah! Isn't that the point? *Is* it your family?'

She takes the string.

'Good girl. And in return, I will have some of that elderberry wine that you were going to offer me before.'

She follows him into the sitting room. 'I really have no idea how to look after a dog.'

'I'd tie him up, we don't want a mess on your father's carpet.'

She follows the instruction, resentfully wrapping the string around the door handle.

Smith sits heavily on the sofa. 'I know you are concerned for Robert.'

She unscrews a bottle, pours the wine, passes him a glass, and leans against the corner of Robert's bureau.

'But don't worry, he's doing important work.'

Staring at the patterns in the carpet, she realises for the first time that the angular lines actually depict animals and human figures, like paper cut-out doilies. How strange she's never noticed it before. 'Why is it all cloaked in such secrecy? I know you can't say much, but why did you keep Kitty in the dark for so long?'

Smith stands up, takes the wine bottle and tops up his glass. 'I must admit, this is surprisingly good. Why don't you have some?'

He's standing too close. There's a sour layer under his scent. Grace turns away, folds her arms, stares out of the window at the narrow strips of flower beds that now host poles and the withered remains of runner beans. A black car passes. A camouflaged lorry follows.

'I must go to my room now. I'm sure Kitty will be back soon, Mr Smith.'

He unbuttons his waistcoat, holds the glass up to the light: an affectation that makes her want to laugh.

The puppy whines; little black eyes staring at Grace.

'What will you call him?'

She knows without giving it a second thought. 'Sancho'.

The puppy wags his tail.

'You are very fortunate you know, Grace, to have been rescued by the Fishers.'

Grace wants to argue that it was Leyland Cornell who lifted her up and carried her to safety. And Hariti who cared for her.

Smith's blue eyes feel like searchlights on her. 'I'll see myself out, Grace.'

December 1943

CHRISTMAS DAY. SHE'S WOKEN from another nightmare: her bed was on fire, floating in a vast sea, slowly sinking. She yearns to feel Hariti's arms lifting her, carrying her to the warm spot in her bed. Half asleep, she wanders to Hariti's room, finds her pyjamas under the pillow and changes into them: soft cotton top and a drawstring to tighten the baggy bottoms. She's feeling belligerent so keeps the pyjamas on to go downstairs. She expects to be told off – with a raised eyebrow at least – but Kitty is sitting at Robert's bureau sorting papers. She looks up and smiles. 'You look nice, darling.' The fire crackles. It's usually Grace's responsibility to light it.

Sancho's claws click-click on the tiles in the hall; his cool nose nudges Grace's hand.

Kitty stabs a letter onto a vicious spike then picks up a square, flat package. 'Darling, put on my new gramophone record would you?'

Grace is staggered: standards really *are* slipping. Grace removes the brown wrapping paper. A Decca record, a swag with the words 'Christmas Songs' over a red bell.

'Oliver is bringing a turkey around this afternoon.'

'How on earth—'

'We will all come through this in the end, Grace. Now, the record if you please.'

Grace slides the disc out of its sleeve; she still finds it extraordinary how just a fine groove cut in black shellac can hold – silently – the secret of sound. She winds the side handle and angles the needle.

'Oh darling, please, not that dreadful song, put on the next one.'

Grace turns the record over. 'I'm going to try phoning Nancy this afternoon.' She hasn't heard from her for an age, in spite of writing to her every month. She's probably taken up with some GI or other.

'That's nice, dear. Give her my regards.'

Sancho settles in front of the fire. Kitty takes her place in the armchair as the mournful voice fills the room. She closes her eyes and starts to sing. '*Stille Nacht, heilige Nacht, Alles schläft; einsam wacht…*'

March 1944

LEYLAND HAD COME AGAIN in the night. Sancho's barking hadn't roused Kitty: she must have been out on her secret war work or deeply asleep. He followed Grace up the stairs, kissed her forehead, made some excuse about being locked out of his digs and fell asleep as soon as he'd slumped into the armchair. He left as pale pink tinged the edges of ribbon clouds; the pillow on the back of the armchair showing the ghostly indentation of his head.

*

Wearing Hariti's pyjamas, Grace sits at her little desk, stares out at the grey sky. The early morning promise of sunshine has dissipated. She'd better try to finish reading her book – a history of Western civilisation – but the world feels so criminally insane that it all seems pointless. The Red Army is making gains, the Americans are bombing Berlin, Churchill has announced he's isolating Ireland to contain anti-Allied sentiments. She wonders how Leyland will feel about that: being neutral must be difficult. Some Irish have joined the fight against the Nazis, but the Irish accent isn't exactly popular in England just now.

Sancho is barking. The front door slams. Odd. It can't be Kitty, she always closes the door carefully. Maybe she left on one of her mysterious missions in a bad mood.

Heavy footsteps on the stairs. She shudders, instinctively looks around for a weapon. Her silver scissors are lying next to a newspaper cutting.

A knock. The door creaks. 'Good morning, Grace.'

She doesn't turn around: what a bloody nerve Smith has coming up to her room when she's alone in the house. The latch on the window is rusty. It would be her only escape. She imagines floating like a bird, circling down to the dark water.

'Is there anything wrong?'

Squawking gulls wheel in a dogfight above a two-masted boat. 'Should you be coming up to my bedroom uninvited, Mr Smith?'

He drags a chair across the room. 'You need some fresh air: why don't you go out, walk the dog around your back garden. What did you name him, again?'

'I'm fine, thank you.'

He rolls up his white shirt sleeves. 'Grace, you are clearly an intelligent girl, and you take an interest in what is going on in the world.'

He's too close; horrid sweat, overlaid with a strangely flowery scent. She gets up and sits on the end of her bed.

He pulls something out of his pocket. 'You need to be careful.' She realises he is holding her National Registration Identity Card.

'Where did you ... give it back to me.'

'I asked Kitty to let me see it. Robert was well connected. Actually, I'm rather impressed, I wouldn't have thought he had it in him.'

'What are you saying?'

He gets up, tapping the card in the palm of his hand. 'You really don't understand, do you?'

'You have no right.' She grabs for the card.

He steps back. 'Gently, Grace.'

The scene is so ludicrous she has to laugh.

'You need to be careful. Shopkeepers might not see through it, but if anyone were to look more closely ... you know the authorities are on constant alert for fifth columnists. We aren't only at war with Germany. There are people with a different agenda. Are you following me?'

And now the penny drops. 'I have no idea who—'

'The Irish, for example.'

'I haven't a clue—'

'Take care who you choose to mix with. I wouldn't want to see you on the wrong side by association. Penalties can be harsh.'

He examines the card, melodramatically holding it up to the light. 'Stay at home, speak to no one, wait out the war. You should concern yourself with your music, that is where you'll find peace. I have left some boxes of tinned food in the hall, dried meat, bones for the dog.'

'Please don't feel you have to use up your precious rations.' She knows she shouldn't goad him, he could – evidently – cause her a lot of trouble.

'I'll have some coal delivered.' He puts a hand on her shoulder. 'I have to go away for a while. Don't worry, others are keeping an eye on you.'

She takes a deep breath. 'Have you any information about Hariti?'

His laugh is disconcerting. 'You imagine I have more influence than I have, my dear, I'm just a servant, doing my best for you and Kitty.'

Grace stares at his black shoes, forces herself to look up. Maybe she's underestimated him.

'You will take care, won't you?'

The door latch drops back into place.

July 1944

A GOLDEN SUN SINKS slowly behind the city skyline. From chimneys all over the city smoke rises straight, each representing a hearth, and around each fire – she imagines – a family: every one with its story, secrets, pain, loss; a tireless, relentless cycle. Maybe one of those hearths in this smouldering city is home to Hariti. It's wishful thinking: in her heart Grace knows Hariti would never have just got up and gone, leaving her alone.

Day dies, night is born, night dies. Is there no escape? Hariti would say there is: *moksha*.

*

Grace wakes, a scream in her head. Another nightmare: the same old theme, but this time she was staggering through a field of brittle yellow stalks taller than her … again, being chased … dazzling heat … her hands and feet bleeding.

She hears it again … so it wasn't in her dream. A moaning, it's coming from downstairs. She reaches for her dressing gown, lights a candle; flickering shadows as she goes down the stairs. Kitty is sitting up in bed, rocking, the ends of her hair catching in the iron bed frame. She looks like a spectre, her eyes staring ahead. She's moaning incoherently. A repeated name: Oliver.

'I'll telephone him, Kitty, don't worry.'

*

Sitting on the stairs. The clock unhurriedly measures more than an hour. A car braking, a door slamming. She hadn't needed to wait up:

he has a key. In his hand a blue ribbed-glass bottle. He climbs the stairs ahead of Grace and closes Kitty's door, shutting her out.

Back in her room, Grace turns on the ballerina lamp. She'd better close the curtains.

August 1944

THE DOORBELL JANGLES. Sancho raises his head, growls. Kitty brushes floury hands on her apron and rushes out. Grace fills the dog's drinking bowl from the tap. Smith seems in a good mood, places his briefcase on a chair, bends to stroke Sancho's neck. 'Grace is looking after you, I see.'

Grace rests her hands on the lifeless lump of bread dough. 'Why ring the bell, Mr Smith? You have a key.'

Kitty slides the kettle onto the gas ring. 'Oliver has it for emergencies.'

Smith takes off his jacket, drapes it over the back of a chair. 'How are you, Grace?'

She punches the dough. 'I'm fine, thank you, Mr Smith. How is your war?'

'The end is in sight.'

'Tell that to the people sitting under the doodlebugs.'

Kitty turns. 'Grace! Manners, please.'

'I'm sure Mr Smith can take a playful challenge from me.'

'Well as long as that's all it is. I'm so sorry, Oliver, I've no idea what's got into her these days.'

A placating smile. 'I'm sure it's hard for her, being confined all this time.'

Grace cuts the dough into six pieces.

Kitty pours boiling water into the best teapot. 'Grace, be a good girl and get down the cups and saucers, please.'

Smith holds the back of a chair. 'Kitty. I've come with news. Obviously, I can't say much, but I *can* tell you that Robert is out of danger and should be coming home soon.'

Kitty tugs at her apron strings. 'I'm sorry, Oliver, I've just remembered, I have to collect something from the butcher before he closes.'

'I could walk you—'

'No, no, it's all right, Grace will entertain you.'

Why the drama? Kitty should be happy, surely. Smith is only trying to help.

The front door slams.

Smith pulls out a chair. 'But no sightings of your Indian friend, I'm afraid.'

'I have some reading to do, Mr Smith, please let yourself out.' She places a tea towel over the rolls and heads for the stairs.

*

Tension in the sky. Cumulonimbus, a dark underbelly heavy with rain.

The stairs creak. Quick, firm footsteps. The latch clicks.

'Grace, we need to talk. There are things you need to understand.'

He puts his briefcase on the bed, throws his jacket next to it; the sleeves fall open, crucified on the pink bedspread. 'Your father has had a difficult time.'

'You know, don't you? Why he disappeared. Why Hariti—'

'All I am prepared to say is that he had a moment of moral weakness. Then he returned to India, to serve his country.'

'I don't understand.'

'You will, one day.'

'But Hariti?'

'I also have to tell you that Robert is not well. The Japanese … I can't explain more than to say he's being shipped home.'

'Oh god. Will he be all right?'

'I'll make sure you are looked after. I'm around for the next few days. I have arrangements to make.' He sits on the bed, strokes the cover. 'Have you seen your friend, Mr Cornell?'

The change of subject catches her out, she feels her face reddening as if in guilt for a crime she hasn't committed. 'I haven't seen him for

… I don't know how long. And he isn't my friend, as you say, he simply rescued me—'

'I hear your Miss Lockhart is in Sussex.'

Grace feels her pulse quickening. 'She's neutral. You can't touch her.'

He laughs. 'Grace, you have some strange ideas about me.' He opens his briefcase, takes out a pile of magazines and drops them on top of the cuttings on her desk. 'I saw these and thought of you.'

Life magazines: ironic in a world of perpetual death.

He picks up his jacket, smooths it over his arm. 'I hope in time you will learn to trust me, Grace.'

KITTY HAS GONE WITH SMITH to Waterloo Station. Robert's return means Grace will be free at last, free to go to Nancy. But first there's the locked drawer. She's confused. All these years she's suspected it contains a secret about who she really is … but what if it's nothing, as Robert once said? She's always needed to trust in him. But what if … if she isn't Grace? She'd have no right to be in this family, in this story, in Hariti's life. And isn't trying to find the letter a betrayal of Hariti, a rejection of *her* beliefs?

She tugs at the bureau's roll top. With no idea what she'll do if she does manage to find the key, she searches the room: on the mantelpiece, in the cigar box on the side table, in Kitty's knitting basket. Sancho pricks up his ears as she curses. She starts up the stairs, but before she is halfway up she hears a car pulling up outside. She's familiar with the way Smith's Austin splutters as the engine cuts out. Voices. Keys rattling. Any second, Robert will step over the threshold, put his hat on the hook, slide his walking cane into the umbrella stand and give her that secret smile he saves just for her. And she'll feel she belongs again.

Sancho whines, sniffing at the letterbox.

The lock turns. Robert stumbles as he enters. He's shockingly thin and almost bald. Kitty is holding his shaking arm. He stares at the floor.

Smith takes his other arm and they lead him into the sitting room. They turn him around and he folds into his chair like a pocket knife.

*

For days she stays in her room, venturing downstairs only to find morsels of food or to let the dog out into the back garden. Closed doors. Whispers on the landing at night.

*

Grace needs the toilet. She clicks on the ballerina lamp and lights a candle for the dark stairs. As she reaches the landing, a bedroom door opens. Robert – head down – is shuffling forward on his stick. He's making no attempt to cover up a yawning gap at the front of his blue-and-white-striped pyjama bottoms. He opens the toilet door, turns on the light.

She sits on the attic stairs and waits. From downstairs, faint dance music on the wireless. Kitty is talking excitedly. Smith laughing.

Roaring water flushes. Robert leaves the toilet door open and the light on: he's forgotten his pyjama bottoms. Tap, tap.

Kitty is climbing the stairs. 'Robert?'

Tap, tap.

She hurries along the landing carpet. 'Oh dear, Robert, darling. Look at you. Let's get you back to bed.'

In the toilet, Grace locks the door and lowers the seat.

Cheyne Walk, Chelsea
21st August 1944

My dearest Nancy,

I love your postcard: that silly seagull perched on an angel's head! And thank you for the birthday message, even if somewhat belated! I miss you too and worry so much about you.

And now – as they say on the wireless – Here is the News from London.

Robert is home! At least he was, but he was not at all well. He didn't speak except to swear loudly at the most inappropriate moments. Kitty has been distraught. In the end, Smith arranged for him to be admitted to a special hospital.

Hariti is not home, alas, although Smith believes she's alive. When I think back, I know you were right all those years ago, you sensed something between Hariti and Robert.

I am so sorry I haven't been able to come to you but I will as soon as I can.

We hear news of the Allies in France. The beginning of the end, surely.

I have to admit Smith has been a good friend to the Fishers, in spite of my initial distrust. His loyalty has been quite impressive. It would have been very hard without a man around.

And talking of men, I was thinking of that Leyland Cornell the other day. You'll remember him, no doubt. I think you took a shine to him.

I'm staring out over the Thames wishing I could spread my wings and fly over the rooftops, across the sea to you. I'm glad you are out of London. It's horrid with those evil bombs. Have you heard? They sound like a lorry with a noisy engine and when they run out of fuel they simply fall to the ground. It's all rather terrifying. I was queuing at the shop a few days ago and we heard one coming. We all looked up and watched it heading for us. We knew if the engine stopped it would fall on our heads, and that would be the end of that. It spluttered overhead. I daren't think where it eventually landed but we heard the explosion half a minute later. No one in the queue said anything. We all knew we felt the same thing.

People are sending their children away again. Such heartache. Why doesn't that vile man realise he'll never win?

I must finish this letter.

Now I feel sad. Write to me!

Grace x

SITTING IN A POOL OF LIGHT from the desk lamp, Grace searches the magazines for pictures of animals. She doesn't know why, she finds them comforting: life beyond the madness of men, she supposes. The King with his corgis at his feet.

She picks up her scissors.

Smith had arrived earlier, clutching his blue bottle of medicine. Grace had expected Kitty's good mood to last, but the terrors have returned. It must be awful to have had Robert back, then taken away again. Thank god Smith can come around so quickly. What devils must be in Kitty's poor head.

She hears it. The unmistakable creak of the fourth step. She turns the lamp off.

Silence.

Another faint creak.

Silence.

Her eyes are fizzing with spots of light in the total blackout of the room. She must have imagined it. She lets out her breath.

The latch.

'Hello?'

A whisper: 'Grace, are you awake?'

She switches the lamp on. 'Why are you creeping—'

'We need to talk.' Smith closes the door quietly. 'There is so much to say. May I pull up a chair?'

'You can't keep coming up here. This is my private—'

'Kitty is suffering. Have you never considered … two wars, her life in India, Robert's absence, the little girl dying, the confusion with you—'

'What has any of this got to do with *me*?'

'Oh Grace, you sound so selfish. She gave you a new life—'

'Kept me away from my *real* family, you mean.'

'But you say you remember nothing. What sort of game are you playing?'

Grace feels the impact in her stomach. 'What do *you* know about my family?'

'I *can* tell you that without Kitty you would have been lost. And without me, *she* would be lost, so you see …'

Unexpectedly he bends down, pulls at his laces, slips off his shoes, then stands, comes up behind her. His voice is quiet but hard as shrapnel. 'You owe me … if nothing else … some common courtesy.'

She jumps as his hands rest on her shoulders.

'I have always done my best for you, Grace. Had your best interests at heart. You engendered fatherly feelings in me when you were little. I lost a child, too. A long time ago. You didn't know that, did you?'

'No, I—'

'And you never thought to ask. Were you never curious about me?'

'You are *their* friend, not—'

'For a while, I did consider the idea of reincarnation. That you might be … We had a professor who was impressed by oriental philoposhy. In the end, I realised it was just wishful thinking.'

Fear rises in her stomach, tightens her chest. What is he suggesting? She has to move. He senses, tightens his grip. If she challenges him he'll overwhelm her. She tries to calm her breathing. She has to find the right moment.

'And then we have your corrupt infatuation with women. It really is *too* bad.'

'Hariti—'

He laughs. 'I shouldn't hold my breath, if I were you.'

Her fingers tighten on the scissors.

'I think it was your sixteenth birthday – well, my fatherly feelings changed, you see, Grace.'

'How bloody *dare* you—' She tries to spin around.

He thrusts her body forward onto the desk.

Air slammed out of her chest.

Heart beating in her ears.
A gasp, a desperate dying breath.
Spasms of icy fear. 'You … can't—'
He presses harder.

*She's floating, floating … in the eye of a bird … a yellow field … a little girl
running … golden wheat swaying …*

Poker-hot, stabbing pain. An ocean of rocking.
The glue pot falls. Glass explodes.

Rocking … on … and … on …

Mo-ther, Mo-ther … drowning … choking …

She's released. Her shaking hand raises the scissors. Her trembling body
collapses to the floor.

*

She wakes. She's on the bed. Her teeth are chattering. She realises with
a shudder that he's still in the room. The armchair creaks as he gets up,
lays a blanket over her. 'You'll get over it, trust me. You can't report
this. You do realise that, don't you? Kitty – and Robert for that matter
– would be in serious trouble. No one will believe you. You don't have
papers. You will be interrogated … and then shot as a spy.'

The door closes with its mournful squeak.

Dark.

Light.

Dark.

Daylight again.

She lies, still in torn clothes, curled like an unborn baby. The terrible pains have slowly turned to pulsating aches. She slips into half sleep, groaning. She turns over, hands gripped between her legs.

Kitty calls from somewhere below, but never comes upstairs.

*

Gentle fingertips stroking her face. Hariti. Telling her she has to survive, has to continue on her path. Have faith. She will return.

Grace pulls the blanket over her head.

*

Steaming water roaring into the bath. Epsom Salts. Condensation on the mirror.

She stands slowly, shaking, unbuttons the torn pyjama top. Bruises on her neck. She lowers herself into the water. Heat enveloping her. How easy it would be to submerge. Leave the pain behind. The shame.

... a dark wood, moonlight, stitch in her side, blinding light. She hears a scream. It's travelled far, over hills, through a dark forest ...

She opens her eyes. Silence. Cooling water over her belly, purple bruises on her breasts.

In her room, she picks up the scissors. Rasping. The blades cut. And cut. And cut. A mass of fair hair falls around her feet.

October 1944

KITTY IS AT ROBERT'S BUREAU. She looks up. 'What have you done, you silly girl?'

Grace lifts the lid of the piano, sits on the stool.

'Your hair was an asset, dear. Now you look quite ordinary.'

The scratching of Kitty's pen nib on the blue notepaper. It gnaws like a rat inside Grace's head.

Her hands are poised above the piano keys, reflected in the black lacquer of the fall board. Mrs Blumen is telling her off for biting her nails down to the quick. Suddenly she crashes down onto the keys and fills the room with violent, discordant chords.

Kitty screams. 'For god's sake!'

Grace wipes tears with hardened finger tips. Why didn't she fight harder. Stab him. Over and over. Why didn't she insist they tell her the truth years ago? Open that little drawer. Release her?

'Whatever has come over you? Go down to the cellar and get some coal, the fire is nearly out.'

Grace watches her fingers – like a stranger's – tapping out clean, clear rhythms, pizzicato: controlled turmoil.

The notes fade, a heartbeat slowing.

Sérénade grotesque.

*

In the cellar she gathers tins of beans, peas and spam. It's been months since the coal hole was opened.

The house shakes.

A curtain of dust floats down from the floorboards above.

She'd not heard a siren or the low pulsing drone of the doodlebugs. Kitty is unravelling one of Robert's old jumpers.

'Kitty, did you hear—'

'No need to worry, it'll just be another of those gas mains exploding.'

'I'm not a child.' Grace places the food cans on the piano lid. 'I'm going to chop up that old cot.'

Fury in Kitty's eyes. '*Don't* you dare—'

'Well you won't be needing it again.'

Kitty tugs at a row of stitches. Tears on her carefully powdered cheeks.

'I'm sorry, Kitty.'

*

… giggling girls in red dresses, arms stretched in Hitler salutes … one tosses an orange at the young German sitting on the top of the tank as it roars along the Embankment … everyone is laughing … the tank turns … caterpillar tracks tear up the cobbles … Grace screams …

She wakes on the sofa. Singing coming from the kitchen: Kitty in one of her strange moods. Grace crosses to Robert's bureau. The roll top is raised. She tugs at the little drawer's ivory handle. It's locked. Of course.

Kitty carries in a tray. Teacups rattling, false warmth. 'I've made us a lovely cup of tea, Grace.'

'Do you have the key to this drawer?'

'It's Robert's desk, darling.'

'I know, but I need—'

'Even if I did, why would I open it? Some things are best left—'

'A real mother would have protected me.'

Kitty sits back in the armchair, reaches for her cigarettes on the side table. A shrine to Robert: a pipe resting on a tin of Edgeworth Sliced, a slim silver penknife, a heavy glass ashtray. 'I've always done my best for you, dear.'

Grace sits at the piano but closes the lid, rests her fingers on the cool black surface. 'Best for you, you mean.'

Kitty levers open the penknife with her thumbnail, takes the bowl of the pipe in one hand and scrapes. A hint of oriental perfume, but also of desiccation, of ruin.

Grace closes her eyes.

Kitty knocks the bowl against the ashtray.

One, two, three.

Then the scraping.

Knocking, one, two, three.

Scraping. Knocking. Scraping.

Brixton
October 1944

SMITH HAS GIVEN HER money in a sealed envelope. She is not to ask questions, just hand it over.

On Vauxhall Bridge, passers-by pay no heed to the woman vomiting into the gutter. Grace straightens up, walks on: Kennington Park, Brixton Road. There's the hardware shop on the corner, an archway leading down an alley. Washing lines strung across the yard from balconies, collarless shirts hanging in surrender. Blue drainpipes stretch up over the white-painted brick walls, branching off at each floor. The same blue paint on the iron stairs. Metal ringing under her footsteps.

Level two. The flat's number is easy to remember: her age. Her life's course is about to be changed at number twenty-four. She has to go through with this, then she'll be free. She will not stay in London. Kitty will have to rely on Smith. She's paid her dues, settled her debt with her karma. Time to live her own life.

The door opens. A tall woman wearing a colourful scarf. She has a lovely smile and a voice at least as posh as Kitty's. 'How do you do.'

Grace hands over the envelope, hears herself saying, 'How do you do.'

'Do come in.' The woman takes the envelope without looking inside. 'Let's have a cup of tea.'

The room is sparsely furnished. Three chairs precisely placed around a sturdy dining table.

'You don't have to tell me your name, dear.'

Grace holds the back of a chair, says the first one that comes to mind. 'Nancy.' Is this the best she can do? Might she be traced? It's okay, there must be hundreds of people called Nancy in London.

'I'll put the kettle on.'

While the woman is in the kitchen, Grace looks around the room, anxiously wondering where the operation will happen. She examines a picture on a wall: a tall man in RAF uniform. The fireplace is empty, the grate polished.

Above the mantelpiece, a painting of a man walking along a desert road, the title: *Road to Emmaus*.

Her nose and throat are still burning. Her breath probably stinks too.

The woman carries in a silver teapot and smiles. 'I beg your pardon, I don't have any milk. Can you take it black? I do have a little lemon.'

'I haven't seen one for years.'

The woman sits down. On a side table, a bunch of knitting needles in a flower vase: they look long and very sharp. Grace shivers.

'Here we are, dear.' The woman places a quarter slice of lemon on Grace's bone china saucer. The sharp fragrance of citrus invades her fragile senses.

'The photograph—'

'My son. We all have to make sacrifices.'

They lift their cups in unison.

'You're a doctor in—'

'I have a cousin who owns a shipping company, he can get just about anything. Last week he brought me a grapefruit. Imagine!'

'Where do you do the, er …'

The woman pats Grace's hand. 'Don't you worry, it starts here but mostly you'll be at home. You *do* have someone to look after you, don't you?'

Grace's cup rattles as she tries to place it in the shallow indent of the saucer. It just won't fit: there must be a saucer – somewhere in the world – made for this cup, and presumably another cup for this saucer.

She stands up. 'I don't think …'

'That's perfectly all right, Nancy. Come back if you change your mind, but don't leave it too long, dear.'

The alley smells of urine; the street is clouded with fumes from a bus standing at the bus stop. She runs for it.

Chelsea
November 1944

'IT WAS DELIVERED FROM HARRODS this morning, Oliver is *so* thoughtful.'

Kitty hasn't been so animated in years, fussing and chatting, treating Grace kindly: it's all rather disorientating.

'He was disappointed, Grace, if I'm honest with you … he said that if he ever found out who the father was … but we forgive you, Grace. This war is *so* maddening.' She holds out the parcel, a determined smile. 'I remember my own first months in India with only Hariti and the servants.'

It's strange having Kitty in her room. Grace sits on the end of her bed next to an old leather suitcase: one of Robert's with a serpent embossed under the handle.

Kitty folds the sleeves of a cardigan. 'I'm sure if you choose your dresses carefully you'll get away with it for a while. You'll have a lovely time in Rye, you won't be able to go to the seaside with all the mines, of course, but you can look in all the shop windows, and I'm sure Nancy will take care of you. And after, when Robert is back, we can be one big—'

'*Don't* you dare say it.'

'You'll be back to your old self in no time.'

'You've never been truthful with me.'

'I have no idea what—'

'Then give me the key to the drawer.'

'You know I can't do that.' Kitty smooths the cardigan. 'And you needn't worry about me. Oliver will look in now and then, and I've got Sancho.' She places the cardigan in the suitcase.

'Then I'll just have to force it open.'

Kitty pats the cardigan, her voice frighteningly quiet. 'You know I would *never* allow that.'

However dreadful this situation, at least it's compelled Grace to escape. Smith told her Hariti is alive, somewhere, and one day Grace is certain fate will bring them back together. Now she's reclaiming her life. Going to Nancy.

'Aren't you going to open your present?'

'You know I'm not keeping the baby.' Grace is determined. She'll make her mark in the world through music, not washing nappies. She doesn't have any maternal instinct. She's unnatural. Rotten to the core. But Nancy loves her, and there is Hariti, the light at the centre of her being.

'Well if *you* won't …' Kitty pulls the pale blue ribbon and unfolds the brown paper. Nestling inside layers of tissue paper is a tiny blue cardigan. 'Oh Grace, look, it must have cost him an arm and a leg. It's really lovely: silk ribbons sewn into the hem. And there's a card. '*You will make a fine mother, Grace. Your friend, Oliver Smith.*' Such a thoughtful man.'

Kitty passes the card. Grace folds it, folds it again and tosses it onto her desk.

Kitty sits on the edge of the bed. 'Grace, we were never great talkers. I need to say … where do I start? In my day you stuck by your man no matter how hard life got. If your father were here, and in his right mind … he would say he forgave you … as I do. I just want you to know … I understand.' She wipes a tear and stands briskly. 'Now, don't forget your little bag of toiletries: when you go into the nursing home you'll need your make-up.' She's at Grace's desk. 'It seems like only yesterday that we heaved this old thing up the stairs.' She laughs. 'Robert was pulling it and I was pushing from below. We really didn't think it would go around the corner, we thought we'd have to cut the banisters but Grace was an insistent little girl. I don't imagine we'll ever move this again, it will have to live up here for the rest of eternity.'

Waterloo
December 1944

SEAGULLS SWOOP LIKE STUKAS in the cavernous expanse of Waterloo Station, twisting and turning effortlessly. The last time she was here she was a lost child, holding Hariti's hand.

Iridescent pigeons nervously strut the platforms, skilfully dodging legs: khaki, navy blue, pin-striped, stockinged. Some gather on the dirty brick ledges and the roof's ironwork, watching with beady eyes, quietly cooing.

On a poster, an anxious soldier asks: *Is your journey really necessary?* Yes, it *is*, if she is to survive. All over the planet, millions of people are suffering far more. Somehow, this thought doesn't reassure. The Buddha – she remembers Hariti saying – started his journey in suffering.

Kitty insisted that Grace travel first class but the old woman is out of touch with the cost of train travel these days. Grace slips the pale green third class ticket inside her right glove for safe keeping. The carriages are crowded but thankfully a soldier lifts her suitcases onto the luggage rack and offers his seat next to the window. Grace holds the cello case between her legs. Another soldier leans over, pokes his head out of the window. Shrill, warbling whistles, a door slamming, the carriages jerk. A young woman on the platform runs to keep up with the soldier, her blue hat flies off and she calls, 'I love you Charlie, I love you …' The train hauls out into weak sunlight. No one seems affected by the melodrama that's just unfolded, that's tightened Grace's throat. A train full of men. All in uniform. Parallel, alien lives.

The train curves around a bend. Steamy, sulphurous smoke billows in. She's back on the bridge with Hariti. The eclipse.

A soldier leans over her, pulls the leather strap from a hook and slams the window shut.

Backs of houses. A lone figure bent in an allotment, straightening his back, waving a bon voyage to the men pressed around her, men prepared to give up their lives for an ancient idea: homeland.

The soldier opposite is reading a newspaper. Grace tries to read the wavering print, a headline about a killing in Palestine attributed to the Stern Gang. What an appropriate name for a bunch of thugs.

She stares at the grey, oppressive sky. How can all these men rocking in time with her not be crippled by fear, knowing they face death without the certainty of rebirth? How can they tease each other, laugh, share cigarettes? She can hardly bear to think of what she will have to go through when it's her time.

They aren't all fresh-faced youths, either: many must have seen 'action' before, survivors of Dunkirk, perhaps. Who knows what they have done under duress, or how war will change them before they return home.

The train lurches, rattling over points.

What will Nancy think? There's no way Grace will be able to hide her body as it distorts into a disgusting lump. She'll tell Nancy it was just a flirtation. She's bound to reject Grace. Feel betrayed.

Grace hauls her luggage off the train at Ashford. The Rye train is less crowded, her cello has a seat of its own. Facing her is a young couple. The man is in RAF uniform, an accent, probably Polish; he might even be a Jew, one of the lucky ones to escape Warsaw. The woman is turning the pages of a Baedeker, pointing out good restaurants. One day she'll show him all the best spots in the West End. She boasts she has never ventured into the East End where the 'disreputable' people live. Grace guesses – judging by a trace of accent – that the East End is exactly where she comes from.

Rye can't be far now.

Nancy is not on the platform. Double-clicking of slamming doors echoing along the train. Grace heaves the cello onto her back, picks up her suitcases – one large for living, the small one for 'later' – and heads for the exit. Queuing soldiers stand aside to let her pass, one removes his cap. 'After you darlin'.' Another calls, 'What you doing tonight sweetheart?'

She passes in front of them. 'Bugger off.'

The soldiers laugh.

She shields her eyes.

There she is!

Nancy waves.

Grace crosses the road as fast as she can. 'Nancy! I hardly recognised you with your hair tied back.'

'You've cut all yours off!'

She's imagined this reunion for years – throwing herself into Nancy's arms, tears, laughter – but Nancy leans forward and kisses her on both cheeks. 'How was the beastly journey? Give me one of your cases.'

'I thought you'd be on the platform to meet me.'

'It's a small town, people gossip. You must be so tired: the sea air will do you good after all that London smog. They have such lovely tea shops here.'

They walk up a cobbled lane, holding onto a black iron railing to steady themselves. Halfway up, Grace pauses to get her breath.

Nancy is chattering nervously. 'There's a rumour that Rye was the only port on the south coast where the trawler men refused to go to Dunkirk. Or was it Hastings? I don't know if it's true. Come on, one more street to go.'

Two steps up to a front door; Nancy pushes a key into the lock. 'Here we are, home from home.'

The hall walls are lined from floor to ceiling with shelves packed with books.

Nancy leads her down a narrow corridor to the kitchen, bustles from sink to kettle to cupboards. 'I love your cute English ways: why does the pot need its own spoonful of tea? Let me have your coat.'

'I can manage.' Grace hangs her coat over an apron on the back of the door. The kettle whistles. Nancy pours water into the teapot, slips a knitted cosy over it. 'I'll show you your room while it brews.'

Pale green carpet muffles their footsteps. Nancy turns a white porcelain door knob. An ornate brass bed dominates the room. Stiff pale blue sheets folded over. 'Come and have a look at mine.'

'I thought …'

'I admit I have the better view.' She opens the door opposite.

Grace crosses to the window. A patchwork of grey flint walls and undulating pantiled roofs.

Nancy sits on her bed. 'How are things in London? Met any nice men?'

Grace turns to face Nancy. 'You know that men don't—'

'Good lord, Grace! Have you … oh my god … you've got yourself … how on earth …'

Grace tingles with shame.

'Was it that rascal Cornell? Come here, you're going to tell me all about it.'

'I'm frightened.'

'Oh Gracie, don't worry, you're here now.'

'I'm not keeping it.'

'There's plenty of time to—'

'I'm going to my room now.'

Rye
January 1945

'MY RATION BOOK IS in my suitcase, sorry, I'll go back.'

'No need Grace, the fishmonger always keeps a few extra scraps for me.' Nancy holds Grace's elbow as they climb down the icy steps, cross the road and follow the path to the harbour. 'I've got some potatoes left in the sack and a neighbour gave me some sprouts the other day. Everyone helps out here.'

'I don't want to be a burden.'

Nancy joins the queue at the fish shop. Grace can't stand the smell and walks off along the harbour wall. She'd built up such hopes of seeing Nancy again, but there's an awkwardness between them. It's bewildering. Maybe their connection was all just a childish infatuation. Does she really have *any* idea who Nancy is?

She walks with her head down, staring at the white splatters on the concrete, past seagulls poking around a pile of nets.

And then she spots him. Somehow, she's not surprised. His legs are dangling over the side of the jetty and he's whittling a piece of wood. 'Good morning, Grace. How nice to see you again.'

'What are *you* doing here?'

'Have a cigarette.'

'I don't smoke.'

Leyland pats the concrete. 'Well, maybe you'll join me.'

'I'm quite all right standing, thank you.'

'I told you, I live between Rye and Hastings, you were clearly not listening.'

'Don't you have a war to fight? Oh, I forgot, you're neutral.'

He ignores her biting tone. 'I like your new hairstyle, a bob suits you.'

'It must be hard for you doing nothing while the world—'

'How is your mother? Survived the inconvenience of the Blitz, I hope.'

Grace stares down at the boats lying on their sides on the mud banks. 'She has a friend looking out for her. She'll be all right whichever way this turns out.'

'Yes, I've heard. He's not a very nice man by all accounts.'

'How—'

'I'd be wary of him, If I were you.'

'I haven't seen you since—'

'You lent me your armchair one night.'

'That's right. What were you up to, Leyland? I don't believe for a second that – what was it? – you'd lost the key to your digs.'

'And what brings you here? Ah, yes, your friend Miss Lockhart.'

'You're avoiding my question.'

'How *are* you, Grace?'

'I must go.'

'We'll bump into each other again, I hope: it's a small town.'

'So I've heard.'

NANCY IS CLEARING AWAY the tea plates. 'It's nearly six o'clock, your call will be coming in soon.'

'I don't know what she wants.'

'She's an old woman, Grace, hear her out.'

As a distant church bell strikes, the telephone rings in the hall. Grace picks up the receiver.

'Grace, darling, hello. How are you?'

'We are all fine, thank you.'

'How is the—'

'I don't know. I haven't asked it.'

The line crackles. 'Wait … this is important.'

Grace stares at the round disk in the middle of the dial, the top half in black, like a night sky, the white letters floating like stars. 'I'm still here.'

'I know you said you'd give it up to another family—'

'There's no use trying to change my mind.'

'I know, darling. What I want to say is … let *me* take the baby.'

February 1945

A MOMENT OF SYNCHRONICITY: worshippers from three churches emerge onto the cobbled streets. Protestants wander among grey headstones – the churchyard is already host to snowdrops and lesser celandine – Baptists stroll out from the white-painted brickwork chapel, Catholics emerge from a small church set back from the pavement.

Nancy steers Grace away. 'Let's go to the Gun Garden.'

A garden of guns? They pass through a stone archway onto a grassy knoll. Three ancient cannons on wooden carriages point over a low wall across the marsh; white bird droppings dribble down their black pitted barrels. At the far end of the 'garden' is a modern cannon garlanded with flowers.

The Union flag hangs limply from a white pole.

'All this land is reclaimed, you know, Grace. The sea used to come right up to the cliff here. See that camouflage in the distance? They're the Bofors guns on Harbour Road.'

'I can see this would be the perfect location to guard against invasions: Napoleon, the Spanish—'

'You might be right, clever little Gracie.'

'We should go home.'

'It's a beautiful day, let's enjoy the sun while we can.' She strikes a match, lights a cigarette, a sharp phosphorus tang in the air.

'I ran into Leyland Cornell.'

'I catch sight of him in town now and then, I don't think he's ever noticed me.'

'I wouldn't be so sure about that.'

A small gathering on the grass: men in dark suits, some with medals; women in spring dresses. The men laugh as one of them lifts a young woman onto a high stone wall. She's blushing in her modest wedding dress, a military dress-coat over her shoulders.

Grace leans against a brick buttress and closes her eyes. The thing inside her is stretching as if it can sense the dappled light and the salty breeze coming up from the marsh. In this moment, everything feels … inevitable. For all of history, men have been pitting themselves against each other, fighting over territory. There's nothing a woman has ever been able to do about it. Her war-baby will try to suck what it needs from her until she's an empty shell. But she's determined. She won't have any of it. Kitty will have to sort it out, get a wet nurse, powdered milk, whatever. Grace will claim her freedom, and maybe Nancy might love her again.

'Who's the father, Grace?'

She opens her eyes. 'I can't, Nancy.'

'We share everything. You can trust me with your life, you know that. So, it wasn't Cornell?'

'No!'

'So who? Who did this to you? Do you even know his name?'

The crowd has hushed. A harsh voice barks an order. Men line up behind the gun and Grace wonders why everyone is covering their ears.

A sharp voice: 'Fire!'

Seagulls launch into the air. Instantly, the shock wave hits her. She falls to her knees, holds her belly and bursts into tears.

'Gracie? Oh my god, my love, what's wrong?'

THE BABY HASN'T MOVED for days. Grace is beginning to think she's carrying a casualty of war.

Vomit slides disgustingly over plates, cups and glasses piled in the kitchen sink. 'I'm sorry, that's absolutely repulsive.'

Nancy strokes her back then swills the dishes with cold water. 'I should have washed up last night. You need to walk.'

'I'm not going out.'

'Put your coat on, it won't show.'

During the night a fine dusting of snow has fallen, covering the steps. Nancy holds Grace's arm as they go down, cross the road and take the harbour path.

'Oh god, Grace? Am I hallucinating? Can you smell bacon?'

'Are you deliberately tormenting me?'

'But you can't live on fresh air, you'll—'

'Nancy, he's there again.'

'Oh Grace! You are *so* innocent.'

They approach the man sitting on the harbour wall. He looks up, slips his whittling knife into a leather sheath. 'Miss Lockhart, if I'm not mistaken.'

'You rogue. Are you following us?'

'I live nearby, I have a studio in Brede. Miss Fisher has had the misfortune to see my work in London.'

Nancy turns. 'You're a dark horse, you never told me you two had dated.'

'It wasn't exactly a memorable occasion.'

Leyland scowls. 'I guess I deserved that. Can I buy you both a cuppa?'

They follow the path to a wooden shack: its front panel is open and inside a woman in a head scarf knotted under her chin is turning sizzling rashers of bacon in a pan. 'Young ladies, I'd be careful of this one.' She winks and turns back to the stove.

Leyland clips a sixpence onto the counter.

Nancy leads Grace to a bench, squeezes up to her as Leyland carries three mugs. 'Park yourself here, mister. You'd better tell us about your art.'

Reassuring heat from the mug seeps through Grace's woollen gloves.

Leyland taps a Woodbine from a packet. 'I'm exploring old legends, it's surprising how the same stories appear over and over again.'

Nancy prods him. 'Give me one of those, will you?'

'Every culture has a story of lovers in trouble. Tristan and Isolde, for example.'

Grace turns her mug around to avoid the chip. 'And the musicians who exploit them.'

'Wagner, you mean?'

'Music doesn't need to be so literal.'

'Some of it is beautiful. It's like a tapestry, themes weaving in and out.'

'You seem to know a lot, considering—'

'That I'm a lowly artist? Or Irish?'

Nancy laughs. 'Give me Glenn Miller any day. So sad the way he died.'

'One more wreck at the bottom of the Channel.'

'That sounds a bit callous. He lifted all our spirits in dark times.'

'So you'd argue that art should exist to make us feel good?'

'Did you know this girl is going to be famous, she plays the cello divinely. I'm envious: you both have creative powers, I just have an allowance!'

Leyland frowns. 'Give me your allowance and you can have my irrelevant artistry any day.'

'So when are you going to show us your work, allow us to be judge of your talent?'

'Art is dead. I've just bought a camera, the Germans are good at engineering. Now I must leave you. I hope we'll meet again soon.'

He walks away, his hands deep in the pockets of corduroy trousers.

'Gracie, he's a dish. And rather infatuated with you!'

'*You* more like. I'll give the tea lady her mugs back.'

'*And* he has a nice bottom.'

March 1945

IN THE ANGLED DRESSING table mirror, Grace inspects her breasts: she's convinced they're getting bigger and to her horror she can see – just discernible under pale skin – blue veins like writhing serpents.

*

In the evenings, they sit in armchairs facing each other, shoes kicked off, turning pages of old magazines, listening to the wireless or to the Professor's record collection. Nancy chats away brightly, sharing local gossip, determined that playing at being happy will make it come about.

'Did you hear, the Home Guard caught four German spies who'd asked for cider after closing time in a pub in Lydd, and they didn't even know what "one and a tanner" meant. Hilarious! So much for German efficiency.'

'Worrying, though.'

'Later the police found a radio transmitter in a suitcase. They're certain to be hanged for espionage.'

'How strange, that wearing a uniform makes murder a lesser crime.'

Nancy is determined to be at the confinement, but Grace will never allow it. The day will soon arrive when Grace will get into a taxi and be gone. The name of the nursing home is folded with a ten-shilling note in her purse. Until then, Grace wanders like a ghost. She avoids the Gun Garden. She wears her coat in all weathers, walks with bowed head along the cobbled High Street, down the hill and under the arch of the medieval gate.

On the flat grass of reclaimed land she stands, imagining the dykes miles away breaking, the sea rushing towards her. She wouldn't move. She'd simply stand there. On the ancient sea bed, accepting her fate.

Hastings
April 1945

THE TAXI DRIVER GLANCES in the rear-view mirror, a shrivelled cigarette sticking to his bottom lip. He parks over a puddle and watches Grace struggling to get out with her small case.

She slams the door. 'That's the spirit, thanks for your help.'

He leans out of his window and lets a stream of brown spit dribble into the gutter, then grates his gears and drives off.

A fine drizzle dampens her hot face. She must sit down. The step is cold, the pain coming in waves. A nurse is by her side, picking up the suitcase. 'Come along, we can't have you making a fuss in public.'

Competing smells in a tiny room: lavender and disinfectant. A corner of the white sheet is folded back, a perfect right-angle triangle. Beneath the hard mattress the iron bedstead squeaks as she sits.

'Get undressed. There's a gown in the wardrobe. The doctor will be in to see you soon.' The heavy door bangs shut.

Above the bed, a gold-painted Jesus on a wooden crucifix: blood dribbles from hands, crossed feet, and the feminine slit in his side. In the wardrobe: a single pink nightdress hangs limply on a padded hanger. She undresses down to her slip and stands by the door to take off her bra, then slides her arms into the nightdress and quickly gets under the sheets, goose pimples tingling up her arms.

The contractions seem to have stopped. She's such a fool for making a fuss. A false alarm. She'll go back to Nancy in the morning.

*

Cliff-edge. Clenching fist. At last it relents; an overwhelming longing she can't name. In the moments of calm she tells herself she's being self-indulgent, that plenty of people have suffered real loss. She just has to hang on, get through.

*

A polished voice: 'Miss Fisher, I presume.' He flicks a switch; the lampshade throws filigree shadows around the room. 'I'm Dr Rodgers.' The sour-faced nurse follows him in.

Grace tries to sit up. The doctor places his hand firmly on her shoulder. 'No my dear, stay lying down. I've had a chat with your mother on the telephone. Your baby will grow up proud knowing that your fiancé died fighting for his country. You were both a little hasty jumping the gun – if I may say so – but it's happening all over the shop. I suppose it's understandable, but still, there are consequences.'

'She's not my—'

'Your mother seems determined that *she* will have your baby. I find it highly unusual: in my experience it's the grandparents who feel the most shame. I urge you to reconsider: I can find a home, there's plenty of demand, especially if it's a boy. Your lack of judgement could still bring happiness to a childless couple.'

She screws up her face as the contraction grips. 'I want it out.'

'We'll have a quick inspection, discuss it later … nurse, how regular is she?'

'Not at all, doctor.'

'How the hell does *she* know? I've been alone for hours.' The doctor flicks the sheet aside as if performing a magic trick, points to her knickers. 'Nurse, get rid of those would you.'

The nurse tugs at the garment. 'I *told* you to get undressed, miss. Baby can't get out through these, now can he?'

She tosses the knickers onto a chair, then wraps a band around

Grace's arm and starts to pump at a rubber bulb, looking at the upside-down watch pinned to her uniform.

The doctor drones on. 'She's leaking, it doesn't always come in a gush, it's sometimes like this, yes, and pinkish discharge, we're well on the way. Now, Miss Fisher, when you feel a contraction coming on, you must go with it.'

He prods hard. Grace cries out.

'The head is nicely engaged. What's the BP, nurse?'

She mumbles some figures.

He nods. 'What a privilege to give birth in times like these.'

She pants. 'How long—'

'I'll be back in the morning, your uterus will spend the night working its magic on the cervix. Whatever you do don't worry, it'll only make things worse. Think about what I've said about giving baby a better future, there's a good girl. Rest: you'll need all your strength.'

Grace has no idea what a uterus or a cervix is, but something must be wrong, the doctor doesn't understand. This much pain can't be right.

*

She's lost in swirling agony. She calls out in the dark. No one comes. She tries to stand, her legs wobble, she falls to the hard parquet floor, crawls into a corridor.

Squeaking rubber shoes. Stern voices.

*

Morning light at a high window. A moment of clarity. Whatever happens this will be over before it's dark again. The nurse bends forward, lifts Grace's knees. The gown slips open. 'Stop moving, girl.'

Dr Rodgers enters briskly. 'Good morning, young lady, I hope you had a productive night. This is one of my students, he'll be observing.'

A young man moves around so that he can peer between her legs.

The doctor puts on rubber gloves, snapping them over shirt cuffs. He bends over her, a cloud of suffocating, astringent scent. 'We'll get her shaved, nurse. So, Miss …' he looks at his notes 'Fisher.'

It's building again. Dizzy panting. From a distance an animal cry.

'The more you worry, the more you'll make the labour hard for yourself. Nurse, we'll leave the enema for the moment. I'll be along later. Relax, young lady, let nature take her course, she knows what she's doing, there's my girl.' He lightly pats Grace's lump.

She screams, 'I'm not your bloody girl.'

'No need to get into a tizzy. Thank you, nurse.'

She's falling into black. *All Things Bright and Beautiful* … A soft voice. From where? She wants to die. Let go. Sweat drips into her eyes. She's a gaping wound. Heart pounding in her ears.

… sharp, tall stems cut her hands … every step too painful to bear … above, a bird's cruel black eye … below, a little girl in a dirty white dress running … falling …

'She can't let go, her sphincters are too tight.'

Grace survives but the next one is building. Worse …

A for Albatross …

Something's wrong. For god's sake get it out. Get it out.

The glue pot shatters. Cold steel in her fist.

'We have some medicines that will help with the discomfort.'

A knife edge. Sharp. Blinding light. Her feet find the shore, a moment to catch her breath. The dreadful wave coming, coming.

B for Buzzard …

'She's not letting baby come through.'

Leyland's arms wide open. Like Jesus. Blood dripping from his palms.

C for Carrion Crow.

She opens her eyes. A woman stroking her face, a different voice: a warm breeze, soft, Irish, like Leyland's, whispering. 'Now, child, the head is nearly out, just a little more, you're doing so well.'

Tears pour into her hair. Her ravaged body convulses and turns inside out.

An alien cry.

Hands help her to sit up. The kind nurse straightens pillows, wipes Grace's face with a warm flannel. 'We want you looking your best for your baby now don't we.' She twists a lipstick's gold tube: a red phallus pokes up. She leans forward and slides the tip along Grace's lips. 'Now press together. There. Mummy needs to make a good first impression!'

A rattling scale pan. Horrible nurse slides the marker along a balancing bar, passes a bundle to kind nurse. 'You are going to love this little lad, he's adorable.'

Horrible nurse gathers white enamel dishes filled with wads soaked in blood, balances them on one arm like a waitress, scoops up another pan covered with a cloth – it must be hiding something of great secrecy and shame.

'Here he is, a beautiful boy and thanks-be-to-god, the right number of toes and fingers.' The bundle is tucked along Grace's left arm, close to her stony heart. Dark wavy hair glued to a greasy head. Black eyes staring up at her. A strange calm surrounds him. A sense he's travelled from far away. Hariti's singing in her head as she spins around in bright sunlight, arms spread wide. Is this it? The moment Grace is meant to feel a rush of motherly love?

Mother–Daughter–Baby. A cord cut. A line broken.

The kind nurse is smiling. 'He's all yours, every perfect inch of him.'

Chelsea

THE KETTLE MURMURS on the stove as it approaches boiling point.

The baby is balanced over Kitty's shoulder. 'Grace, we must sort out a few things.' She pats his back with a gentleness Grace has never witnessed.

Her breasts still hurt despite Kitty's folk remedy: two cabbage leaves washed in cold water. If it weren't for the pain, Grace would have laughed at Kitty's stupid superstitions, but she'd been reassured by the cup shape of the leaves and went straight to her bedroom and pressed them to her burning breasts. Relief was instant, if mild, so she bound them in before she could change her mind. 'There's nothing more to say. I'm going.'

'Well, names, for instance. I have a few suggestions.'

'It's up to you.'

'Grace. It's not *natural*.'

'Why don't you assert his Englishness – name him after one of your beloved Shakespearian characters.'

'Actually, that's a good idea.' Kitty holds the baby out in front of her, looks into the grumpy face. 'He's *so* lovely, Grace. What a pity Hariti left, she would have loved him, she'd probably say he was a reborn soul: what do they call it?'

Grace knows Kitty is trying to engage with her. She slides *The Shropshire Lad* into her handbag. 'It's called reincarnation. And you know perfectly well why Hariti left.'

'I don't think I showed her enough appreciation. It's only when someone isn't there …' She lays the baby on a clean nappy in the middle of the table. 'If the war's taught us anything, it is to appreciate

God's blessings.' She hums, lifts the kettle with a grunt and carefully pours boiling water over the glass feeding bottle in the sink. 'He's such a lovely boy.' With a tea towel, she lifts the bottle onto the draining board. 'You *are* a clever girl, Grace. It's a blessing that you stuck to our agreement: he's better off in his family.'

'I've paid my debts.'

'You don't really believe in all that nonsense, do you?' The baby starts to whimper. Kitty nuzzles his sweaty neck. 'Time for dinner, little one. Grace is going in a few minutes so it'll just be the two of us … oh look, he's smiling.'

'If you didn't believe in Hariti's *superstitions*, why did you keep me?'

'There was nowhere else for you to go.'

'You never believed I was your daughter.'

'Oh Grace, let's not disagree. There are things you were too young to understand … even now—'

'That's so convenient.' Grace crosses her arms. Her body is pulling towards the baby. Her mind is appalled at the nightmare memory of Smith. Her soul is crying out for freedom. 'What aren't you telling me?'

'Robert and I did what we thought was best. And good has come out of it.'

Grace takes a deep breath. What is the use? Fate was playing with her, delivering her to the Fishers. But also to Hariti, and for that she will always be grateful. Even if she never sees her again. In this life.

On the shelf above the fireplace, Grace notices two silver picture frames. They've been there for years but she's never paid them much attention. One holds a sepia picture of a swaddled baby in a cradle against a painted backdrop of rushes by a river. In the second frame, a young Kitty stands in an exotic garden, squinting, and holding a posy of flowers. Behind her, much taller, is Robert. In the distance two naked Indian children squat on a hard mud road and stare towards the camera with astonishingly wide, dark eyes.

Kitty looks up from stirring a pan of milk. 'That was in Simla. He's a towering presence in my life, Grace. No one will ever take his place. I'll be incomplete until he's better and can return.'

Grace peers at a smaller dark-wood frame: two young people each side of a lamppost, leaning on it, laughing. One must surely be Kitty. It's obviously in a foreign street but Grace is not sure what makes it seem so. She's never asked before who the young man is. It suddenly hits her. 'It's Smith!'

Kitty licks the bottom of the teat and stretches it over the bottle's ridge, then shakes some milk onto her wrist. 'Shouldn't you be getting off, darling?' She holds the bottle under the cold tap. 'You don't want to miss your connection.'

'Just how long *have* you known him?'

Kitty tests the milk on her wrist again. 'Oh, forever. Before India. We all travelled out on that dreadful ship ... full of women husband-hunting.' She smiles at the baby. 'I know you will never believe this, Grace, but I thank God for bringing you into my life.'

Grace closes her eyes for a moment, tries to calm her breathing. 'What happened to Hariti's statuettes?'

'I tidied them away somewhere.'

Grace picks up the small suitcase. 'Confident she wouldn't return?'

'If you must know ... I didn't want reminding—'

The baby cries; Kitty picks him up, rubs her hand in circles over his back, starts to sing.

Words have all been exhausted. Kitty has found a way to live with the contradiction: that she doesn't believe in reincarnation, that she kept Grace in spite of it. Now she has her reward. Smith's dreadful spawn.

Kitty holds up the baby's thin arm, makes him wave. 'What do you think of calling him Orlando?'

'It's no concern of mine.'

SEVEN

Croydon
2000

A NURSE PULLS BACK THE SHEET. 'Time to get your legs moving, sweetheart, never goin' to get you dancin' out of here if we don't start now.'

Another nurse is leaning on the window sill, staring out at the dark branches of a tree, her tangled blonde hair clearly not properly combed. Grace calls out, 'You've got a crow's nest in there, my dear,' but no one hears. The first nurse lifts one of Grace's legs and manipulates her feet into tartan slippers. She slides her arm around Grace: horrid smell of cheap perfume. Tangled-hair nurse takes the other arm and together they heave Grace onto her feet. Looking down, Grace is amazed to see a bag half full of yellow liquid hanging off her leg. Balanced between two shoulders, she watches her feet being dragged to the end of the room. She's always hated her feet. Not like Nancy's: perfect, strong, a ballerina's. Her bearers are huffing and puffing like a couple of steam locomotives. What's the matter with them, she's light as a feather.

Tangled-hair nurse starts to turn her. 'Let's get her back to bed.'

First nurse nods. 'Your son's comin' this afternoon, Grace, that'll be nice won't it!'

'But when's Hariti coming?' No answer.

She's back in bed, alone. How did that happen? No sound in the room, just the damned tick – tick – tick.

*

What the devil's wrong with her eyes. She can't seem to focus. Two men, or is it one? Side by side, holding the rail at the bottom of her bed: ghostly accusers. She's sorry but it wasn't her fault. She'd never asked to be a mother. What do they want from her? A dying breath? She's not afraid. Hariti is waiting.

*

Grace's bloated arms lie in parallel on the white sheet, like branches stripped of their bark, creamy white with a tint of sappy yellow.

A nurse puts her arm around Grace's unfeeling back and leans her forward; she has a lovely Irish accent, it's hard to imagine *her* blowing up hotels for the sake of a flag. She straightens Grace's glasses.

Orlando pushes open the door. He's whistling some tuneless song. He winks at the nurse. So crude. Surprisingly, she smiles back and touches his arm as she leaves: she really shouldn't encourage him. He swings the rucksack off his back, slides the toggle. To her amazement, a dark nose appears, then a head, then paws. Caesar wriggles out like a snake sloughing its skin. He licks her face and, getting no response, finds a space at the bottom of the bed, turns around and slumps on the pale blue bedspread.

Orlando strokes Grace's arm; hairs stand on end. He tells her not to worry, she's getting better.

The other boy … holding her hand. But he's on the wrong side, and all he seems capable of saying is, 'It's okay, it's okay.' He holds Grace's stare, then asks if she knows who he is. She not bloody senile. She remembers the weight of him, always restless.

*

A plastic spoon forces its way into her mouth. Grace grunts. The nurse wipes her chin with a tissue. She strokes Grace's forehead, tells her to stay calm.

Grace doesn't have the breath to explain.

Hastings
April 1945

NO LINES CONNECTING HER to antecedents. Or descendants. She's a slave to no one. She'll never trust again, especially bloody men. So why are her footsteps echoing on the icy flagstones of this dark street in Hastings? She's on her way to meet a man she hardly knows while Nancy is waiting for her in Rye.

She can't get the image of the baby – Orlando, as she must think of him – staring across the kitchen at her. The forced wave, a look of utter bewilderment, as if – even at just a few weeks old – he understands the nature of abandonment.

She must sort out the ration book. Kitty could get the extra milk, orange juice, vitamins and so on. The Ministry of Food are keen to keep the baby production line going. But then, there's something odd about her papers, isn't there?

Leyland is leaning against a wall in a swathe of light from an open door.

He drops his cigarette on the pavement. 'What happened?'

'I'm sorry, the train was delayed and I missed the Hastings connection. I'll have to go back soon to catch the next one. Nancy will be worried.'

'Come.'

They have to duck to get under the lintel. Leyland reaches over the bar to shake the barman's hand. 'Joe, allow me to introduce you to Miss Grace Fisher.'

Joe shakes her hand. A soft accent she can't quite place. 'Hello dear, do go sit yourself down.'

Their chairs scrape on the wooden floor.

'His name is really Joseph, Jewish, got out just in time.'

'How did you meet him?'

'In Paris. I'd gone to paint, but ended up picking grapes in Bordeaux. Joe worked for the vineyard. When the war started—'

'What about his family?'

'Don't ask him.'

'That sounds rather ominous.'

'He's obsessed about the Jews having a homeland.'

'Everyone needs a home.'

'Forget I mentioned it, it's all very indiscreet of me, you never know who you can trust.'

Joe, walking with a slight limp, carries over an uncorked wine bottle. 'I've got a lovely bit of cod in tonight.'

'We'll just have some of that.'

Joe pours, leaves the bottle on the table and returns to the bar.

Grace sips: cool, perfumed, slightly sparkling. 'This is lovely.'

'The vineyard is still producing good wine – it's something the Nazis care about.'

'I wanted to ask you – you seem to know a lot of people – what are the chances of finding Hariti?' She tips her glass, drinks half her wine in one gulp. 'Kitty insists she ran away with all the food stamps.'

'Mr Fisher also disappeared around that time, if I'm not mistaken.'

'It was all very odd. He was sent on some sort of mission. Came back a broken man.'

'London is an easy place to get lost in if that's what you want.'

She struggles to find words, tears welling. She lifts the wine bottle and fills her glass. Leyland has hardly touched his. He leans forward. 'I'm sorry, that was insensitive.'

She shakes her head. 'I haven't eaten anything for a while.'

'We should get you home.'

'I have to get to Rye.'

Leyland pushes the cork into the bottle, slides it into his coat pocket.

They walk into the dark. Her teeth chattering.

The motorbike engine settles to a constant drone. The wobbling aura of light stabs into the dark tunnel of trees arching over them. In spite of the heat on her legs she shivers and tightens her arms around his coat.

Brede
April 1945

EVEN BEFORE SHE OPENS her eyes, the smell of damp tells her she is not at home. She remembers: they'd missed the train by minutes. Pale, silver light through threadbare curtains. She eases herself up, leans back against the dark wooden headboard, scans the room: a washbasin with a jug on a marble top, a small fireplace in a corner, a wardrobe jammed tightly under a black beam.

She's still in her underwear, the straps of her suspender belt are threaded under her knickers. Her stockings are folded over the back of a chair, her coat, cardigan and dress are hanging on wooden pegs on the back of the door, and her shoes are neatly placed under the washstand.

The warped floorboards are icy cold to her bare feet, like walking on a frozen sea. She shivers, slips on her dress and cardigan and lifts the wooden latch. The door opposite is padlocked. She holds the banisters on both sides and makes her way downstairs into the middle of a large room. To her left, the kitchen: a black range, logs piled in a corner, a shallow stone sink, a cupboard set into an alcove, wooden planks laid across trestles for a table. On a shelf a wireless, its plaited electric cord looping across the wall to a single electric socket.

The other side: a tidal mark of brown stains on the whitewashed walls; an old, threadbare oriental carpet lying over flagstones; an old sofa sprouting wiry, golden hairs through badly patched holes, and sprawled on it Leyland, wearing only a white vest and underpants, his eyes closed and his breathing deep. A rumpled blanket on the floor.

She stands over him, catches his scent, sweet and private. A scar on his chest, just above his vest. It can't be a war wound. Further down, his vest dips above the navel. Dark hairs curl above the top of his underpants. It's freezing: she's amazed he can sleep. She picks up the blanket and lays it over him.

Two laceless boots discarded by the door are covered in splashes of paint. Her feet slip easily into them. She takes an old tweed jacket off a peg, turns the long-shanked key in the lock. The old door scrapes the stone step.

His motorbike leans at an angle in the entrance to an open-sided barn, its chrome sparkling with frost. Brambles covered in silvery spiders' webs grow over the low stone wall surrounding a rough, grassy area. She walks to the centre of it, under a canopy of branches, and closes her eyes. For a moment she is the last person on earth, with just one lone bird and its miraculous song high above: *S for Skylark*, reputed to never stop singing while they are on the wing. Or is it that they never land? But then, how would they breed? She can't remember. Maybe she's thinking of the albatross.

Frost-frozen grass crackles behind her. His hands rest on her hips. She steps away. She's a ravaged landscape. A no-man's land.

'Grace, I've been thinking. You should come and live here with me.'

She hears the hard, cynical edge to her laughter.

'We could be useful to each other. You need to leave the past behind, Grace.'

'Now you're sounding like Hariti.' An upside-down shirt and two vests hang from a line strung between two trees, their frosty shapes glinting. 'I have a strong instinct to run.'

'This place needs a woman's touch.'

She turns, and in an unguarded moment strokes his bristly face. An absurd gesture of gratitude. He was there at the start. He's always turned up when she was most in need. She can choose to be suspicious or to accept her fate. 'I'm hungry.'

'There's smoked bacon in the larder and probably an egg or two in the hutch. I'll ride over to the village to get supplies a bit later.'

'I have to get back to Rye.'

'We could pretend to be married. It'd be convenient.'

Grace imagines Nancy's sceptical look: she'd call him a fast worker. What on earth *is* Grace doing here? Is she really considering his ridiculous proposal? It *would* be a place of refuge, but too reckless, too self-destructive.

*

He's gone to the village shop. The house feels safe. How many generations, births and deaths, have been witnessed by these whitewashed walls? She rinses two breakfast plates in cold water at the stone sink, using an old piece of shirt for a dishcloth. She pulls the plug and dirty water pours through a hole in the wall; she hears it sloshing on the ground outside. Maybe this is the answer: reducing her life to utter simplicity. There is beauty in the idea, like abandoning the polyphony of an orchestral work and returning to the purity of the Baroque.

The insect buzz of the motorbike grows to a loud spluttering as it turns into the barn. She leans against the front door frame. He lifts a brown paper bag from the saddlebag. 'I've been out hunting, Mrs Cornell.'

'You'll be lucky.'

He kisses the top of her head as he passes into the kitchen and places unlabelled tin cans on the table.

'How on earth do you know what's in them?'

'They have codes stamped on the bottom, look: this one has the letter 'P', it must be peas.'

'Or peaches.'

'I didn't think of that.' He rotates the can. 'Or it could be a 'd' for—'

'Duck!' A shiver: the alphabet game.

'By the way, I bumped into our neighbours – the Fletchers have the cottage down the lane – and they insisted on coming around to meet my new wife.'

'Oh god, Leyland, I've been in the same clothes for days. This is all too much. We hardly know each other.'

'Don't worry, I put them off, but we'll have to invite them soon or people will talk, gossip spreads like wildfire in these parts. I told them we were married in London a few days ago and will have a proper honeymoon when we have the funds.'

'You didn't say we couldn't afford it?'

'They won't be interested in our history, they'll spend the whole time talking about themselves, don't worry.'

'I have to go, Nancy will be worried.'

'There's a phone box on the corner of the lane.'

'I'll get a lift somehow.'

'The postman is an old friend. George. I'll arrange it.'

*

Cigarette smoke fills the postman's van.

'Can we stop for a moment, I'm not feeling well.'

The van slides on the muddy verge. Grace struggles out, climbs the bank. Her head is aching. She squints. Romney Marsh is a vibrant green. Sheep wander with heads down, their lambs nearly fully grown. Life goes on in spite of humans killing each other all over the planet.

George calls impatiently, he has a very important job to do.

*

As she slides her hand along the black railing, her shoes ring on the cobbles. How many people have steadied themselves on this rail over the centuries? Lives folding into each other. Fate. Karma. She'll have to pay for abandoning Orlando. In this life or the next.

Nancy will be worried but Grace is not ready to face her. She walks past the house into the Gun Garden. The last time she was here it was spring and she'd felt a hostage to fortune.

The land stretches out, mostly flat, with a pale ochre line like a rucked-up blanket. She sees clearly how this would be the perfect location for the Germans to launch a counter-invasion. The newspapers say they are in retreat but one never really knows what truths are hidden by the powers-that-be. She sees them against the metal grey sky: swarming formations of German bombers, white parachutes floating down like dandelion seedheads.

Footsteps behind her. She turns.

'Grace, you're back.'

'I'm sorry—'

'Leyland telephoned. I was watching, I saw you pass.'

'How have you been?'

'Oh, tickety-boo. Worried about you.'

'Can we walk?'

Women bustle along the High Street carrying bags and baskets. A board outside the butcher's shop announces early closure; a shop window full of dolls with accusing stares.

Grace senses Nancy's melancholy. They walk aimlessly out of town. She's not sure what the point is of being in Rye, she doesn't really belong here, but the alternative is London, or to accept Leyland's mad offer, and she's not sure she can deal with his secrecy.

A line of elms casts faint shadows across the road. Over the hedge, large camouflage nets arc over the Bofors guns.

'We'd better go back, Nancy.'

'Let's turn around at Tillingham Bridge.' A pillbox. Ominous dark slits in the grey concrete. 'Leyland is expecting you to return.'

'I don't know where I belong, Nancy.'

'He's far too furtive for my liking.'

'I guess it's hard being a foreigner.'

'Then why isn't he in his precious Eire?'

A shout: 'Halt! Who, er … who goes there?'

They turn. A young soldier is pointing a rifle.

Nancy takes the lead. 'I am so sorry young man, we've obviously interrupted your call of nature.'

He looks down at his unbuttoned trousers. His face reddens. 'You better move.' His rifle jabs the air, directing them towards the wooden barricade topped with barbed wire set across the road.

Nancy takes Grace's arm. 'Better do what he says, I'm worried he'll let that thing off – the rifle I mean.'

An elderly man with three stripes see them approaching, drops a cigarette butt. On the other side of the bridge two men are pushing a large cable reel.

Grace whispers, 'What are they doing?'

'It's supposed to be a secret but the whole town knows. They put dynamite under the bridge. Now they're having to undo it all again.'

The sergeant demands to see their identity cards, insists they reel off their numbers, then hands the cards back.

Nancy can't resist teasing. 'So tell me, Mr Shilling – Grace, you know the butcher don't you – what was that performance for?'

A man in khaki stoops as he exits the guardhouse. 'Ah, welcome my children.'

Nancy releases Grace's arm. 'Hello, Vicar, I didn't expect to see you in a place like this.'

'These men are doing God's work.'

'Let me introduce my friend, Miss Fisher.'

His handshake is surprisingly firm. 'Pleased to meet you, Miss Fisher. Will we be seeing you at St Mary's on Sunday?'

'I'm only visiting.'

'I believe I've seen you in the area before.'

'We must be getting on, Vicar.'

'May God be with you.'

They walk back past the pillbox. 'Nancy, what do you think was going on there? The vicar looked a bit guilty.'

'Probably a bit of black market.'

'Where would Jesus be in this war? I'd guess he'd be a conchie.'

'He'd certainly be against the capitalists.'

'What, all that turning tables over in the temples?'

Nancy hesitates. 'How was it? You don't have to tell me, but if you want—'

'I have to look forward.'

'You can't go back to Cornell. I don't trust him. I won't let you. We'll be a couple of old maids. Scandal of the town.'

Rye
May 1945

It's almost too amazing to be true. Hitler is dead.

*

Grace is polishing a candlestick: a sharp, oily smell of Silvo. Everything in its rightful time and place. She flicks the cloth over her shoulder, turns the dial of the wireless through a cloud of hisses and squeaks. The door knocker echoes in the hall. There's a gypsy encampment out on the marsh. She prepares to offer polite refusals to bunches of heather.

The shock hits her in the belly. Smith. In a strange echo of the past, he holds out Sancho's lead.

The dog rushes forward, tail wagging. Smith jerks the lead hard and spits out: 'Sit!' The poor dog places his bottom on the pavement.

'He's too much for Kitty now, you have to accept responsibility for *something*.'

Before Grace can answer, Smith has pushed past her into the hall.

Nancy calls from the kitchen, 'Who is it?'

Smith strides down the corridor. 'Ah, Miss Lockhart, I presume. I'm not sure we've met? I'm Mr Smith, an old friend of Grace's family.'

Nancy has expertise in these social situations. She puts out her hand. 'How do you do, Mr Smith.'

'So this your house?'

'We would offer you tea, but there's no milk I'm afraid, or sugar, or lemons of course. And now I think about it, we've just run out of tea.'

'I wouldn't want to put you to any bother. Grace, don't leave it too long before you visit your mother, and remember, contact me any time you need help. I'll see myself to the door.'

Sancho lies at Grace's feet, stretching his paws like a sphinx.

THE BUTCHER CUTS A CUBE of lamb, wraps it in greaseproof paper. 'It's all over now that 'itler's done 'imself in, 'bout bloody time.' Women in the queue are talking excitedly about an announcement at three o'clock.

Sancho sniffs the sawdust floor. Nancy takes the package from the butcher and hands over her ration book.

Out in the narrow street, Nancy is excited. 'Gracie, can you believe it!'

Grace is glad, of course. No more nightmares of Nazis on the streets, no more fear from the sky, but she doesn't seem able to feel joy. 'What about the Japs? There's no sign of that ending soon.'

'You have to learn to *live*. Let go. The world will never be perfect.'

'What will become of *us*?'

Nancy laughs. 'Oh my Gracie. We'll be able to travel. We'll go to America.'

The idea of crossing an ocean sends fear tingling up her spine. Why? Isn't this exactly what she always wanted? On the pavement, a dancing shadow, and Grace is a little girl, her shadow trying to step on Hariti's. 'I just want to take my cello out of its case without feeling guilty.'

'You will, Grace. It's up to us now to make the world a better place.'

Two boys in shorts and a girl in a dirty dress run past them, carrying armfuls of wood and a doormat in their spindly arms. Nancy calls, 'Hey, where are you lot going?'

'Pipemakers Arms, Miss, they're 'aving a bonfire.'

Further down Watchbell Lane soldiers have gathered, singing, spilling beer from tankards. It's not even opening time.

Women standing on chairs are tying up coloured bunting from house to house: seemingly endless triangles made from old striped pyjamas, cotton sheets, muslin and calico. How long have the upright women of Rye been sewing in secret, a communal act of faith?

The morning clouds have drifted away. They walk without speaking, pausing now and then for Sancho to sniff the ground. They arrive at the greengrocer's in time to see him carrying a wireless into his shop, the brown electrical flex snaking over a display of earthy potatoes and early carrots. A car has been abandoned in the middle of the road, its black doors open like the wings of a cockroach preparing to fly. A small crowd waits patiently for the wireless set to warm up.

The volume is turned up full. Churchill's headmasterly voice is unmistakable.

We may allow ourselves a brief period of rejoicing …

*

People are pouring into the afternoon sunshine. Nancy is swept away by a group of rowdy sailors. Sancho barks but no one is afraid, not today. Grace can't resist the tide of hope lifting her. She is hugged by grinning housewives, old men freed of their craggy pessimism, and young men in blue and khaki, determined to ignore their injuries.

At the bottom of the town, a crew of women in aprons is fussing around children seated at a long row of trestle tables in the middle of the street. One dishes out slices of apple pie, another follows, a tin of Carnation milk in each hand, happily pouring out the precious hoard.

*

When Grace eventually finds Nancy, it's getting dark. She's dancing in the arms of a tall man in a pinstriped suit. She sees Grace and waves. People are gathered around a huge pile of wood and broken furniture. Three sailors drag a mattress on to the top. The crowd has abandoned itself to unrestrained singing. *We'll keep a welcome …*

Someone unscrews a jerrycan. Whoosh. Sancho whines. Flames snake into the heart of the structure, smoke curls and billows.

Panic grips Grace's chest. She has to escape. Flames flickering on ecstatic faces. She runs to the shadows, up the cobbled path, clutching the iron railing, a stitch in her side, Sancho pulling like a husky.

A distant bell. She's not heard it before: haunting, a seafaring clang, clang.

She reaches the top and pulls Sancho back to get her breath.

A window is open. A scratchy record, a familiar voice floating into the lane. Marlene Dietrich. Grace remembers Kitty playing it:

Bei der Kaserne
Vor dem grossen Tor
Steht 'ne Laterne
Und steht sie noch davor

A hand on her shoulder. She jumps.

'You look pale.' Smith holds out a plate. 'Here. Have one of these.'

Acid bile rising.

'Grace. Today of all days we should forgive and forget.'

Words are trapped in her gullet.

'You tempted me and I gave in: perhaps I shouldn't have but what happened, happened. And it's made Kitty very happy. Orlando is a lovely boy. You should get to know him.'

With seemingly no control of her body, her hand reaches out and takes a triangle of dry beige bread.

He squats, ruffles Sancho's neck. 'We must have a chat about your Mr Cornell one of these days.' He turns, puts the plate on a low wall and is gone.

Her arms hang helplessly by her side, the sandwich squeezed tight, doughy bread with its fishy filling oozing between her fingers.

LEYLAND HAD TELEPHONED. She'd accepted his invitation. Truth is, she doesn't really care. She's like a piece of flotsam. Jettisoned. Aimless. What else is there to do with her life? He'd suggested supper with his neighbours – the Fletchers – good people, salt of the earth. He'll be in town to pick her up.

*

He kickstarts the motorbike. Grace stands on a pedal, holds her skirt down as she lifts her leg over the pillion seat, puts her arms around his leather coat. The motorbike judders over the cobbled lanes. Out on the road she relaxes, leans into corners with him, rests her head against his back.

He shouts over the noise of the engine. 'We have to pretend to be married.'

'We can't ... we'll never ...'

'Trust me.'

The sitting room seems brighter. He's whitewashed the walls, but the damp stain – a persistent high-tide mark – still shows through.

'They're due any minute. I'm going to change out of my overalls. There are candles around somewhere.'

He takes the stairs in twos. Grace finds the candles wrapped in greaseproof paper in the musty wall cupboard. She lights all twelve – to hell with the waste, the war is over – and makes little pools of wax for them on the rough wooden table. The room glows with honeyed light.

Leyland bounds down the stairs: black corduroy trousers and a dusty blue shirt with billowing sleeves. 'How do I look?'

'Piratical! Why do you always padlock your room?'

'It's a darkroom. You could ruin things if you barged in.'

'I'm not in the habit of *barging in* anywhere.'

A knock. He makes a flourish as if holding a sabre. 'Repel boarders!'

He opens the door. An elderly woman holds out a bottle of wine. 'My dear Leyland; and I assume this is your unfortunate wife.'

'Grace, let me introduce Charles and Mary Fletcher.'

Charles Fletcher's hand is fat and puffy. 'How do?' He holds Grace's gaze a little too long, then gives a small nod and releases her.

Mary Fletcher's hand is bony. 'Welcome to Sussex. We've known this miserable rascal for years. It's wonderful to see him happy at last.' She turns to the table. 'Oh my poor dears, have you got no electricity?'

Leyland offers a chair. 'There is only one three-amp socket, we don't need—'

'We can't have that … Charles, pop over to that shed of yours and get the flex.' Mary touches Grace's arm. 'Don't you worry dear, you need all the comforts you can get in this desolate place. Your husband is very naughty bringing you here.'

Leyland extracts the cork from the wine bottle. Red wine glugs into glasses. Mary babbles on, sipping carefully. Leyland finishes his in one gulp. Charles returns with a coil of twisted flex and a string bag of lightbulbs. He surveys the ceiling, then stands on a chair – with no apparent sense of intrusion – and hangs one end of the flex over a nail in the black beam, puts a bulb in the holder, then trails the flex over to the socket by the fireplace chimney and pushes the plug in. The room is instantly flooded with a violent yellow light.

Mary claps her hands, 'The wonders of civilisation!', and blows all the candles out. A haze of waxy smoke hangs over them.

Charles takes a glass from Leyland. 'Aye up.'

Grace is determined to be the pleasant hostess. 'I detect a northern accent, Mr Fletcher.'

Leyland interrupts. 'And a northern chip.'

Mary pats his arm. 'Leyland Cornell, behave!'

Charles exaggerates his accent. 'Thee's al'right luv.'

Mary chatters on, apparently contentedly. Does she know she's the centre of attention? Perhaps she's just being kind, keeping the conversation going, endeavouring to create a light-hearted atmosphere.

Grace asks Charles where he was originally from. Mary speaks for him. 'Sheffield, had a bad start, didn't you, Charles.'

He stares into his glass. 'The war messed up many people's education.'

'Well let's hope the world will be a better—'

'That's what we thought the first time.'

Leyland's voice is already slurring. 'We'll assert our rights over those who control us.'

Mary shakes her head. 'I'm sorry, Grace, he's talking about Ireland again.'

'Actually, I'm referring to the ruling classes, but I take your point.'

'Well you'd better not get me started on your country's disgraceful neutrality.'

'If we'd sided with you, Hitler would have had the perfect excuse to invade, then where would England be?'

'And that de Valera. Nazi sympathiser.'

'If we hadn't been forced to beg, borrow and steal to stay afloat—'

'And he sent condolences on Hitler's death! We won't forget *that* in a hurry.'

'It would have made no difference to us which of you lot won, the Irish would be swapping one master race for another.'

Mary's face is reddening. 'You can't compare … that sort of talk is treason.' She turns to Grace, more control in her voice. 'You'll have to take a position on the Irish question if you are going to manage your husband.'

A squeak from outside, maybe some poor rodent being caught by an owl. The wind has risen; a cold draught on her legs. The squeak again, then a shutter bangs on the wall.

Leyland starts to get up but he doesn't look too steady. Grace holds his arm. 'I'll do it. Stay here.'

The dark is a relief. She pins the shutter back, looks through the window at the convivial scene and sees a look pass between the Fletchers. She senses something; an undercurrent, some truth disguised by polite, teasing conversation.

She returns, leans hard against the door to close it.

Mary raises her glass. 'Well, this is all very nice! Leyland tells me you are a musician, Grace, how splendid.'

Grace tells anecdotes about Mrs Blumen, the nail clippers in her carpet bag, and how Mrs Blumen was booed in a concert. Grace knows she's talking far too much. She needs someone to stop her.

Leyland isn't finished. 'England is history. Your British Empire is crumbling.'

Mary rises to the bait. 'Well, I wouldn't say it was *my* Empire.'

'The people will rise up, claim their homeland … all over … the Middle East …'

'You mean the Jews? I agree, it's time they had their own—'

'No, Mary. The Palestinians.'

'Oh dear, I fear we are entering another quagmire! We don't want to be the cause of marital discord. Come on, Charles, it's late, we'd better leave the happy couple to some peace and quiet.'

They gather at the door, Mary kisses Grace on the cheek. 'Leyland is a very lucky man. Do call in if you need help, any time at all.'

'You are too kind.'

Leyland re-lights one of the candles.

Grace turns off the electric light. 'Leyland, you promised—'

'I'll take the spare room.' He leads the way up the stairs. 'Mary is sweet, but dear God can she talk. I thought they'd never leave.'

'You were a bit hard on them.'

'I'll go to Rye tomorrow to get your things.'

'I must have my cello.'

'I'll put Nancy's mind to rest. I can put the cello on my back. There won't be room for you. You stay here.'

His abruptness makes her stop one step short of the top landing. 'I don't know about this, Leyland. Nancy will think you've abducted me.'

'I can handle her.'

'Can she handle *you*?'

'This is all rather surreal, don't you think?'

One more step and they are facing each other on the landing. 'As long as you behave, Leyland.'

'I understand. People like you and Nancy—'

'You know nothing about *people like us*.'

He kisses her forehead. 'You are right, you are a complete mystery … except … I did undress you that first night.'

'Not all the way, I'm grateful to say. You'll have to get my dog, too.'

'I can tie his lead to the pillion, give him a good run for his money.'

The image of poor Sancho with his ears flapping in the slipstream makes Grace laugh. 'Goodnight, Leyland.'

*

A glow from the corner fireplace. Leyland must have made a fire and stoked it up before the Fletchers arrived. Standing on a small rag rug in front of it, she undresses down to her slip, feels tears – unaccountably – welling up.

The house creaks in the dark. He's pacing next door. The wind is picking up.

A light tap on her door. 'You awake?' A wavering shadow cast by a candle flame. His ghostly figure in vest and underpants. 'My room is freezing.'

He crosses the room, puts the candle holder on the bedside table, slides under the bedclothes. 'We need to talk. I always want truth between us.'

'That's an easy thing to say.'

'I mean it, Grace. I respect you.'

'And you did rescue me from being run over by a London-bound train.'

'Yes, that is also true.'

'You don't believe in reincarnation, do you?'

'I don't know what I can offer, Grace, but there is something significant between us; something precious when so much has been destroyed. Why did you stop playing your music?'

'Kitty wouldn't allow it.'

'I love the cello.'

'You may live to regret saying that.'

'One thing I promise you, Grace, is this: I will never lie to you.'

'There will always be secrets.' Silence. She's not sure if he's still awake. 'Why are you doing this – looking after me?'

'Would "Fate" do as an answer?'

She laughs. 'I wouldn't have put you down as the mystical type.'

'I can't explain it.'

He turns over, puts his hand on her belly. She jumps. 'Leyland—'

'Sorry, my hands must be cold.'

'I can't—'

'Don't worry. Our friendship is based on honesty and respect.'

She focusses on her breathing. His hand is resting on her soft belly, her void; where a child had taken comfort from her heartbeat. A baby now free of her.

'Grace, if things do go downhill, you might have to come to Ireland with me.'

The candle splutters, regains some strength, then dies into the dark.

His breath puffs on her shoulder. The room lightens a little: maybe there's a moon behind the shutters. She stares up at the dark timbers: there are sure to be spiders, just waiting to drop onto her face when she falls asleep.

… exploding glass … the room shimmers with uncanny light … sour oily paraffin … smoke curls on the ceiling … the curtains in a flaming dance …

She's alone. Dawn light. She hasn't had that nightmare for ages.

Leyland returns with a cigarette and a box of matches, gets back into bed, strikes a match: a calming cloud of smoke. He offers the cigarette.

'No thank you.'

'You were whimpering in your sleep.'

'I had a nightmare.'

'Not surprising, given what we've all been through.'

'We? I have no idea what *you've* been through. I know nothing about you, really.'

'Well that's not true, Grace. I'm an artist—'

'That's not what I mean. You could be a spy, or a refugee, or a … I don't know what. And I don't know why you are interested in me. I can't give you anything. I don't even know who *I* am.'

'Grace, I will make it all better, I promise. I have to go away again soon but I want you to wait for me. We'll find our own way to be happy. I will get a job and bring in money. I just need time.'

Brede
June 1945

SHE HUMS AS SHE LAYS two thick bacon rashers in the frying pan. They've managed their platonic relationship for nearly three weeks.

The door scrapes and Leyland comes in with logs balanced along his bare arm. He kicks the door closed and stacks the logs at the side of the stove. 'Morning, lovely lady.'

'Morning, Mr Blarney.'

He hasn't remembered it's her birthday, but why should he? Just because – on the summer solstice eighteen years ago – he found her on a railway crossing.

The familiar tooting of the post van's horn.

Leyland goes out to meet George and returns with a small parcel, a letter and a postcard.

'Have you known George for long?'

'He's a survivor ... the Great War.'

'I would have thought that would make him rather hostile to the Irish.'

'Yes, I see that, but he says all war is pointless.' He tucks the parcel under his arm, examines the postcard.

'So it's not a present for me then?'

'Tubes of paint, I've been waiting for zinc white for months.'

He drops the postcard on the table. Halfway up the stairs he opens the letter.

'No bacon for you?' She picks up the postcard.

'Sorry. I'll have to give you a lift back to Rye. Could you make a couple of sandwiches?'

The postcard is addressed to 'Miss G. Fisher, care of Mr L. Cornell'.

There's no message. She muses on the idea implied by 'care of', then turns the card over.

A surge of adrenalin. The image of a carving: a figure in black stone, a grizzled face, and in each hand a half moon. Rahu.

Rye
July 1945

Love Lane is an ironic place to feel so alone. A tunnel of trees. On such a hot day, it's a relief to be in the shade of the magnificent horse chestnut. From the size of its trunk Grace imagines it must be at least a couple of hundred years old. The history it's witnessed! Rooted to the spot, patient.

She loves the way Sancho runs ahead, sniffing the hedgerows, turning back to check Grace is still following, then loping ahead again. She's suspended, accepting that she'll never feel again the nerve-tingling thrill from years ago when she lay with Nancy as bombs fell on London.

Sancho stops suddenly, his whole body alert.

Behind Grace, a tinkling bell. A boy on a red bicycle wobbles past, probably taking a telegram to some unfortunate family. In spite of the war ending in Europe people are still dying.

A few seconds later, footsteps. Sancho growls.

Grace puts the strap of her handbag over her head, crossing it over her chest.

'Mrs Cornell!' Charles Fletcher is out of breath. 'I thought it was you. How are you?'

'I'm fine, thank you.'

'I haven't seen you down here before.'

'The town can be a little claustrophobic.'

He crouches to stroke Sancho. 'We haven't seen Leyland for a while. Do you come to Rye often?'

'He's away a lot. I have a friend here I stay with.'

'It's not the liveliest place for a young lass ... coming all the way from London, it must be very dull.'

'Well, I have plenty to read.'

'I have a particular love of poetry ... here.' He pulls a little book from his jacket pocket. 'I think Dickinson would suit you, listen: *"Hope" is the thing with feathers.* Beautiful, don't you think?'

A shiver. The marbled light seems to lift off the path and float in a blur. She leans against the railings.

Sancho whines.

Mr Fletcher gently touches her elbow. 'Are you all right, lass?'

'Yes, sorry, it's the heat. I'm fine.'

'Take it. I've read it hundreds of times.'

'No, I couldn't—'

'Go on, lass.'

'That's so ... thank you ... so kind.'

August 1945

They drop their umbrellas into the stand just inside the entrance to the tearoom. Sancho shakes his wet fur, sending a spray onto a row of customers' coats hanging on hooks.

Nancy nudges Grace. 'Look at those GIs flirting with the waitress.'

The blushing young woman turns away from their table and drops half a scone on the floor. The Americans laugh and she stutters an apology. The accent, familiar from the movies: 'No big deal, lady.'

Sancho lunges forward and the scone is gone in seconds.

The waitress frowns. 'You can't bring that dog in here.'

Nancy pulls Sancho to heel. 'We'll sit over there.'

'It's against the rules.'

Nancy strides to the back of the tearoom.

'Nancy! You're such a troublemaker!'

'Silly woman.'

'Please don't draw attention to us.'

'And where's your protector when you need him?'

'Wales apparently, looking for a job.'

'Doesn't Kitty help you out?'

'She did say she would send some money but nothing ever materialises. She's probably heard I'm living in sin with a Fenian, and worse than that an artist.'

'Well, it's right he's looking for work, it's what a man should do for his woman.'

'For a rebel you have some traditional ideas, Nancy. I'm not his woman.'

'*He* might be thinking differently.'

'Anyway, I expect he'll be back soon.'

She lights a cigarette, 'Is he good in bed?'

'Nancy! It's not like that.'

'I haven't forgiven him for stealing you away from me.'

'I'm with you, I hardly spent more than a few weeks with him. He's always off somewhere.'

'He's far too flirty with me, considering.'

'You're in a naughty mood today.'

A short bald man pushes through swing doors. 'I believe my waitress told you that dogs are not allowed in my establishment.'

Nancy laughs. 'Your *establishment* is it? What? You think this is the Ritz?'

'There are rules.'

'We'll have a pot of tea for two please.'

'If you don't remove the dog, I'll call the police.'

Sancho growls.

A GI from a nearby table scrapes back his chair. An American accent: 'Captain Bridges at your service, ma'am, do we have a problem here?'

Nancy crosses her legs. 'Good morning, Captain, one of my countrymen to the rescue.'

He offers his hand. 'Delighted. And you are from?'

'Washington. And you, sir?'

'Delaware, ma'am. How can I help?'

'You're far from home.'

'Can't wait to get back to my wife and little boy, to tell the truth.'

Grace watches the pride, the sense of purpose in his whole physical being: he's a father, he'd die for his child, why else is he over here? A moment of panic … she calms her breathing. Orlando is better off with a woman who lost a child to a river than with her.

'This silly man is insisting that our dog leaves the premises. It's raining and it would be cruel to tie him up outside, don't you agree?'

The Captain turns to the proprietor, hands him a coin. 'Leave this with me, sir.' The man looks at the coin, shakes his head and walks back to his kitchen, mumbling.

'This is a contravention of the rules.' The Captain winks. 'They may be silly, but we all have to follow them. Behave now.' He turns back to his table. The officers laugh too loudly. Nancy pulls on the lead. 'Sancho. *Sit*.'

The waitress avoids eye contact as she places two cups of tea on the table. Grace notices scars on her left arm. Who knows what she's been through. Maybe she was bombed out in the Blitz and lost her whole family. Perhaps her new husband was sent abroad to die in a stinking muddy field, a tractor turning the soil newly fertilised by rotting corpses, the farmer's crops feeding a starving Europe. And it's not yet over in the East.

'Darling, you're miles away. Shall I order a teacake?'

'Grace. Telephone for you.'

'Who is it?'

Nancy raises an eyebrow and passes over the receiver.

The line is crackly. 'Grace, I'm back.'

'Mr Cornell. How pleasant for you.'

'Don't be like that. I've explained before, I had to go away. But things will be different now. You can come back to the cottage. We'll start again.'

'Start what?'

'George will give you a lift tomorrow. Please come, Grace. Let's see what we can work out.'

*

Grace doesn't believe for a moment that he is capable of sticking to any of his promises, and for the life of her she doesn't know why she's ready the next morning when George knocks on the door.

Brede
September 1945

GRACE TURNS THE DIAL to the Third Programme. The dreamy vibrato of a violin circles the damp walls.

Standing at the french windows, she notices that the blue paint on the rotting wooden frame has been carelessly splashed onto the glass. She's sure the house would prefer to be somewhere warm, like the Mediterranean: France, perhaps, with scorching sun heating the stone walls, baby lizards running into the shade of the vine over the front door, red grapes ripening, bees intoxicated by the nectar of purple wisteria. Poor France. Grace can't imagine what it has endured all these years, with Germans crawling all over it like a plague of lice. And now, liberation! It must feel so sweet. She's heard about the witch hunts, people condemned for siding with the enemy. How fine the line must be between cooperation and collaboration. And how easy it is to judge.

The harp and flute have picked up the theme, poignant, ethereal.

She's in a strange mood: a nervousness, an anticipation, a sense of possibility. The destruction is over. The dark past is dissolving into a brighter future. Surely it can't now matter where she came from, how many lives —

'Are you trying to wake the village?' Leyland is leaning over the banisters.

She turns the volume up.

'You are going to be in serious trouble, young lady.'

'Well, I'm not *your* lady, young or otherwise.' A horn sounds in the distance. 'It's the bread van, Leyland, can you go please, I'm busy.'

'Doing what! You are hopeless!' He stomps down the stairs in baggy underpants, his shirt flapping free over his vest. 'Can't for the life of me imagine what that old Professor taught you.'

She laughs. 'All I know is how to survive … men in particular.'

Men have been drifting back over the past months, but there are still too many families waiting for a father, husband, brother to return, unsure of how the man will be: a blessing or a curse.

The door scrapes. Leyland kicks off his unlaced boots, puts the loaf and a few coins on the table.

She's standing in the centre of the room, swaying slightly as the music swirls.

'Useless woman.' He touches her arm and kisses her cheek.

'No, Leyland, don't.'

'It's okay. I understand. You can trust me.'

'You have too many secrets.'

'It's for your own protection.'

'Which is confirmation – as if any were needed – that you are involved in something dangerous. Makes it even harder for me.'

'It's cold in here, let's light the stove. Can you do it?'

'Leyland, do you think … I don't know how to say it … that now that the war is over, there will be some some sort of cleansing process, lessons learned, new ways of – I don't know, cooperation between countries?'

He picks up a hatchet and with confidence, swings it down onto a log. 'Not in my opinion. This is just the start.'

She sits on the arm of the sofa watching him create a pile of kindling. It's both agonising and thrilling. Passion and fury in each accurate strike.

The concert has come to an end. The announcer is talking about Elgar's *Enigma Variations*. She turns it off, picks up her book, flops onto the sofa.

Leyland feeds the stove, stretches and sits down next to her. 'What are you reading?' He leans over. 'Emily Dickinson, we did her at school.'

'Mr Fletcher lent it to me.'

'She was undiscovered in her time, you know.'

'There's one about a bird … sent shivers up my spine.'

'Show me.'

She turns a page, reads aloud: ' *"Hope" is the thing with feathers* / *That perches in the soul* …' A catch in her throat.

'If only I could paint like that ... it's soulful.'

'That's tender, Leyland.'

'Poetry … art … it doesn't just reflect what we are; it's about our potential. Look at how we're moved by the Renaissance half a millennium later, and the revelations of the Impressionists, and the revolutionary Surrealists.'

'That's more passion from you in one sentence than I've heard since I've known you.'

He scratches his unshaved chin. 'Be serious, Grace. This war might be over, but we're on the verge of a new struggle. We must be prepared.'

'But now that Japan has surrendered—'

'Grace, how about we get married. Properly this time, it would help us both.'

'That sounds very utilitarian.'

'I don't mean—'

'I just want to hide. I've had enough conflict to last a dozen lifetimes.'

'I know I'm not what you really need. You don't even know yourself do you? And that's sad.'

'You know me better than I do, now?'

'You've been lost ever since I found you.'

'That could be quite poetic if it wasn't so patronising.' She strokes the book's cover. 'Anyway, you're not the type for marriage. I know you have battles to fight. I don't know what they are and I don't want to know. All I can hope for is to conquer Bach. Anyway, I can't abandon Nancy, she's always been there for me.'

He lies back, one arm crooked behind his head. 'I'll ride over and get her this afternoon.'

'Stop teasing, Leyland.'

'I'll pick up some rations and we'll have dinner for three – by candlelight this time!'

'You are a riddle wrapped in a what's-it, however that phrase goes.' She prods his ribs. He exaggerates falling forward onto the carpet, rolls onto his back, his arms above his head in surrender. She laughs, puts her book down. She sees the truth of him: inside this troubled man, a vulnerable boy. A realisation creeps over her, a sense of what life would be like without him. She can't say she loves him, but his presence is necessary for her to feel … to feel she belongs.

She stands up, steps across him, looking along his body: that male shape, slack, but evident. It's too familiar. But how does she know? From what Hariti told her about *lingam*? If only she could lay to rest the nightmare of Smith. Far worse has happened the world over. Now there is peace. A new beginning. Dare she? She knows exactly what will happen.

She kneels, her skirt billowing over his legs.

He holds her stare.

She won't take her knickers off, she'll never go that far again. She slides her fingers inside the elastic waistband, carefully eases his under-pants down; he raises his hips to help. He's starting to grow. He's saying she doesn't have to, that he's there for her anyway.

'Shush for once, Leyland.' She puts her hand around him, warm as she knew it would be. Her breathing is short, she's feeling dizzy but she continues to stroke. He moves his hips and moans until pungent wet spills onto his panting belly. She releases, relieved it's over. She wipes her hand on the tail of his shirt. 'Don't make assumptions, Leyland.' She stands, wants to laugh, it's all so bloody ridiculous. Surreal, even.

He sits up, pulls up his underpants and tucks in his vest and shirt, a wet patch quickly spreading.

They sit quietly side by side on the sofa. Not touching.

'Grace, I'll get Nancy. It'll make you feel better.'

'I'm sure she'd like that, Leyland.'

From across the fields, church bells start ringing. After all the years of silence, their sonorous tones tighten her breathing.

'Do you ever think about your boy, Grace?'

'I'm not cut out—'

'I know. You're a musician.'

She can smell him on her hand, salty-sweet.

He sighs. 'I must find some money.'

'And a clean shirt.'

At this very moment in Chelsea, parishioners – she imagines – are being summoned to St Luke's. She remembers sitting next to Kitty in the pews. She loved her white cotton socks. Sometimes the bells played 'Oranges and Lemons': it always made her feel sad for some reason. Orlando will be growing up hearing them. Kitty will wash his face, tidy his hair, tie his laces, teach him how to say nicely 'How do you do?'

'Anyway, what could I ever give a child?'

November 1945

THE MOTORBIKE PURRS into the drive; the engine splutters and dies. Grace watches from the kitchen window: Nancy laughing as she lifts her leg over the pillion, her hair a terrible mess from the ride, Leyland's hand on the small of her back as they walk towards the cottage.

*

Lunch is courtesy of one of Leyland's many furtive friends, who has given him a colander of tiny silvery fish from the River Brede. He drops them into batter while the wireless feeds them sombre news of the Nuremberg trials. He transfers the fish into a frying pan of hot lard.

The overgrown cottage garden, it turns out, is not quite the paradise of weeds she'd assumed: there are patches of herbs and salad leaves, some bitter, some tasting a little like soap, but with the addition of sharp vinegar they taste vital.

*

They've moved their kitchen chairs onto the rough stone verandah and watch Leyland swinging a scythe.

Nancy sips her elderberry wine. 'He's quite the Robinson Crusoe, we should keep him, don't you think?'

'Apparently he's got work somewhere. He'll be going off again. I really can't be here alone.'

'It's idyllic.'

'Not many opportunities for a concert career.'

'Very few of us have the luck to live the lives we imagined we would.'

'I hear they've cleared Winchelsea beach, we could go for long walks.'

'Aren't you happy, Grace? He adores you.'

'Don't take any notice of me. And don't read too much into me staying here with him.'

'Everything is temporary for you, isn't it?'

The comment stings. She feels red rising to her cheeks. 'Leyland is determined you'll stay overnight; you will, won't you?'

Nancy drains her glass. 'He doesn't stand a chance with the two of us.'

*

Leyland takes his shirt off and stands at the sink wiping the dishcloth under his arms. 'Nancy can have the spare room.' He dries himself on an old army towel.

*

Sitting up in bed, he lights a cigarette from the candle flame and watches Grace undress down to her slip.

She slides under the sheet and blanket. 'Where did you get that scar?' Pale light from a half moon illuminates the smooth hairless wound.

'I got caught on a hook in a cold store: makes me look even more piratical, don't you think? Nothing to fuss over.'

'I can't imagine how you found work while so many in the country can't.'

'I ran into an old friend.'

'What sort of place is it, where you do this job of yours?'

'On the docks.'

'The docks? I need a bit more than that!'

'It pays for my digs and ciggies. Not what I was educated for, but it will do for now. How are things with you and Nancy?'

'I don't know what I'd have done without her.'

'Is it love?'

'That's very to the point, Leyland. For one thing, Nancy looks after me. I don't have to hang around here waiting for you to return.' Grace isn't sure how to explain. Nancy is part of her, but she'd never use the word 'love'; in truth, she doesn't really know what it means. The only person she has ever totally, deeply trusted was Hariti: her soft smile and big brown eyes; holding on to her in clouds of steam and smoke; her singing surrounding Grace in a bubble of perfect security.

'I'll go back with Nancy tomorrow. While you're away.'

'You understand, don't you? I do have to work.'

Outside, a shutter squeaks. 'They'll blow off one of these days.'

He gets up and opens the window, letting in a rush of cool air. Grace pulls the blankets up. He leans out and latches the shutter back against the wall; luminous clouds obscure the moon. He turns back. It looks so incongruous sticking out like that – especially in wavering candlelight – but threatening too.

His body is cold near hers. In spite of his reassuring words, he can't hide his desire.

'I don't want to push you, Grace, if you don't want—'

'There's a void at my centre, Leyland.'

'I understand. Let me be your compass.'

The ridiculousness of his cliché makes her laugh.

His hand rests on her belly; fingertips stroke, a small circle, gradually moving down. If only she could allow it … if only she could be normal.

'You can trust me, Grace.'

He reaches her hairs. He's gentle, knows not to push too far.

Floating clouds, the smell of tar, perfume of wild flowers.

He's lifting her up in his arms.

Hariti's voice. 'Her heart is beating, Mrs Fisher'.

The exploding glue pot.

'No, no. Leyland, stop.'

Nancy's sitting room has a wonderful acoustic, probably thanks to the thick stone walls. Grace positions the cello's spike in a groove between two polished floorboards. Scales first, quick runs up and down, staccato and legato. Mrs Blumen would be pleased with Grace's renewed dedication: she used to say that proficiency at scales gives one the deepest feeling for melody. Whatever happened to her? She must ask Kitty.

Grace rubs the amber block of rosin along the bow, tests the tension, places her fingers in the familiar pattern on the neck and draws the bow. The prelude to the first of the Bach suites.

The mournful sound floats through the open back window, past Nancy who is busy pruning roses, down the cobbled streets, across the harbour and out to sea. To Hariti, wherever in the world she might be.

'We really should make a recording of your playing, Grace.' Nancy is leaning on the window sill. 'It's sounding very professional.'

'Not on your life.'

*

That evening, Nancy brings out her father's recording machine from an alcove cupboard. She lifts the lid: two large reels, shiny brown tape threaded on a complicated path around little silver capstans. A row of ivory buttons. One red. A plaited cable leading to a lozenge-shaped microphone.

Rye
December 1945

SANCHO IS HOGGING THE rug in front of the glowing fire. Footsteps outside. He raises his head and barks. Nancy calls from the kitchen, 'It'll be the post for you Grace, probably that postal order from Leyland.'

'You are so naughty!'

She opens the front door to George, who holds out a parcel, a letter and a postcard.

'Looks like you've got friends in London, Mrs Cornell.'

'Thank you, George.'

She notices the postcard and her heart races.

George bends down to stroke Sancho. 'There's more good news. Did you hear about young Roy Miles?'

'I can't say I—'

'He was captured retreating to Dunkirk, see, seems he spent most of the war in the coal mines in Poland. His poor mother hadn't had news of him for years. She lived in hope but I think she believed he'd gone.'

'Goodness.'

'Well, he was freed by the Russians, see, and spent weeks with a group of Frenchmen in a lorry.'

'How horrid, how do you know all this?'

'I'm getting to that, see. He sent a letter to his mum when he got to Paris to say he was safe.'

'Thank goodness. She must be relieved.'

'The funny thing is, he cadged a lift with the RAF and got back to Rye before the letter. His mother was in the butcher's when she saw him walking down Ferry Road right as rain, and she fainted from the shock.'

'One never knows what life will throw at one next.'

'Indeed, miss.'

'I must go. Thank you for the parcel. I hope Mrs—'

'All's well that ends well.'

Grace puts off looking at the postcard. She unpicks the parcel's knotted string. Inside, a bundle of newspaper cuttings and a picture scribbled in wax crayon. Grace recognises Kitty's fine italic handwriting below the embossed Cheyne Walk address:

20th December, 1945

Dear Grace,

I thought you'd like news of life in your old home. All is generally fine here.

Robert – you will be relieved to hear – has returned from hospital. He has good days and not such good ones. Time will tell.

The other day I managed to bake a cake for Orlando: your old mother baking! And for months I've been squirrelling away ingredients in order to make a Christmas cake. It's hard to believe the boy is two and a half years old now.

I thought you might like to have your cuttings. You so loved sitting at your little desk, didn't you, whiling away the hours. I have added some more newspapers and a few magazines in case you want to snip some more pictures.

Orlando made a drawing for you. It's all a bit sketchy, as you can see, but he told me what it was: a little boy at his bedroom window watching an angel in the sky and his mother watching from another window. He's quite the artist. Unfortunately, he can't sing to save his life, although he can make plenty of noise when he wants to. I am not always sure I can cope, but the moment passes and we get back onto an even keel, so there really is no need to worry about us.

Darling, I do hope all is well with you and your friend Nancy, and I do so hope we shall see you in London one day in the not too distant future.

Oliver sends his best wishes and says he'll write.

Your loving mother, Kitty

Grace drops the letter onto the sofa, picks up the other envelope: she doesn't recognise the writing. She turns it over and back again, squints at the postmark. Nancy passes by, strokes the small of Grace's back. 'You could open it, then you'd know who it's from!'

Grace takes the letter opener from the mantelpiece and slices.

Dear Grace

I am sitting at Robert's magnificent bureau and – forgive me – using his writing paper. He stays in his bedroom most of the day.

I am not used to writing personal letters; I have not had much call for such skills. I have been getting reports that reassure me you are living a comfortable life with Miss Lockhart.

Kitty will have written to tell you about Robert.

Sometimes he's his old self, but mostly he's lost in a fog. It is strange watching him grow fond of Orlando. Kitty constantly asserts that the boy's father must be someone from your circle of bohemian friends. She needs to believe this, and I hope you will continue to allow her to think it. The truth would be devastating, and you owe them some consideration.

Contact me if you need any assistance. I occasionally have business in Hastings and could drop by.

Yours sincerely
Oliver Smith

She closes her eyes, tries to calm her breathing. The letter drops to the carpet. Will he forever be casting his dark shadow over her? She will *not* be trapped. She will *not* be made to feel guilty about the boy. She turns her attention to the postcard. It is dog-eared, with a pinhole on the top edge. An Indian woman carved in stone is squatting under an arch. Her hair is centrally parted and a bead necklace hangs symmetrically between her rounded breasts. Sitting on the knee of this goddess is a child with a strangely adult-shaped head.

Grace knows who this is from before she turns the card over.
The Ashmoleum Museum. Relief plaque depicting the Goddess Hariti.

THE TELEPHONE BOX STINKS of urine. Grace picks up the receiver, slots in coins, dials and presses the silver 'A' button. The coins drop. 'Leyland, is that you?'

'What happened? I've been waiting for ages outside this bloody box.'

'I'm so sorry, there was an old woman making a call. It stinks to high heaven in here, I think a cat—'

'How's Sancho?'

'Leyland, it's been ages—'

'I know I said I'd write but it's been mad here. I'll be able to send you some money soon, once I've paid for my lodgings and my tab.'

'Where are you?'

'I had to go abroad.'

'*Abroad!*

'I'm in Liverpool now, looking for work again.'

'But where abroad?'

Insistent pips. She presses in another coin. 'I have no more money. I need to talk to you. Give me your address.' The line has gone dead. 'Leyland? Leyland? Bugger!'

Through the window a soldier holds up his wrist and taps his watch.

She listens to the whining tone, places the handset in the cradle and pushes the door open. Her anger makes her brave; she puts on her best accent. 'You're an uncouth lout, I must say.'

She half expects him to hit her, and she wouldn't care if he did. He is just a young man. He bends his head and mumbles, 'Sorry ma'am.'

Grace wants to hug him but instead holds the door open.

'WE REALLY SHOULD GO, Grace, show our faces.'

'No, I hate them whispering behind our backs.'

'Don't be silly, it's the Christmas service, and anyway, everyone will be thinking about their dinner. You can choose the denomination!' Nancy gives Grace a hug. 'Come on, let's have some fun.'

'You are so naughty.'

*

They walk the few yards to St Mary's Church. The flying buttresses look like the legs of a giant insect clinging to the Rye hilltop. Inside the porch, a soldier guards a rick of rifles leaning together in a corner.

Bach is being massacred. It's not just all the wrong notes, the organist can't keep a predictable rhythm.

As expected, Leyland has not made contact since the aborted telephone call.

The vicar is praying for all the souls who have died in the war. Is he including all those facing execution in Nuremberg? He's evoking the infant Jesus to forgive their sins. How can one baby become a Messiah and another a Nazi?

Nancy senses Grace's mood. 'Let's get out of here.'

They join the queue, shake hands with the vicar, and finally make it out into the cold, sharp fog.

Nancy takes Grace's arm. 'Come on, the old scandal-mongers are watching, let's give them a show.'

She forces Grace into a skipping run.

EIGHT

Croydon
2000

THE IRISH NURSE FLOATS IN, glances at the clock. Humming, she turns Grace onto her side, puts something under her, rolls her the other way, then onto her back. The tune is haunting and familiar. *She walks through the fair* … Leyland's song.

The nurse fills the water jug at the sink, tells Grace she's getting stronger every day. Tomorrow she'll be going out in the wheelchair.

Grace remembers: alone with the constantly crying baby in the freezing cottage in Brede. Deprived of sleep, she has no idea how she'd stopped herself from throwing him against the wall.

The nurse raises her into a sitting position, plumps up the pillows and carefully slips Grace's glasses onto her nose, before placing a book into her good hand. She says Orlando found it in the hospital library. Grace's mouth is dribbling again.

The nurse says she'll be back in a minute. The book falls flat on the bed sheet. She can't raise her hand far enough to lick her fingers to turn a page.

*

Grace feels the bed sagging, opens her eyes. She's still alive, then.

'I found these two envelopes in a wooden box of postcards. Do you recognise them?'

What a stupid question.

From the larger one he brings out a document. 'Your adoption certificate. The date is 1938, before the war. So Kitty wasn't your biological mother.'

Long after the war had ended, Grace had found out. All the lies about her papers being dodgy – that was Smith's ruse to keep her captive, hold her in fear of the authorities.

A smaller white envelope. Her name on the front. Of course. He extracts a newspaper cutting.

'What's this, Mother?'

The room fills with her desperate moaning.

'I'm going to read it out.'

> *The Bell Inn, situated at the crossroads of Five Acre Wood, Epsom, was the scene of a terrible fire on Tuesday morning.*

Rye
June 1949

SANCHO STANDS ALERT at the top of the steps and sniffs the salt air. Nancy holds her skirt down as they descend. 'The flood's receded but it's still rather muddy, be careful, Grace.'

'It's supposed to be summer.'

'Have you had any news from—'

'I don't want to talk about him.'

'I'm not surprised; I've given him up for dead.'

The people of Rye have gradually adapted to peace, but there's a constant grumbling – especially in the shops – about rationing continuing years after the end of war. Slowly, tourists are becoming more evident. Shopkeepers are happy to take money from the grateful French, Dutch, and even from the occasional intrepid German.

Grace practises her cello for hours every day, and she's recently started learning Elgar's unpopular Cello Concerto: the key of E minor creates a mood which resonates with her, a sense of alienation and sorrow, not something people want right now.

They stop by the harbour to watch the gulls squabbling over the nets. Grace pushes her hands deeper into her cardigan pockets. One seagull is poking its head into an old tin can. 'Look Nancy, the poor thing will get its silly head stuck if it's not careful.'

'Tell me, where is Leyland now?'

'I don't care.'

'Come on, let's get a cup of tea.'

The shack is open. The same woman serving. 'Hello dears, cuppa?'

'Two of your finest please.' Nancy picks out a silver sixpence from her purse.

The woman stirs the large metal teapot, places two chipped mugs on the counter, cuts a currant bun in half and spreads butter. 'Here, have this on me, you look a bit peaky.'

Grace carries the mugs to the bench. 'I used to wonder about Leyland, how far he'd be prepared to go for his precious Eire.'

'You listened to your instinct about him.' Nancy breaks off a bit of bun and tosses it to Sancho. 'He's unreliable, and that's why you're living with me.'

'Okay, first of all, I'm not with you because I'm running from him.'

'We could go to America. He'd never find us there.' A seagull, its sharp eyes on the bun, waddles towards them. 'My father has influence.' Nancy lights a cigarette, smoke whips wildly around her head. 'Any news from London?'

'That was another life.'

'Has your father recovered? We could go and see them. Go to the pictures: it's been years.'

Grace wonders what she means to Nancy. More than friends, but not lovers. And why is that? Grace is no longer the naive young girl that Nancy was drawn to. But there are times when they look at each other from opposite armchairs, stockinged legs tucked up, the wireless murmuring, the fire crackling, when she feels a tingle of energy ripple up her spine. Hariti would have called it the rising of the *kundalini*.

'Sometimes...', she leans her head on Nancy's shoulder, 'it all feels so pointless.'

Nancy slips a record from its sleeve, a present from the Professor all the way from America. *The Voice of Frank Sinatra*. She holds it rather carelessly, lays it on the gramophone turntable, winds the handle and lifts the needle.

Grace, cross-legged on the sofa, is re-reading Emily Dickinson. The orchestral introduction fills the room. An unseasonably cold north wind is hurling sleet against the windows. Sancho stretches in front of the fire, looks up anxiously as a log crackles.

The music drones on. As Grace suspected, the 'Voice' irritates her, it's far too pleased with itself.

When Nancy's head slides sideways to rest on the wing of her chair, Grace tiptoes over to change the record, chooses Tchaikovsky's *Pathétique*, a strangely inappropriate name for such a passionate composition.

Sancho is suddenly alert, a low growl gathering in his throat. The door knocker raps. He is up, barking. Nancy stirs, wipes her eyes.

A gust of wind as Grace opens the front door. 'Bloody hell, what are you doing here?'

'Aren't you going to invite me in?'

She stands back. Leyland steps into the hall and removes his hat. 'Hello, Sancho old boy.' He takes off his oilskin coat and hangs it over others on the hall stand.

'Give it here, you fool, I'll put it near the fire to dry out.'

He follows Grace into the sitting room.

Nancy sits up. 'Miracles will never cease.'

Grace places the coat over the back of a chair, angles it towards the fire. 'Nancy, how about making us all a nice cup of tea?'

Nancy wags a finger at Leyland. 'I'll be back in a minute. Don't you dare whisk her away.'

Leyland stands with his back to the fire. 'This all looks very cosy. How is everything?'

'I thought you'd gone back home to your precious Republic.'

He raises an eyebrow.

'You think I don't read the news?'

'Look Grace, I know I've left you alone for far too long, but I couldn't help it. I've got work now. I'm saving money. I promised I would make things better for you, didn't I?'

Grace sits back down on the sofa and leafs through the pages of her book.

'I don't blame you for hating me.'

'I've never depended on you and I never will.'

'It's not been easy for me, Grace. I've missed you so much.'

She gets up, turns the record over, places the needle back in the groove, Allegro molto vivace.

As she passes, he catches her wrist. 'I have exciting news, I've bought a boat. We could test it out. It's not exactly a yacht but she's sturdy – an old fishing boat. She's got a mast and sail and a motor. You'll love her, we can go on adventures, start a new chapter. What do you say?'

Teacups rattle. Nancy places the tray on a low table.

Leyland kneels. 'I'll pour. You're looking well, Nancy.'

'I *am* well, and happy. We are all well and happy. Thank you *so* much for your concern.'

He passes them each a cup on a saucer, then spoons sugar into his own and sits cross-legged, stroking the dog. 'And how are you, my old Sancho?'

Nancy sits back. '*Our* old Sancho is fine.'

Grace laughs nervously. Nancy looks at Leyland for longer than is comfortable, then catches Grace's eye. 'I have to abandon you, I'm afraid. I'm off to bed. I'll see you in the morning, Grace.'

Leyland stands up. 'Goodnight, Nancy, I'm sorry for all the trouble I've caused you. I know you care for Grace, and I'm grateful to you for looking after her while I've been away. It will be better now.'

Nancy pauses at the door, looks like she's about to say something. Then she's gone.

Leyland kneels in front of the fire. 'I like her spirit.' He picks up the brass pan, shovels grey ash from under the grate and sprinkles it onto the coals. 'Grace, we need to talk, but I'm tired. Can we go to bed?'

'You *can't* expect to just walk in—'

'Listen, Grace—'

'You can use the sofa. Just for tonight.'

'Thank you. Then I can show you the boat. I need to go to the cottage to clean it out. You could come too.'

'Goodnight, Leyland.'

'Does he have plans?' Nancy blows cigarette smoke into the wind whipping across the harbour wall.

'He's at the cottage. There are lots of dead rats, apparently.'

'He'll feel at home, then.'

'I don't know why he wants to take me out in that damned boat. Can't you come, Nancy?'

'Not unless it's big enough to take me across the Atlantic. You'll be fine.'

'Something has to come to a head soon, we can't drift on like this.'

'Frankly, I'm surprised he's come back. Where's he getting his money from?'

'I don't know.'

'Grace, you *will* be careful, you know what I mean? Go to the doctor. You don't want to end up—'

'That is not about to happen. Come on, let's walk, Sancho is restless.'

LEYLAND REACHES UP FROM the boat. 'Come on, Grace.'

'You don't expect me to get down into that?'

'You won't sink her, just step down.'

'I know I won't sink it, you fool.'

Sancho is barking at a man further down the jetty.

Nancy pats Grace's bottom. 'Go on girl, don't let the side down.'

Leyland waves his hand impatiently. 'Leap of faith. Don't you trust me?'

'You really don't want to hear the answer to that!' She takes off her shoes and passes them to Nancy, reaches out with a bare leg.

The boat sways.

He points to cushions on the slatted wooden bench running along the side, then nods to Nancy who interprets his signal to lift a rope off the mooring. He ducks into the little cabin. The engine's throaty purr vibrates through the boat. They slide in a sweeping curve away from the jetty, seagulls flocking behind. In a reversal of the natural order of things, it's the land that floats, bobs, tilts.

They chug towards the sun; sparkles of light on a million little waves. Slowly, Grace gives in to the gentle movement, trusting the white-painted overlapping planks bent into beautiful curves, the solidity of the rails and blue-painted mast.

The coast is passing on the left: is that port or starboard? On the path, a couple are strolling behind two yapping dogs. In a cove, a child is piling pebbles into a heap. Further on, a man swings a baby up into the air. It's all so ordinary, like those London Underground posters painted in flat pastel colours inviting people to escape to the countryside: so serene, so English.

Leyland cuts the engine. A sudden quiet except for a gentle rippling against the side of the boat; little puffs of spray dampening Grace's face.

'Leyland, we need to talk.'

He's holding his camera, scanning the horizon.

'What are you up to?'

He steps over coiled ropes, sits beside her. 'I want so much to find you, Grace. I always have.'

His words rile her. 'What a bloody patronising—'

'I admire you so much, your survival instinct.'

'You know nothing about me.'

His fingertips gently stroke the back of her neck. He starts to sing, *She walked through the fair …*

All the music she's ever heard is crowding in, saturating her: the heartbeat of the cello, haunting Marlene Dietrich, Mrs Blumen's thrilling arpeggios, Kitty singing Clara, church bells tolling. And flowing and weaving through them all is Hariti, spinning light into sound.

'In my clumsy way, I'm trying to tell you I've always loved you, Grace.'

The ridiculous words feel like a punch. She closes her eyes; a haze of red; she knows it's just blood in her eyelids but it feels mystical, timeless. The gentle movement of the fragile vessel, an acorn cup, defying – by some strange law of physics – the power of the ocean trying to suck them down. There's another voice, light, from beyond: *All Things Bright and Beautiful.* Sobs rise from her belly.

'Oh Grace. It's okay. I'm here now.' A kiss on her cheek, her neck. He guides her to lie along the bench. 'You're safe with me.'

His body arches over her, blocking the sun.

A is for Apple, the forbidden fruit.

And B? Blue sky.

C? She's above, in the crow's eye, watching the speck of a bobbing boat below, in a vast shimmering sea.

*

She sits up, smoothes down her dress. A brazen gull watches from the stern rail. Rigging slaps the mast.

He's standing by the cabin, squinting into the camera viewfinder.

He'd kissed her tears. 'Is this all right …'

'Is this all right …'

'Is this all right …'

She'd needed … But what? To belong.

And now? His pungent smell on her.

She stands up, holds the rail, makes her way along the side of the cabin.

He lowers the camera; a tender smile. 'I think you slept.'

She raises her hand to shield her eyes. 'What's that poem?' She's feeling strangely calm. No depths, no heights.

'Are you all right?'

'A painted ship or something.'

'*Day after day, day after day, We stuck, nor breath nor motion / As idle as a painted ship*—'

'That's it, *upon a painted ocean.* I found it rather frightening when I was young, but now I'm here … I don't know … we tell ourselves such ridiculous stories but really, we're all pretty insignificant.'

The wind rises from nowhere. 'Come to the cabin, the current is changing.'

She follows him inside. The engine stutters and growls to life.

'I'd like to go further down the coast to Hastings: are you up for it, Grace?'

The horizon swings; wind skims the boat like a flat pebble.

'What do you say, Grace?'

'I feel a bit shaky.'

'Are you okay. I mean—'

'Take me back.'

*

Nancy reaches down, takes Grace's hand as Leyland lifts her by the waist. 'You look a bit green round the gills. Not such a jolly tar, then.'

The boat sweeps away towards the estuary.

They walk to the end of the jetty, arms linked.

'I have just the thing for you, Grace, tomato juice with ice, lemon and masses of Lea and Perrin's. That will clear your head.'

Three cigarette butts squashed on the jetty. 'That man watching … did he say anything to you?'

'Probably one of my admirers, overcome with shyness.'

'Nancy, be careful.'

She laughs. 'We have Sancho to protect us.'

'Leyland has to leave for a while.'

'We're safer without him.'

'I don't need protecting.'

August 1949

'Bloody thing.' Grace twists her body to reach the suspender belt at the back. A car horn. She smoothes down her slip and skirt.

Charles holds the passenger door open.

'Mr Fletcher, it is so kind of you to lend us the car.'

'You're all right, lass. We have to look out for each other.'

She slides onto the cracked leather passenger seat. Nancy is pulling on leather gloves, shakes Charles's hand, takes ages thanking him before taking her place behind the steering wheel. She starts the engine and the car purrs down the lanes, past the flood plain and out onto the London Road. She passes her cigarette packet. Grace lights one for her and passes it back. 'This car makes me feel like royalty.'

Constant humming. Gentle rocking. Telegraph poles flashing past.

Grace wakes as her stomach convulses. She manages to wind the window down just in time. She's so bloody stupid. He'd said he knew what he was doing, that she'd be safe.

The car bumps off the road onto a track. Nancy pours hot tea from the Thermos flask over the vomit streaked along the car. 'Maybe you're hungry. It's hours since we left. We should have brought a picnic.'

Grace leans against the farm gate; two pigs are churning up clods of earth with their snouts. From behind, Grace feels Nancy's arms around her, a warm protective body against her back. Two ducks waddle over and dart in to grab worms. She laughs but can't stop the tears.

'Grace?' Nancy turns her around, presses her into her old woollen jumper. 'It's okay darling. I guess I know what's happening.'

Nancy knows the route without having to refer to a map. They cross Westminster Bridge and turn left at Parliament Square. Grace is surprised: so many buildings still in ruins, huge piles of bricks stacked up against walls.

Wisteria still winds through the railings in front of the house.

'I don't know why I agreed to come.'

Nancy lifts the lion-head knocker. 'Because you're brave. Because you need to face the past.'

Kitty is wearing a straight-cut woollen suit, surprisingly gaily coloured in flowing greens and yellows. 'Darling!' She kisses Grace on the cheeks – she's never done that before – then holds her hand out to Nancy. 'What a pleasant surprise. I was so delighted to get your letter.'

And there he is. Peeping from behind Kitty's legs. Short trousers. Grey shirt.

'Allow me to introduce my son. Orlando, say "How do you do" to Auntie Grace and her friend Miss Lockhart.'

Nancy crouches down and offers her hand. 'I'm so pleased to meet you.'

The first miraculous words from the being that Grace had carried inside her over four years ago: 'You sound funny.'

'I'm from America, we speak proper English over there.'

Grace is astonished. She feels so stupid, she'd not allowed herself to imagine the baby growing up, but here he is, a shy smile behind long, jet black hair. She picks up her case. 'We'd better freshen up.'

'Of course, come in. Your room is just as you left it, Grace. I do apologise, I'm so disorganised these days.'

Nancy pats the boy on the head. 'Don't put yourself out, Mrs Fisher, we'll be fine.'

'Dinner is at seven, I'll ring the bell.'

Brass drawing pins are still pressed into the walls of the dormer window where she'd put up her cuttings. Her desk has been cleared.

'I've always loved your room, Grace. Look, your ballerina lamp is still beside the bed.'

Grace stares at the river: a boat with a dirty sail, timeless barges. 'I'm so tired.'

Nancy sits down heavily in the green corduroy armchair, a cloud of fine dust rises in the late afternoon sunlight.

Grace curls up on the bedspread. 'I'm sorry about Kitty.'

*

… dancing bubbles in watery shafts of light … surrounding, enfolding, lifting Grace towards the sun …

Nancy's body is curled around her. She kisses the back of Grace's neck. 'You were trembling.'

A tinkling bell sounds from downstairs.

'It was probably just a past life.'

'Do you really believe in all that?'

'Yes and no. We'd better go, Kitty doesn't like people being late.'

In the dining room, Grace repeats the old routine, laying out the bone-handled knives. Nancy follows her with the forks.

Kitty calls from the kitchen. 'Please take your seats, I'll be there in a jiffy.'

The little boy is watching from the door. Grace smiles and he runs off. A waltz is playing on the wireless. Grace turns the needle along the dial through clouds of static, past Hilversum, Lisbon and Marseilles to a lively clarinet leading a band.

Kitty carries a large saucepan, the boy close behind. He starts to dance to the music, his hair flailing wildly. 'I'm sure Nancy doesn't want to listen to that noise, Grace: re-tune it to the Third Programme, there's a good girl.'

'Nancy is very broad-minded, aren't you Nancy?'

Kitty's face reddens. 'Please do sit down.'

'Thank you, Mrs Fisher.' Nancy pulls out her chair. 'This is a real treat, stew with dumplings.'

'I'm sorry it's mostly vegetables, the butcher just can't get anything at short notice, you'd think there was a war on.'

The boy slurps from his spoon.

Nancy breaks bread into her bowl. 'It's delicious, thank you.'

Grace detects Kitty's discomfort: breaking bread into one's food is so common.

'How is your husband, Mrs Fisher? I understand he's—'

'To tell the truth, things have been easier since he went back to the hospital. He knows no difference, it's merciful, really. Orlando misses him though.'

The boy is tapping his knife on the edge of his plate. Kitty touches his hand. 'I'll have to cut his hair soon. I don't think I mentioned, Grace, he's achieved a place at Robert's old school. Strings were pulled, no doubt.'

Grace sips the over-salty stew; it needs some of Hariti's secret spices.

Kitty chats away happily to the clinking of silver cutlery. 'I understand your father is in America, Nancy. Do you have other family over here?'

'Only Grace.'

In the distance, a dog howls. Deep inside, a fluttering. Surely, it's too early to feel it, a little fish in an ocean, floating far from home.

*

The boy has been sent to bed.

Kitty takes off her apron. 'I'm sure Orlando would love you to say goodnight, Grace. He's in Hariti's old room.'

Grace is not at all sure about being alone with the boy. She creeps up the stairs, opens the door. Light from the landing falls onto the bed. She listens. He's asleep. A relief. She starts to leave.

'Mummy?'

'No, it's Auntie Grace.' She crosses to the bed, sits on the edge.

Innocent brown eyes stare at her. 'I thought you were my Mummy.'

It is surprisingly hard to deny him. 'She'll be up to say goodnight soon.' He is better off with Kitty, but she feels a surge of sadness at leaving him stranded on such a loveless shore.

'We could pretend.'

'Pretend what, little boy?'

'That *you* are my Mummy.'

'I don't think that would be a good idea, you have a Mummy already.'

'Mr Fisher shouts at me, I don't like him. He's not really my Daddy.'

She strokes hair off the boy's forehead. 'He hurt his head in the war. It's not his fault. Anyway, he's gone back to hospital now. You're perfectly safe.'

'Uncle Oliver buys me toys, he's nice.'

Grace's throat tightens. 'I'd better get back to dinner, I'll see you in the morning, goodnight now, sweet dreams.'

Downstairs, silver moonlight slants into the echoing hall. It seems like no time has passed since the night she and Nancy returned from a walk, fearful of the Luftwaffe. The black Bakelite telephone is in exactly the same place on the cool marble hall stand; Nancy asking to be connected to a number in Rye, Sussex.

In the sitting room, she crosses to the bureau, strokes the roll top, which she's sure will be locked. She takes her place next to Nancy on the sofa.

Kitty lifts the lid of a wooden box. Cigars line up like soldiers, releasing a rich, sweet perfume. 'If my husband were here I am sure he'd offer you one of these, Nancy.'

'Oh, no thank you, Mrs Fisher, they are far too strong for me.'

'He was everything to me.' Kitty takes out a cigar and holds it under her nose. 'Poor man. He never met his daughter, he was too busy serving his country.'

A knock on the front door. For a moment, history folds in on itself as Grace hears Hariti's footsteps in the hall.

Kitty rushes out.

Nancy is frowning. 'Are you all right, Grace?'

'I'll survive. It's right that I witness this … this charade.'

Kitty returns. 'What luck! We have a surprise guest.'

'Good evening all.' Smith removes his black hat. 'I am so sorry, I didn't know Mrs Fisher had guests. How nice to meet you again, Grace. Are you well?'

Grace's face is burning. She looks down at her hands gripped tightly in her lap.

Kitty takes his coat and hat. 'Do sit down, Oliver. I don't remember if you have met Grace's friend, Miss Lockhart?'

Smith shakes her hand. 'Momentarily, in Rye, when I delivered the dog. Your father is an American diplomat, if I remember rightly.'

Kitty plumps a cushion. 'Mr Smith is an old friend of Robert's. They were at Cambridge, he and my husband worked for the government in the war, all very hush-hush, wasn't it Oliver.' She goes to the sideboard, picks up a tray. The bottle of port has already been opened. Four glasses.

Nancy pretends normality. 'Are you still doing your important work for the government, Mr Smith?'

'I had a very low-grade position in the Civil Service.'

Kitty pours, passes the glasses. 'I am sure Oliver doesn't want to talk about himself all evening. We want to know about *you* and your delightful time in quaint Rye.'

Smith smiles. 'I work in shipping now.'

A distant patter of feet; the door opens. Orlando's eyes are red, he sees Smith and runs over, 'I had a bad dream.'

Oliver opens his arms. 'Orlando is afraid of the dark.'

Grace gulps her port, peppery, over sweet, and holds her glass out for a top-up.

Smith strokes the boy's hair. 'Such an innocent.'

FOR A MOMENT SHE'S disorientated. Before she opens her eyes she remembers: Nancy helping her undress down to her black satin slip, getting into bed, this same bed where so long ago she had dared to touch Nancy, feel herself melting into her, into her hair, into her skin, her sweat, her smell.

She turns over. Nancy is sitting on the edge of the bed rolling her head from side to side, stretching her neck, the impression of creased sheets on her back.

'I can't do this again, Nancy. I want it over with.'

'There are people I know.'

'How—'

'I'll help you.'

'We can't stay here.'

'I'll get our cases packed.'

Kitty is already sitting at the dining table daintily using the tip of a knife to separate a kipper's crumbling flesh from its skin. 'There you are darling, I didn't expect you up so early.' She waves her knife towards the sideboard. 'Do help yourself.'

'We've decided to go early, Kitty, to get out of your hair.'

'Oh must you? Orlando will be so disappointed, he knows not to come down before nine.'

'The traffic—'

'Nancy, won't you have a cup of something first?'

'Thank you, Mrs Fisher, but we'll hit the road, it's a long way back. Please don't get up.'

Kitty stands up. 'Well, it was delightful to meet you again, and do drive carefully, people are so reckless these days.'

On the doorstep, Kitty crosses her arms.

Nancy puts the cases on the back seat, slides in behind the wheel and starts the engine.

Grace buttons her coat. 'I'm concerned for you, Kitty.'

'Don't worry about me, darling.'

'How are you managing?'

'Oliver is a great support.'

'The boy is bound to work it out in the end.'

'Every family has a token auntie or uncle these days. The war has scrambled so many families. Let the boy have his innocence for as long as possible. One day I'll tell him that he was adopted, but by that time he'll know he's been loved and cared for, so where he came from won't be an issue.'

The chasm between them is too wide. 'The truth is the only thing that will satisfy him. In the end.'

She pats Grace's arm. 'You mustn't worry. It's not the life either you or I expected. Fate has brought me unexpected happiness. Orlando is a delight. I'll always be grateful to you … you understand, don't you, Grace? It's best this way. And Oliver absolutely dotes on him, which is *such* a bonus. Now you'd better go, your Nancy is waiting.'

*

By the time they pass Biggin Hill it's raining hard and the little wiper blades are struggling to keep the windscreen clear.

'Your mother's got a lot on her plate.'

'I don't think she has much choice really.'

They pass the aerodrome, the ghostly shape of a parked aircraft materialises on their right, its nose pointing towards the sky. Grace lights a cigarette for Nancy. 'Do you think you'll ever go back home?'

'There's nothing for me there.'

Grace passes the cigarette. 'What about your father?'

Nancy winds her window down a few inches and blows smoke into the slipstream. 'America is … I don't know. Too pleased with itself.'

The rain is a real downpour now, forcing Nancy to pull over onto a small track. She turns off the engine and the wiper blades freeze in position. In seconds, the windows mist over.

Grace winds hers down a little; she's feeling sick again. 'Where do you think we are?'

'I've got a map in the boot.' She gets out, pulls her coat over her head. By the time she gets back in she's soaked. 'My god!'

Grace laughs.

Nancy spreads the map over the steering wheel, traces her finger along coloured lines. 'Bugger. I think we're here … look.' She taps the map.

'But we are miles off track then.'

Nancy rests her head on the back of the seat, closes her eyes. Her neck is pale, smooth, vulnerable.

Rain drums on the car roof.

Grace wakes with a stiff neck; the rain has stopped. Through the drizzled windscreen she can see Nancy, a few yards ahead, staring at something.

It's a relief to get out of the car: the air is fresh and an earthy smell makes her feel suddenly optimistic, as if the rain has washed out the foul taste of London – and her past. She threads her arm through Nancy's and follows her gaze. A savage ravine is being cut between hills: throbbing engines of a digger, a mechanical shovel disgorging black smoke, a line of men swinging pickaxes.

'I bet there are a lot of Irish down there. Maybe your Leyland found work after all.'

'I haven't seen him since that day he sailed off into the sunset, I hope he turned right at Land's End and kept going – until he reached his precious Eire.'

Arm in arm, they walk slowly back to the car; mist rises from the warming tarmac.

Rye
September 1949

Gas flames hiss under a saucepan. Nancy is stirring slowly with a wooden spoon.

'What's that wonderful smell?' Grace peeps into the saucepan: 'Blackberries!'

'I picked them earlier when I was walking Sancho, it was beautiful in the lanes this morning.'

'I slept in, sorry, I'm so tired these days.'

Nancy had tried … had written the name and telephone number of a doctor in Hastings who would 'help'. Grace had carried the strip of paper in her purse for weeks. Once, she had gone into a telephone box and picked up the receiver. She couldn't do it. The memory of a vase of knitting needles frightened her too much. Some days she tries to convince herself that this time, she'll do better. *Be* better. Find in her heart a kernel of love for a little child.

Nancy spoons jam onto a saucer, blows on it. 'Grace, prepare yourself for some news.'

There's no sign of a telegram on the table, or a letter. Maybe someone telephoned and she'd slept through the ringing.

Nancy fills the kettle, places it on the stove. 'I was in the grocer's, and I spotted him across the road. I mean Leyland, of course. Head down, looking rather furtive if you ask me.'

'Did you speak to him?'

'Here, test this.' She offers the jam-covered spoon.

Grace blows on the spoon: the perfume of damp earth and sunshine. She puts her tongue on the dark red congealing jam. 'Oh my god. Divine.'

'I'm afraid I invited him to supper.'

'*What?* Nancy!'

'You two need to talk. He needs to know.' She places a funnel over a jar and pours the hot lumpy liquid. 'He asked lots of questions … his main concern seemed to be any male company you might be keeping, he's clearly not threatened by me. Then he had the nerve to start flirting. I sent him away with a flea in his ear.' She moves the funnel to the next jar. 'Sorry, you're right, I shouldn't have invited him.'

*

Nancy has gone to bed, claiming tiredness. Grace has nothing to say to Leyland. She'd stupidly trusted him. What's the matter with her? She knows he's a man with a secret life. What was he doing on that footpath when he found her? Why did he pop up out of the wartime fog to guide her home, nail boards across her bomb-damaged window, appear on the harbour wall in Rye? He's been a shadow all her life. At this point, Hariti would have talked about guardian angels and the dance of cosmic energy.

And where is *she?* No more postcards. Maybe they weren't from her after all.

She opens the front door and stands on the step. If he does turn up – and that is by no means guaranteed – he'll have to eat something cold: she's not about to put herself out to cook.

An owl hoots; she guesses it must be down by the edge of the woods on the London Road. Another calls closer by. The distant owl hoots again. Now she hears it: the familiar purr in the distance, gradually becoming a growl.

He parks the motorbike, follows her in without speaking. She leads him to the kitchen, where he paces up and down, scratching his stubbly chin. He rips the greaseproof paper off a jar, dips his finger in, hooks the warm jam into his mouth, stands by the window idly sucking his finger. 'I'm sorry I haven't been back for a while. Things haven't been easy.'

'I'm going to bed. You can use the sofa.'

She folds her cardigan over the back of the chair, undoes the buttons of her dress, stands by the window and shivers. Clouds race past the thin sliver of a new moon. She recognises the constellation, Orion, a warrior with a sword belt. She steps out of her slip, leaving it like a puddle on the floor.

Nancy's footsteps on the landing.

Grace unclips her bra and pulls on her cold nightdress. A low murmur of voices downstairs.

*

She wakes in a fright.

'It's only me, Grace. Nancy has just told me.' The springs of the bed creak. 'Darling, I'm back now for good.'

'There's really no need. Nancy and I are quite happy here.'

'I've been talking it over with her.'

'Yes. I can imagine you have.'

'I have a plan. We'll all go to the cottage, live together, grow our own food, we could get some more chickens, a pig or two, ducks even, live a happy life away from all these prying eyes. Let's throw our lot in together. With Nancy's allowance we'll be secure.'

'You've worked it all out.'

'Think about it, she can't have babies, and when we have ours we'll be one big happy family.'

Nancy has never mentioned that she is infertile: what sort of story is she weaving? If it's true, it's no wonder Leyland is so drawn to her: pleasure without consequence.

'I know this is not very romantic, I should go down on bended knee and so on, but I've been in another world. I can't say more, but please believe me, I'm here for you, Grace. We could get married, properly this time.'

Grace lets out a cruel laugh. In a strange way she can see it makes sense. She knows she's broken, twisted. She yearns for a sense of belonging, for security. If she were to marry Leyland she could focus on her music; they'd all get their needs met.

He strokes her cheek. There is no mistaking it. The smell on his fingers takes her straight back to a night when falling bombs made the ground shake in staccato rhythms.

'What do you think, Grace?'

Hariti's sweet voice, conspiratorial: *One day you'll marry him*.

'We're not really right for each other, are we, and besides, we're far too unconventional.'

For the last few nights she's allowed Leyland to share her bed, on the clear understanding that he keeps his distance. It's his fault that this worm inside her is becoming a living thing; he can bloody well stick around to look after it.

He turns onto his back; his snoring stops for a few moments, then becomes little puffing sounds, like a train waiting in a station.

Leyland has an instinct for rescuing. He'll make a good father. With Nancy involved too, maybe this could work.

A fine ribbon of silver light from the half moon.

Her reputation as a musician is spreading. She's started giving piano lessons to some of the little brats of Rye's upper class, and she's even been invited to play a chamber recital at Lamb House: a concert for reconciliation. Bach and Elgar, purity and sentiment, German precision and English pastoral. She loves the passion of the Russians – Tchaikovsky is her favourite – but it wouldn't be diplomatic to include him on the programme with how things are in the USSR.

Leyland turns again. Even in his sleep his hand reaches for her, pulling her nightdress up until it rests on her belly. She carefully removes his hand and turns away.

*

The bed sqeaks. The door creaks.

This pregnancy has made her hearing super sharp: she can detect his feet padding on the landing carpet, his hand turning the white ceramic handle of Nancy's door. Surely it's impossible to hear sheets rustling, a bedstead bending to his weight, fingers rasping through bushy red hair, blood pulsing, a moan, and a sigh.

Something is scrabbling in the ceiling: rats, probably. She doesn't mind them, they have to find warmth somewhere, she just hates their long, thin tails.

*

The sheet lifts; a waft of cool air, an arm around her. Nancy kisses Grace's shoulder. 'You awake, darling?'

'I'm starving.'

'We need to talk …'

'I need bacon.'

'… so that we all know where we stand.'

'Words define, delineate. I may not want that.'

'Oh god, you English are so … what's the word? … inscrutable!'

'I feel controlled enough as it is.'

'You know I love you, Grace. Since the first day I saw you sitting shyly in my father's study.'

'But you don't need me.'

She strokes Grace's hardening belly. 'Is baby okay?'

'*It* needs bacon.'

Nancy laughs.

GRACE IS DRAWN TO HER bedroom window by raised voices outside. A neighbour is arguing with Leyland from her doorstep. He looks up, sees Grace, shrugs, and leaves the woman shouting at his back. She hears him bounding up the stairs.

'Come on you lazy things, Charles will need his car back later today, we've got to get a move on.'

Nancy calls from her room. 'Leyland, we'll never fit everything in.' Her door closes. Muffled voices. Then silence.

He's on the landing. 'Grace, pow-pow, sitting room, three minutes.'

She bundles her bedclothes into the middle of the bed ready for the laundry van and wonders if she will ever return to this room.

Downstairs, Sancho is padding around the suitcases stacked around the cello case. Nancy is tying string around a cardboard box. Leyland has a finger on the knot. 'Darling, there you are. We have a problem, I really don't think we'll all fit in, what with Sancho and the cello and all. I'll take this lot up to the cottage and you rest here nice and warm. We'll get the range going and the spiders swept out, what do you say? I'll get the car back to Charles and then you and I can go on the motorbike: ace plan?'

'You'll do what you have to.'

'Don't be like that, Grace.'

They carry boxes to the car. The neighbour is still on her step, watching them with a scowl. In the doorway, Nancy kisses Grace's cheek. 'Now you be good, see you later. I've left a portion of rabbit stew in the larder.' Grace gives her a quick hug, feels Nancy pulling away.

The neighbour slams her door hard.

Grace sits down on the sofa. Two more books she'd forgotten to pack: William James *The Varieties of Religious Experience* and the Gibbon that she's had for so long she daren't take it back to the library.

The baby is moving.

What if she *were* to marry Leyland? No doubt he'd still run around the country fighting his battles to liberate the six counties, or some other hare-brained scheme. At least she would have Nancy; they'd be able to miss him together, share bringing up his child.

Wearily, she climbs the stairs. In Nancy's room, she undoes the knot of sheets and opens them out, steps out of her shoes and lies down in the cocoon of Nancy's smell.

Rain taps the dark window pane. The rabbit stew in the larder: had Nancy planned this all along? She turns on her side, bringing her knees up.

… she's running … fiery breath on her back … run, run … over the stile … into black …

*

Watery light. Early morning.

The cobbles are shining wet. She walks aimlessly, stepping into doorways whenever the showers strengthen. 'Where the hell are you, Leyland?' She daren't go far from the street in case he comes back. She passes the town hall as the clock's ancient mechanical Quarter Boys chime, enters the house again, treads the carpeted stairs like a ghost, and returns to Nancy's bed.

*

The impatient rap on the door makes her jump. She's still in her coat. She leaves a damp impression on the sheets and tries to straighten her hair as she goes down to answer the door.

'Mr Cornell asked me to—'

'Oh, George, that's so kind, would you mind waiting a tick?'

'We must go now, see, or I'll be in trouble.'

'Just give me a minute.'

She closes the door, stares at the reflection in the hall mirror, then brushes her hair out. It's just long enough to gather and twist. She pushes in a couple of hair grips to hold the top knot in place, puts the hairbrush into her handbag, picks up the books, calls: 'Coming.'

*

George hums annoyingly as they make their way down the Sussex lanes.

'Do you think we could have the heater off? I'm not feeling too well.'

He slides the control lever. 'Yer 'usband, he's been away a lot, hasn't he.'

'Yes, for work.'

'Difficult these days … for his sort.'

Grace just can't find the energy to rise to the challenge.

'Mind you, I'm not saying they're all bad, some of them are decent blokes.'

'Is that so?'

'I knew one in the Army … a lot of them signed up you know even though they didn't have to … anyway, this bloke, I'll give him his due, he were brave, saved his officer's life, took one in the 'ead he did.'

'Really.'

'I'll never forgive them – the Germans – for what they did … they're born evil, they are.'

'I don't think one can say that, George, they were just taken by the tide of history.'

'Mind you, not as bad as the Japs.'

'Now that we can agree on.'

'We've had a few Krauts coming to Rye on holiday: bloody nerve if you ask me. We should root them all out and shoot the lot of them.'

'The King as well?'

'Why'd you say that?'

'The royal family is of German descent.'

'Oh, right.' He offers her a cigarette. Grace shakes her head. 'That shut me up, didn't it.'

Brede
October 1949

LEYLAND IS GRUNTING WITH each thrust of the spade, shaking earth off potatoes. He pauses, takes his shirt off and tosses it over the washing line.

Sancho watches anxiously, sitting alert between Grace and Nancy on the terrace. Nancy strokes his shaggy fur. 'Your betrothed is strong, considering he's as thin as a beanpole.'

Grace pulls her cardigan tighter. 'He's not my—'

'You know it would be perfect.'

'So *you* say.'

Grace tries to focus on her book but Nancy is in a chatty mood. 'Have you noticed the scars on his back and chest?'

'Can't say I have.'

'Now Gracie, don't be like that. You do feel all right about this, don't you?'

Grace tilts her head back, stares up through the jagged vine, dark against a blue sky. 'It's over three months.'

'Exciting, I think it's starting to show.'

Grace is all too aware of the relentlessnees of the creature inside her, but strangely, she feels that she herself has come to rest. Washed up on a shore. 'We are all very bohemian, and life is short.'

'As long as you're okay.'

'*Rough winds do shake the darling buds of May*, or something like that.'

Nancy laughs. 'Oh yes, our English tutor. God knows where my father dug him up from, he couldn't teach for toffee. What a hoot.'

'And then there was his wooden hand.'

'And the attachments he'd screw on.'

'Yes, for eating.'

'I wonder what he screwed on when he got home to his wife.'

'Nancy! You're so naughty!'

Leyland straightens up, jabs the spade into the ground and walks over. 'I'd kill for a cuppa.' He drags out a chair. 'Have you sorted out what you'll wear for the wedding?'

'If you think you're going to get a ring on my finger you can think again, mister.'

'I'm hiring a car, she's quite a beauty.'

Nancy laughs at something in her magazine, shows Leyland.

Grace closes her eyes. Sunlight warm on her face. The air feels fresh. She's detached. From the laughter around her. From the birdsong nearby. From the baby stroking her. All her worries have dissolved. Hariti would say she's living in the ever-present moment. Maybe the future is just too scary to think about.

December 1949

Tᴄʜᴀɪᴋᴏᴠsᴋʏ's E-ᴍᴀᴊᴏʀ transcribed for cello: as she plays she is part of the sound evolving around her, yet separate from it. The baby dances inside. She puts the bow down, rests the cello against the sofa and lays her hands over her belly. Maybe, just maybe, she'll find a way to manage this time.

Leyland is polishing her shoes at the kitchen table. 'Come on, Grace, take your dress off, I need to iron it.'

'You're deluded. I'll be the witness when you marry Nancy.'

He balances her shoe on his slim fingers. 'Stranger things have happened.' He carefully circles cloth on leather then swaps shoes and takes out a small brush from his shoe-shine wallet. 'Bright as a button. Can't be too perfect for you today. What's Nancy up to? She's been up there for hours.'

'Trying to make herself prettier than me, no doubt.'

'Hurry now, your dress needs ironing.'

'It's velvet, you fool, it can't be ironed.'

'I know what I'm doing, trust me.'

'You've said *that* before.'

He stands behind her and pulls the zip down, his cold fingertips deliberately tracing her spine. She shivers. Slowly, he coaxes the dress off her shoulders, eases it over the bump, kisses her quickly on the neck. Grace steps out. She's wearing the Parisian silk underwear that Nancy lent her earlier.

'You won't be able to wear these for much longer.'

'You've ruined me.'

'Don't let the gossiping old biddies get to you, today of all days.' He turns the dress inside out and lays it on the creaking wooden ironing board. 'This is *our* day, remember.' He pumps the plunger on a little brass pot and a fine spray floats onto the tea towel placed over the dress. He strokes with the iron. A rising mist of camphor, damp and cigarette smoke.

*

Leyland holds open the passenger door of a black saloon and bows as Grace approaches. 'Madam!'

She turns up the lapels of her coat. 'Where did you get this, the undertaker?'

He calls into the house. 'Hurry, Nancy, we need to motor.'

She emerges, the hem of her cream knee-length dress showing under her fawn raincoat. They slide in together on the back seat. Leyland starts the engine. Nancy lights a cigarette.

Grace stares at the trees and hedges flashing by. Nancy leans forward to chat, Leyland laughs. Country roads give way to Rye's narrow streets. The ratcheting sound of the handbrake brings Grace out of her daydream. Leyland opens the door.

'What the hell am I doing here, Leyland?'

He offers his hand. 'Let me help you out.'

Nancy holds out a posy of delicate white flowers. 'Come on, Gracie, we can do this. You look magnificent. I'd ask to marry you myself if I was a man.'

'And I'd say yes.'

Mr Shilling – a bloody apron tied tight over his big belly – stands in the doorway of his butcher's shop. As they pass, his country accent is clear. 'Lambs to the bloody slaughter.'

Leyland laughs.

The lugubrious face of Winston Churchill looks down from an ornate gold frame. His eyes follow Grace as she paces the red carpet in the waiting room.

The Fletchers bustle through the door. Mary makes straight for her. 'My *dear* you look absolutely radiant.' She looks at the bump. 'Leyland doesn't deserve you. And my dear, don't worry, Charles and I have forgiven you for leading us up the garden path: pretending to be married, indeed! We do understand the shame, but now you're making it right.'

Grace can't change her life's course; this baby will grow, be born and be held by Nancy and Leyland. A wanted child. Grace will be hollowed out. Again. But then she will be free.

The usher's white-gloved hands are held together as if protecting his manhood. He announces that they are to follow him.

Leyland holds out his arm. 'My beautiful girl.'

Their footsteps are muffled by red carpet as they troop mournfully past rows of empty chairs. They sit at the front on velvet-cushioned seats. Pale morning light filters through the veils hanging at the french windows. Fold lines on the starched tablecloth. Gold candlesticks. Between the table and the window is an artist's easel holding a matching gold frame. Grace is transfixed by the image of a crucifiction. A Roman guard is standing near the cross, the bright red fabric under his armour matches the red on the tip of his lance.

She's feeling hot, slips her arms out of her coat. The Germans and Japanese have a lot in common with the Romans: an insatiable hunger for territory and enslavement. Grace is in no doubt that if Hitler had won the war, historians in the distant future would be writing about the Third Reich in glowing terms and there would be no Jews or degenerates like her to argue the contrary. The Romans brought order, as Hitler would have done. She understands the yearning for certainty.

She stares at the grotesque depiction of torn flesh, and wonders what Jesus – if he were reincarnated in the twentieth century – would think of the world. Maybe he'd be besuited, like the portly man entering from a side door, striped military tie, his cheeks covered in a network of fine red veins. Jesus driven to drink by two thousand years of men making war?

The man smiles at Nancy. 'Would the bride and groom please stand.' A golden, polished voice: this Jesus would be a baritone, perhaps even a bass.

Leyland stands.

Grace looks at Nancy. 'Go on, you can have him.'

'Oh no, he's all yours.'

The registrar's cheeks grow even redder. 'Oh, I do beg your pardon.' He looks at Grace's velvety bump. 'I am so terribly sorry.'

Grace gets up slowly. 'Not as much as me.'

Nancy laughs.

The registrar's voice intones a welcome, a warning, and an invitation to repeat after him. Grace hears the words about obeying and looks at Leyland. His suit is just a bit too short in the sleeves and hangs loose at the waist; his silk cravat is just a little too flamboyant around his thin neck.

The room is silent. Grace turns to Nancy then back to the polished voice, and the repeated question.

Leyland threads his fingers between hers.

February 1950

THE AWFUL RAINS HAVE CEASED and the floods have abated. Unexpected sunshine is encouraging the fragile tips of snowdrops to emerge among the primroses in the shady hedgerows.

Nancy is swinging Sancho's lead. 'I think he prefers these lanes to being in Rye, don't you? He's so good off the lead.'

'I wonder if he'd ever come to our defence if we needed him.'

As they approach the village pond, they notice Mary Fletcher kneeling by a flowerbed around the stone memorial cross. She slips her trowel into her apron pocket. 'Mrs Cornell, how nice to see you again.'

'How do you do, Mrs Fletcher. You've met my friend Nancy Lockhart?'

'Yes, at the wedding.'

'Nancy, Mrs Fletcher, is an old friend of Leyland's.'

Nancy shakes the old lady's hand. 'A maker of arrows?'

'Indeed! My husband is convinced his ancestors were at Agincourt.' She glances up at the memorial: a bronze broadsword leaching coppery-green into the stone. 'We could have done with their skills this time around.'

'Your husband very kindly lent us the car for our London trip. We're so grateful.'

'I detect an American accent.'

'My father is a diplomat, we travelled a lot. I seem to have got stranded over here.'

'That's nice. And we haven't seen you for a while, Grace. How is Leyland?'

'Spends all his time in his studio, he's supposed to be working towards an exhibition but we never see any sign of his art.'

'And the baby? Can't be too long now.'

'I'm not counting.'

'Well, I mustn't keep you, you know where we are if you need anything, anything at all, you only have to ask.'

'Actually, we're looking for a field to have a picnic.'

'You could try the church, there's a pretty little meadow at the back.'

'We'll do that, thank you.'

They pass under the thatched lychgate and through the graveyard to a sloping meadow where they spread their rug near an ancient yew tree.

'The Druids believed the yew tree had mystical powers.'

'They're spooky if you ask me.' She opens a copy of *Vogue*.

'When the Christians arrived, they built their churches on top of the old pagan temples. Cynical, don't you think?'

'Wow, look at this dress, she looks like a peacock. Amazing!'

A cloud slips in front of the sun; the air instantly cools. Grace shivers, remembering Rahu – a lifetime ago. She lies back, her dress tight over her belly. 'Such a relief to get the weight off my legs.'

Nancy turns a page. 'The Italians are so stylish. Look, what do you think?'

'I just want this thing to stop moving around all the time.'

'Can I feel?' Nancy lays on a hand. 'It's amazing, Grace, I'm sure that's a leg. It must feel awesome.'

'You're welcome to it, any time.'

'I would. You know that.'

'So you like to think.'

Nancy lies back, picks up her magazine, a sharp edge to her voice. 'We're doing this together, remember.'

Grace sits up and rubs her eyes. She studies Nancy: tumbling curls of red hair, slightly damp at the roots above her forehead, long fingers, chipped red nail polish, and under her cardigan and cotton dress the perfect shape of her breasts, and lower, her narrow waist and belly rising and falling, her breathing a gentle tide. Strange to think Grace had once—

'*She*'s rather delicious, don't you think?' Nancy taps a picture.

'She's just a girl! Look at her ponytail.'

'Innocence can be powerfully attractive.'

'Nancy, don't you think, now the war's over, the world seems a sadder place?'

'You're doing your bit to bring about a new generation. New life.'

'Nothing to fight for, I suppose.' Grace lays a hand over the moving limbs. She can't say this baby was made in love, but it'll bind three strangers into an unholy trinity.

'This is the perfect solution. It'll have two mothers. The old structures are breaking down.'

'Maybe if I'd chosen it.'

Nancy pokes her belly and Grace shrieks.

Sancho barks.

March 1950

While she waits for the kettle to boil, Grace stands at the open front door watching Nancy carrying the laundry basket, leaving a trail through frosty grass, pegging up shirts and underwear on the line strung between two ash trees.

The Brandenberg Concerto is nearing its end. Grace lifts the kettle from the range and pours boiling water into the stone sink. She puts another log into the burner so that there will be hot water for a bath later on.

She can hear Leyland pacing in his studio above. He says they can't afford the laundry service and anyway hard work is good for the soul, and so it seems to have fallen to her to be rubbing his shirt collar with a bar of yellow carbolic soap. Grace wrings the shirt, drops it into an enamel bowl, picks out one of Leyland's vests from the pile on the draining board, plunges it into the water, then a pair of black, lace-edged knickers – Nancy's.

The baby kicks. Leyland's baby was made out of carelessness; not out of violence at least. For a few days, Grace seems to have been breathing more easily; the baby must be lower down.

Nancy puts the empty laundry basket on the table. 'I'm dying for a cuppa.' She calls up the stairs. 'Tea up, old man. Five minutes.'

She fills the kettle and puts it on the range. 'How's baby, Grace?'

'What is there to say?'

Leyland clumps downstairs, humming. He pours water into a jam jar, drops in three brushes, then washes his hands in the soapy clothes-washing water.

Grace nudges him with the bump, he turns and smiles, 'How is baby?'

She nods to the jam jar. 'Why are you doing that?'

'Water stops them drying out. Oil and water don't mix, you know.'

'Yes. I know that: look at you and me.'

Nancy laughs. 'Grace, you're impossible.'

Leyland pulls out a chair and sits in front of the parish news sheet. 'I see *Gone with the Wind* is on in Hastings: you tried to see it once didn't you?'

'How do you know that?'

'You must have mentioned it.'

Nancy places cups on the table. 'Remember, the organ that wouldn't work?'

'And the dancing girls.'

'Hey, let's go! We're owed a night out – we might not get a chance for ages judging by the size of you.'

Leyland turns a page. 'I can't come, I have to go out. You girls go and have some fun.'

Grace pulls the plug on the grey water. 'Who's the lucky girl?'

He raises an eyebrow. 'I've got my hands full with you two. Anyway, I heard on the wireless that the weather is about to turn, snow is forecast. You'd better go while you can, looks like we'll be snowed in for a few days.'

Nancy pokes his shoulder. 'Make sure you give Sancho plenty of food, we'll be out all day.'

As the Home Service had predicted, a heavy blanket of snow had fallen overnight, and there were reports of trees and telegraph poles being brought down.

Leyland is locked in his studio developing film; so he says.

Nancy squats next to the fire's glowing coals, toasting a slice of bread on a long-handled fork. 'What a shame, Grace.'

'Bloody weather, I was so looking forward to it.' Another pile of dirty clothes is waiting in the washing basket, root vegetables need chopping for the stew, and bacon needs fetching from the meat safe in the outhouse.

Nancy turns the toast. 'We could go anyway, the snow's stopped now, I bet the buses are still running.'

'There won't be any in this.'

'Come on, Grace, where's your spirit of adventure? Let's at least set off and see how far we get!'

'What if the baby—'

'You're not due for weeks. The exercise will do you good.'

'Well, I've got the energy for it now. I doubt I'll have it in a few weeks' time.'

*

Sunlight streams through the eerily silent woods. Snow has blanketed the road. Grace is wearing her warmest camel coat and a black woollen scarf wound tight around her neck. She's getting a few of those early contractions: Braxton something or other. Who was Braxton, anyway? No doubt a male doctor, the sort who miraculously knows what a woman is feeling. 'What do we do if a bus doesn't come?'

Nancy scoops up snow with a gloved hand. 'Then we'll turn back, but there's always a knight in shining armour. I'm determined to get there, and you know me, I get what I want.'

'Well you can put that snowball down right now, miss.'

A menacing smile.

Grace starts to run as best she can, holding her belly.

Nancy laughs. 'You look like a penguin.'

They flop down on the bench in a bus shelter. Nancy takes out her cigarette packet, strokes her thumb absent-mindedly over the pack's embossed lettering.

'Nancy, where do you feel you belong? You know, where's home for you?'

Nancy lights a cigarette. 'Well, since you ask, I don't really feel American, if that's what you mean.' She blows smoke into the cold wind. 'Men can never say what they feel. We both know he's a bit infatuated with me, but none of that matters, you are the one. If you feel insecure about this—'

'No, Nancy, it's not that, it's me. I don't really know what I *should* be feeling. Men have always felt alien. I'm drawn to them in a way that might not be healthy … I don't know, maybe it's just this pregnancy scrambling my mind.'

'Men *are* pathetic; women are the strong ones. We can make this work. You and me, the axis of power … hey, I hear a bus.'

In the distance, an ominous grey shape emerges from a flurry of snow. A droning sound grows steadily louder. Grace moves Nancy's hand off her lap. 'I don't like it, Nancy.'

'It's a convoy, one of them is sure to give us a lift.'

They stand by the roadside. Nancy waves. The driver of the first vehicle stares ahead and ploughs past; the driver of the second raises a hand but doesn't slow down; then the third and fourth roar by. The fifth vehicle is a little way behind the others. A man in the cab leans over to the driver. The lorry slows; screeching brakes bring it to a halt. A window winds down. 'Good afternoon, ladies, are you stranded?'

Nancy steps forward. 'Captain Bridges from Delaware. I never forget a face.'

He opens the door. 'The naughty ladies from the café!'

'We're waiting for the bus, we're going to a matinee in Hastings.'

'We'll drop you off close enough to walk.'

'That's so kind of you.'

He leaps down. 'Let me help you.' Gripping Grace's arm, he helps her step up on to the footplate, then the tyre and into the cab. Grace has to shuffle up onto a hot metal engine cover to make room for the others.

The cabin smells of oil and sweat. The driver pushes the gearstick forward and the engine roars beneath them. The vehicle slowly catches up with the convoy.

From his wallet, Captain Bridges brings out a photograph. 'My wife. I've not seen her since we married – this was taken in a small village in southern France.'

Nancy takes the photograph. 'Is she French?'

'She saved my life. I see your friend is married. And you?'

'No man has proved to be my match!'

'Fortunately for you, I'm taken.'

Nancy laughs. 'What will you do when you get back, stay in the army?'

He raises an eyebrow. 'I used to be a dentist.'

Grace holds the bump, the heat from the metal engine cover is penetrating her coat, becoming hard to bear.

One by one, the lorries turn in through a gate in a high fence and come to a halt in a yard. The Captain jumps down and offers a hand to them. 'Half a mile down the road and you'll be in Hastings.'

Nancy shakes his hand. 'It was very good of you, Captain. Thank you.'

All along the fence, thousands of little triangles of snow nestle into the diamond shapes of the interlaced wire. Along the top, loops of frosted barbed wire glint in the sunlight. Tarpaulins at the back of the lorries are being drawn back and soldiers are jumping out and forming ranks.

'You must come to the Officers' Mess sometime.'

'We'll be a bit distracted for the next few months.'

'Or look me up next time you're in Delaware.'

*

'No, put your purse away, my treat.' Nancy slides a half crown over the polished counter. 'Two shilling seats please.' The tickets pop out from a slot. 'Here we are.' She rips the tickets apart.

'Thank you.'

'This is so exciting, I haven't been to the pictures for donkey's years. I love that *kerchung* noise the ticket machine makes, it gives me such a feeling of anticipation!'

A man standing in the corner of the foyer looks familiar. For a moment Grace can't place him. 'Hello. It's Joe isn't it, from the café?'

'Never met you, miss.' He lifts his hat a fraction and hurries off with a slight limp.

Nancy raises an eyebrow. 'Nice friends you have.'

The usher's beam guides them down the carpeted aisle. They sink into soft velvet seats.

Nancy pulls off her shoes. 'My feet are killing me.'

'We'd better get back after this.'

The Pathé News has already started. Grace tries to hold on to the images and snatched voices: preparations for a motor show, soldiers walking up a ramp onto a ship, the King offering his hand to someone getting off a train. The world is teeming with activity, while she just wants to withdraw into a bubble of silence.

*

They follow multiple trails of footsteps in the snow. In a café, they order eggs on toast from a grumpy waitress who says they'll have to be quick as she has a family to go home to. When the food arrives, Grace sprinkles salt, shakes the pepper pot. 'Going to the cinema in the light and coming out in the dark feels rather indulgent, don't you think?'

Nancy spreads butter on a huge chunk of bread. 'I am absolutely, one-hundred per cent head over heels in love with Mr Gable.'

'I don't like his moustache.'

Nancy waves her knife. 'Scandal! If I were a man …'

'Look at the sea now, it's really high, I wonder if a storm's on the way.'

Nancy lowers her voice. 'Frankly, my dear, I don't give a damn.'

They laugh. Grace sips hot tea. 'Vivien Leigh is perfect, if I *were* a man.'

'Even if I weren't.'

'We'll have to go to the bus depot soon. We can't rely on getting a lift again.'

'You worry too much.' Nancy presses the knife into her egg, yellow yolk bursts over the toast. 'We could always get a room, they'll be cheaper away from the beach: we could sign in as Mr and Mrs Leigh.'

'Leyland will worry.'

'You must be joking. Anyway, he'll work it out. Snow on the ground, no buses. He'll put two and two together. Relax, live a little. We'll pick up some beer and go in search of lodgings.'

'Oh god, Nancy, I don't know. I just want to be home.'

'Don't worry, the weather won't get any worse overnight; it'll all be slush in the morning and we'll catch the first bus.'

They walk through pools of light sparkling on snow, the sea crashing and sucking on pebbles. Nancy has already finished her beer and is halfway through Grace's.

Ahead of them, the floodlit steps of the Grand Hotel.

'Come on, Gracie, let's see if the bridal suite is available!'

'A broom cupboard will do right now.'

The carpeted lobby is crowded with men in dark suits. White capital letters on a black velvet notice board spell out: 'The State of Israel Conference'.

Nancy puts her bottle on the counter. 'More men dividing up the world. Bloody stupid religion.'

'Nancy! You'll swing one of these days.'

'They've got to catch me first.'

The receptionist puts the telephone receiver down. 'May I help you?'

Nancy's voice is slightly slurred. 'Two of your finest rooms please.'

Grace holds the bump, trying to ignore tightening muscles. The man strokes thin strands of hair across his head. 'I'm afraid we are full, madam.'

'You can't be. We just need one tiny room, we'll fit into an attic.'

'As I said, madam.'

'Your hotel is full of Jews, it's freezing outside and my friend is about to give birth to her own baby Jesus.'

'Might I take your names?'

'Hah! I told you, Grace, you just have to be firm.'

Grace ignores the embarrassing tirade and gives the man their names. He writes them on hotel notepaper, then looks up. 'As I said, madam, we are full, now it would be better for you if you were to leave quietly.'

Nancy's voice is shaking. 'How dare you speak to us like that? My father—'

'I'll be forced to call—'

'If you had no intention of giving us a room, why did you need our names?'

'Well, young lady, if you have nothing to hide you have nothing to fear.'

'May I remind you, *old man*—'

Grace pulls her away. 'Excuse my friend, we're leaving.'

She guides Nancy down a side street. 'You are very naughty rising to the bait, Nancy, you have people depending on you now.'

'I hate their Fascist self-righteousness; the class system in this country stinks. We didn't fight a war for these toadies to still be lording it over us.'

'You said it would be easy to find another hotel. Please help.'

Something in Grace's tone breaks through Nancy's mood and she puts her arm around her. 'Come on, we'll try the next street.'

*

The tiny room is sparse. Nancy sits on the sagging bed. 'That batty old receptionist thought we looked bit suspicious with no luggage.'

'I'm going to find the bath, my back is really killing me, if there's any hot water I'll squander it all.'

The roll-top bath has been roughly cemented into the corner of the tiny room. The Ascot heater roars to life.

Grace balances the hot and cold, and eventually there is enough water to lower herself into the bath. The relief of her weight being taken feels wonderful. The clenching muscle relaxes.

Her mind is clear. The baby has grown out of her darkness and will find its own light. She sees it as Hariti would. A being floating in another dimension, choosing Grace for some unearthly reason. She can do this. Honour the baby's choice. Hariti was always right.

She closes her eyes. Her heart is pounding. A word screams in her head: *Mo-ther!* A jolt of pure fear. She opens her eyes. The water is pink; a strand of concentrated red pooling between her legs.

'Oh god, oh god, please no.'

She stands, yanks the plug's chain, grabs a thin towel. Dark red instantly stains it but the bleeding seems to have stopped. She grabs her clothes and leaves a trail of wet footprints along the corridor's dirty linoleum.

The bedroom door closes behind her and she bursts into tears.

'Gracie, what's wrong? Come here.' Nancy leads her to the bed.

'I was bleeding. I'm scared.'

'Don't worry darling, you've done this before.'

'I thought for a second it had died.'

'I'm with you.'

'It was calling me ... sorry, that's deranged.'

'We're doing this together.'

'I didn't choose this ...' She's sobbing, gasping for breath. 'But I don't want it to die.'

'It's part of you.'

'I'm being silly. It's not coming yet, it was just a scare. But I do need to get home.'

Nancy holds the blouse for Grace to slide her arms into, lifts it onto her shoulders, leaves a kiss on the back of her neck. 'I'd put your knickers back on in case you bleed again. Come on, into bed. We'll go to the hospital at the crack of dawn, baby might be born by the seaside!' She covers Grace with a blanket, undresses down to her coral-pink satin slip and slides in next to her. 'If this bed doesn't crash to the floor it will be a miracle.'

Their laughter shakes the bed frame.

*

She can't sleep. Nancy is snuggled around her, breathing heavily. Baby is quiet. She's grateful. And something else. A sadness. A black hole at her centre ... that this poor baby has been assigned by fate to her. Hariti is laughing, lifting her into her warm bed, telling her that baby chose her for a reason, that Grace needs to accept. Baby moves. Grace strokes the prodding limb.

Nancy groans, turns onto her back. 'What time is it?'

'It's still dark, go back to sleep.'

'You are sweet.'

'But we should talk, soon.'

'You *are* happy, aren't you?'

'Will this work?'

'Your baby will be loved. You won't feel imprisoned, I promise.'

'I don't trust him, Nancy. I know he means well, and I really *want* to believe what he says—'

'Leyland loves you, Gracie. This is just the worry of the birth.'

'Be honest, he loves you … I don't mind.'

'There's a physical thing with him and me. You know what men are like. It'll pass. All of us being together is the obvious solution.'

*

… a burst of shattering glass … silver stars floating in a black sky, and running … running for her life … a pinpoint of flame. 'Wait till I bloody get you…'

She's awake. An explosion, deep, reverberating, a terrible nightmare. The Blitz.

Nancy turns over. 'What the hell …'

Grace is confused. 'You heard it? It wasn't in my head?'

'Must have been a landmine on the beach: maybe they're clearing them.'

'In the middle of the night?'

Voices in the street. Singing? No, crying. Someone drunk?

Now it's unmistakable. Screaming.

Boots on the pavement.

'Oh my god.'

Now on the stairs.

'What's happening, Nancy?'

The door crashes open. Screaming: '*Get up!*'

Nancy scrambles off the bed. 'What the hell? Who are—'

Astonished, Grace watches as a man in a suit – in slow motion – thuds his fist into Nancy's chest. She falls backwards, arms splaying out, hits the bed frame and crumples to the floor. A second man yanks the bedclothes off Grace and hauls her up.

She screams. 'My baby—'

'Get the bitch out of here.'

She's marched so fast that her bare feet hardly touch the floor. Downstairs. People watching. Why don't they do something? The air is heavy with the sour smell of the Blitz. A van's engine running. She's pushed into the back; it moves away fast. She falls. Someone in the dark helps her sit up.

A stranger's voice, foreign accent. *Insha'allah.*

'What? I'm not—'

She's shivers violently.

'It is God's will.'

*

The stranger is silent.

She holds the bump for dear life. How long … minutes … hours?

Tyres screech.

The back doors open. A torch blinds her.

'OUT! Come on, fucking hurry up.'

Hands behind help her step down. She falls to her knees in the snow. 'Don't hurt my baby, please don't.'

The stranger puts his jacket over Grace's shoulders before he's grabbed by his arms and hauled away. She's pulled to her feet. She holds the jacket for dear life. Her arms are gripped tight. She's marched towards a shadowy building.

A door squeaks on old hinges. A standard lamp near a huge curving staircase. She's pushed towards a door in a panelled wall. She stumbles down stone steps.

A cellar, even colder than outside.

Her teeth are chattering like a machine-gun. Her mind is scrambled; she has no idea what she's done wrong, this can't happen in England, there's been a big mistake, someone must come soon to rescue her. She slides her arms into the jacket sleeves, walks in circles to keep warm, around, around, around, mumbling, 'It's okay baby, it's okay ...', stroking the bump, trying to sing in a cracked, shaking voice. *She ... walked ...* She can't remember the words, they are in her head somewhere ... *through the fair ...* A small rectangle of sky high up in the wall, gradually lightening.

Brick arches.

Black holes.

Dusty wine bottles.

Maddening birdsong.

How can such a parallel world exist, teasing, taunting?

*

Footsteps. The lock mechanism ratcheting. Sobs convulse her even before the door is opened. Two men. The thought that she's about to be shot rises in her brain like a razor blade. Warm pee leaks through her knickers, down her legs.

Up stone steps. Corridors. A large room. In the shadows, huge paintings of ugly men. She's led to a chair. Pushed down. The men leave; the slamming door makes her jump.

In the middle of the room a large red rug. A desk. An aura of light from a desk lamp. A man. Thinning hair. White shirt sleeves rolled up. He raises his head.

Grace's fuzzy, frightened mind can't work it out. She's tense with fear but flooded with relief. Someone from the other world. Normality.

Smith closes a file. 'Well my dear. What a mess.'

Aching belly cramps scream a warning into her crazed head.

He stands, walks around the desk.

Her whole being is clenched.

'You seem to have an unerring instinct for trouble. We're curious about the company you're keeping.'

Her breathing is high in her chest. She must control it, not look frightened.

He takes a packet of cigarettes off the desk and lights one, walks towards her, puts it between her lips. She daren't move her hands from the baby. The smoke makes her cough, the cigarette falls to the polished floor. He bends, picks it up and puts it between his lips.

'You are an intelligent woman, Grace. And we have known each other for a long time. I am sure we can clear this up. Tell me what you know, then I can get you home.'

The word 'home' ... tears choke her.

He gently strokes her wet cheeks.

She searches for logic. 'Why are you … what's …?'

He walks around her. 'Now you're going to tell me about the hotel.'

A wave of pain grips her; she tries to slow her breathing. 'We … we went in, the man was horrible …'

'What were you doing there?'

'*Gone with the Wind* … there were men in suits. We'd been for a walk, couldn't get home.' Sobs rise in her throat. 'The horrid man wouldn't give us a room so we went to another. I had a bath, there was blood.'

His voice behind her. 'Blood?'

'It stopped but the baby isn't moving now. Help me, Mr Smith, you know me, you know my mother. Please. There's been a mix up, a terrible mistake.'

He whispers. The smell of smoke on his breath. 'Tell me about the bomb.'

'I heard something … mines on the beach.'

'No, Grace. It was the hotel.'

'A bomb? Oh god. When will it ever end?'

'If the desk clerk hadn't gone out for a cigarette he'd be dead too. He told us about a very insolent red-haired woman and her heavily pregnant friend. He had your names written down. It didn't take long to find you.'

'We didn't … we'd just been to a film. We couldn't get a bus back. Please.'

'Where is your Mr Cornell now?'

'I don't know, he said he had to meet someone.'

'So you *can* confirm he was going out? Where to?'

'I don't know, maybe Mary and Charles … they're our neighbours.'

'Yes, we know the Fletchers.'

What does he mean by 'we'? It doesn't fit. He's just some clerk in shipping. Her mind is refusing to clear, but her life depends on it, she must work this out.

Smith walks to his desk, sits back in the creaking chair, stubs the cigarette in an ashtray. 'We have history, Grace. I know you don't believe me, but I care deeply for you. You've always been someone I've wanted in my life. I thought you felt something too, but then you abandoned our baby …'

'Mr Smith … Oliver—'

'In spite of your rejection I shall still do my best to get you through this, but you have to cooperate, do you understand?'

'It's all a big mistake … what has this to do with me? Where's Nancy? She's done nothing.'

'I need you to tell me everything you know about Mr Cornell and Miss Lockhart. Who comes to the house, who are their friends?'

'But … no one … we don't have friends.' Suddenly, she remembers. 'There *was* a man.'

Smith looks up.

'I met him ages ago, in a café, used to pick grapes in Bordeaux, with Leyland.'

'Don't play with me, Grace—'

'He was in the foyer of the cinema …'

'Yesterday? Here in Hastings?'

She's desperate … she just needs it to end … to save her baby. 'I've met him before, old friend of Leyland's, at least, I think it was him.'

'Describe—'

'Wearing a cap. I remember his name. Joe.'

'Anything else?'

'I spoke to him. It was queer, he said I was mistaken. No, wait, he has a slight limp.'

Smith takes notes. 'Has Cornell ever talked to you about Israel?'

'Israel? No, he's obsessed with Ireland.'

'It must have come up in conversation.'

'Leyland is Irish. And Nancy's American.'

'You needn't worry about her.'

'You can't … what? … she's—'

'You won't see her again.'

'You *can't.*'

'She'll be deported.'

A sob bursts from Grace's chest.

'You really are a Jezebel, aren't you.'

He opens another folder, picks up a photograph. Hazy smoke floats in the lamplight. Think, Grace. *Think.* Maybe Smith is Jewish, it has never occurred to her. She remembers there was talk about Palestine once: when was that? Supper with the Fletchers? That was ages ago. And who said what? Another griping ache is building up.

'We are fighting a global enemy, Grace.'

'Leyland is an artist. A photographer.'

'Yes, very useful skills for a spy.'

'A *spy!* No, no you have it all wrong. He's nothing to do with Israel. It's Ireland—'

'Terrorists collaborate, Grace. You must be aware of that. They see their struggles as part of a global movement. Revolution. Do you understand now?'

Another wave of pain; she gasps for air.

'Please, Oliver … this baby … can we talk about this later?'

His laugh has a vicious edge. 'I said I would always protect your family, didn't I? How can I make you understand how all this has to be?'

'I've done nothing wrong. Leyland … I don't believe—'

'Either you're more stupid than I thought, or you're very clever, Grace. I haven't decided which.'

She's panting now, holding the sides of her chair. 'Nancy's … just a friend … we're not what you think.'

He turns pages in the file. 'I will always be grateful for what you gave me.'

She has to get out, find a safe place. 'My baby … please.'

He leans back. 'So you care about *this* one?'

'You can do anything to me.' She's panting hard, dizzy.

'Your family has been under suspicion for years. Now here you are. I am giving you a chance. It depends on what you say in the next two minutes.'

The pain slowly ebbs, a few moments of relief. She looks around, as if waking from a nightmare and finding she's still in it. 'I don't …' And then a logical argument comes to her, she grabs it like a lifeline. 'Nancy can't be involved, we'd never have tried to stay at the hotel, the one with the bomb, would we?'

'You are so naive.' He picks up the photograph, carries it across to her. It is both familiar and strange. Leyland and Nancy. Arm in arm, smiling at the camera.

'Do you *really* have no idea what's going on in the world? Listen to me. I am trying to save you.'

'That's just some holiday photo.'

'Look at the background.' He holds the top corners of the photograph as if it's drying on a line. Then she sees it. It's the promenade and in the background the Grand Hotel.

'I need times and dates. That trip in the boat, for example.'

She remembers: Sancho excited about a man on the jetty, cigarette butts squashed on the ground. 'You had me watched?'

'Where did he say he was going afterwards?'

'Nowhere … I don't know. He just disappeared.'

'I'm trying to save you, Grace. You rejected me, and I accept that.' He taps his fingers on the manila folder. 'Water under the bridge: so here we are. I'm doing this for Kitty now, not you Grace. I couldn't care less what becomes of you.'

What is it? Something she can't quite get hold of.

'Believe me, the Israelis wouldn't be so considerate.'

Underneath, he's let something slip out.

'It's only because you are Orlando's mother …'

And suddenly, through her brain fog, there it is. At last.

He's talking without looking up. 'You've alerted suspicion from the very beginning: unnatural mothering instincts, unhealthy relationship with an alien, yes, we have been watching for years … you choosing to marry a terrorist.'

'It's Kitty, isn't it!'

He stops, his black, ratty eyes piercing. 'That took you long enough.'

She's up on her feet. Crossing to the door. Banging with her fists.

'There's no way out, I'm afraid, Grace. Now come and sit down and let's see if we can sort out this mess.'

She rests her forehead on the wood panelling. 'All that pretence of being Robert's friend when all along—'

'But it's true. Robert and I go way back—'

'I bet you had him sent to India, so you and Kitty … oh my god. You've been manipulating *everyone*.'

'Back to business, Grace.'

'You're just a …' Another contraction building. '… A cuckoo … a viper.'

'If Mr Cornell cooperates, gives us names, maybe there's a chance for him. But he will have to prove his use, and you are the key to his seeing sense.'

She speaks to the door. Her voice quiet, controlled. 'Just get it over with. Kill me now. I know you're going to.'

He laughs. '*So* melodramatic. Who do you think we are, Grace? We're not uncivilised. I am offering you a chance to give your baby a life. I am doing this because Kitty seems to believe you might be her daughter. No other reason, you understand? I said I would protect you didn't I, now be a sensible girl.'

Hatred – like a living monster – rises inside her, tearing to get out, to mutilate him; the shining scissors in her hand … tear … stab …

She turns slowly, manages to make it back to the chair. 'I'm not cooperating with you.'

'You're in no position to refuse.'

In her head she hears Hariti whispering: death is an illusion … you'll return … Smith can't hurt you.

Grace doesn't recognise her own voice, it has a will of its own and it stops him in his tracks. 'I see you, Mr Smith. You can't kill Kitty's "pretend" daughter, but even more, you can't kill your son's mother.'

He screws the top back on his fountain pen. 'You stupid bitch.' He taps his fingers. 'You can't go back to your life before, you'll return to Kitty, she'll keep an eye on you. You might get to know our son, he's a lovely little boy.'

'You're a fucking Nazi.'

He shouts. 'Get her out of here.'
The door opens, hands grab her arms from behind.
'I'll be coming for you, Grace.'

THE VAN TURNS OFF THE ROAD into a narrow lane.

Ghostly snow-covered trees loom in the headlights.

'Where … where are we?'

The driver stares ahead. 'Shut your fucking mouth.'

A rutted track. Shock waves slicing her body. The lights sweep across a camouflaged caravan. The driver leaves the engine running, gets out, opens the door on Grace's side and pulls her out. She stumbles barefoot through virgin snow. He pulls the caravan door open. 'If you try to escape …', he puts two fingers to his temple, '… we'll blow your fucking brains out.' He pushes. She falls into black. The door slams. Light sweeps across the windows.

Aching pain. She crawls, reaches out, a platform, pulls herself up onto a bed. She's going mad. Poor Robert. All these years believing Smith to be his friend. And Kitty the faithful wife.

*

… floating … high … a soughing wind … patchwork fields below, washed-out green, mustard yellow … a dark, straight slash across the land, a railway line and tiny figures crowding around. Someone has fallen.

The door opens. A blizzard of freezing light.

Smith pulls the blanket off her. 'Shit! What a bloody mess.'

He paces the length of the caravan, stares out of the end window, walks back to the bed. 'I could solve my problems right now. Out there. You understand?'

Grace stares, no longer afraid, he can't hurt her any more.

He turns quickly, opens a cupboard, pulls out a pair of old brown corduroy trousers and tosses them onto the bed. 'Two minutes. Hurry or you and your baby will die here.'

Painfully, Grace pushes her legs into the trousers, holds them up and looks back at the bed: a large wet patch on the sheets. She still has the jacket, given to her a lifetime ago by a kind stranger. She pulls it tighter. On shaking legs she steps out, walks slowly across the snow to a black car. Smith is tapping his fingers on the steering wheel. She crawls onto the cold leather back seat, kneels, leaning forward to relieve the pressure.

He drives too fast, bouncing over ruts and potholes. Grace is queasy but at least it's confusing the contractions.

Sancho is whining in her head. Her arm is squeezed, impelling her onto numb feet. The tarpaulin in the corner of the shed: is his motorbike under it? Smith's boot lands hard and flat, the frame splinters, the door flies open. He pulls Grace inside. Sancho runs up and down, excitedly spreading paw-shaped patches of pee all over the floor. Grace reaches for the banisters, falls onto the bottom stair. For a moment she fears he's about to shoot Sancho, but he takes a tin of dog food from the draining board. The awful stench of dog meat invades the room. He puts the plate on the floor, ruffles the dog's neck.

At the door he hesitates. 'I'll be back.'

The door scrapes, slams shut.

The car engine fades.

Sancho gobbles desperately at the food, his pink tongue pushing the plate into a corner.

A wave of pain flows over her. She lies on the stairs waiting for it to pass. The trousers fall off as she crawls upwards.

A pause. She pants, gets her breath. Nancy. What did they do to you? Where is Leyland? They couldn't have captured him, or there wouldn't have been all these questions.

Just a few more steps. She's on the landing. Pain spasms in her back. She's in the bathroom … squeaky taps, thank god the water is hot. Steam fills the room and condenses on the mirror. She turns the taps off, lets the jacket fall from her shoulders.

The water takes her weight. Her feet bleed as feeling returns in searing waves.

A deep, knotting ache, a ball of convulsion. She's certain now. She is about to die. She will sink below. Bright bubbles will burst out of her. It's familiar. She'll be safe. Free of pain.

Sancho's barking.

Heavy steps on the stairs. Smith is coming to kill her. She's ready. The baby will travel with her. Find their next ...

Boots dropping onto the bathroom floor. His voice close to her ear, soft, warm, balmy.

She's gasping for breath. Floating. The water is draining out. In a moment of clarity she realises he's in the bath behind her, his arms around her. Supporting her. She leans back into him, panting, crying, shouting. His fingers stroke her face, hold her shoulders; his words have no meaning, just the sound, holding her, making her believe.

She can't take anymore, but it gets worse. She's dead. She's nothing. Distant screaming. It's coming from her.

And now ... a different cry.

Sweet merciful relief, oh god, oh god, thank you god. Leyland slides from behind her, lays her back against the soothing enamel. Another spasm. She's too tired to go on.

'Grace, he's alive.' Leyland places the slippery body onto her chest. She puts her hand over him ... so warm.

'I'll have to cut him free. You have a bit more work to do, are you ready?'

His whittling knife flashes, slices through a shoelace, ties the purple cord. A swift cut. He wipes the blade on his wet trouser leg.

Her baby. Separated but part of her. Snuffling like a small animal. So, so vulnerable. She can do this.

A final purging contraction.

He leads her on shaking legs to the bed.
     'They're looking for you.'
     'I know. I'll call Mary and Charles.'
     'Go, Leyland. While you can.'

Chelsea
June 1950

THE BABY SCREAMS AS Kitty lays him in the pram. Little Orlando looks worried, picks up the dummy and pokes it into the baby's mouth, then bounces the pram a little too hard. Kitty puts on her summer coat. 'Grace, why don't you come for a stroll, you're looking peaky.'

'I need to work on the Chopin.'

Grace has returned to the piano with a vengeance, practising with demented energy. She had not wanted to come back to Kitty's but she'd had no choice. The months alone in the cottage after the birth are a blur. She has no idea how she'd survived, or the baby for that matter. He'd cried constantly. And in the dark nights, staring up at the black beams, she'd cried too.

The Fletchers brought feeding bottles, teats, nappies and safety pins, and George brought powdered milk and food in spite of there never being any post. He'd heard that Leyland had gone abroad and everyone in Rye seemed to know that Miss Lockhart's father had summoned her back to America.

Grace holds the front door open for Kitty to bump the pram down the steps.

'Grace, there's a postcard for you. Rather mysterious, I must say. I've left it on the hall stand.'

She's alone in the hall. The grandfather clock has returned to its silent state.

She reads the postcard. *Grace Fisher, care of Mrs Fisher.*

She turns it over. A black-and-white photograph, hand-tinted, of a steam train puffing under a bridge in a rural setting. The artist has washed a watery green over the embankment's flora, and pale blue over a clear sky.

Carefully written under the photograph are a date and time.

She understands.

THE PRAM SPRINGS NEED OILING. *Weeech, weeech, weeech.* The baby seems to like the infernal noise, or perhaps it's the rocking motion. Grace is anxious whenever she takes him out, afraid he'll cause a commotion and everyone will see what a hopeless mother she is; but today he's snuggled under a thin blanket, eyes tight shut, fists held to the side of his head.

People in the street seem in high spirits. Already two women have stopped her to peep under the hood at the sweaty face, and now she's getting smiles from people sitting on the station benches.

The train rattles in and a man in a tweed suit helps her lift the pram into the goods carriage. She lifts the baby out, carries him awkwardly over her shoulder to find a seat. How strange. The familiar patterned fabric on the upholstery from all those years ago, the leather strap for lifting the window, the same netting luggage rack, a soldier had lifted her suitcase onto it as she took the window seat, her cello between her legs.

The lane is familiar, but seems neater, the verges cut back. The church-yard wall still bulges but the graves behind it seem less likely to spill their buried bodies into the road. She leans on the pram handle to lift the front wheels around a tight corner. Overhead, a canopy of startling birdsong, competing, overlapping, weaving together.

And there she is.

Grace kicks the brake lever and runs. 'Hariti!'

HARITI HAS COME PREPARED. She's spread a tartan blanket in the shade of an oak tree. The wicker picnic basket creaks as she opens the lid. There's so much to say, too many words tumbling out.

Grace unscrews the top of an orange pop bottle, fizzy bubbles spill into their Bakelite cups. She picks up an acorn shell. '*Quercus*—'

'I know, I remember, my little clever Gracie. But look at you now!'

'No one would talk about you. It was as if you'd never existed.'

'I don't know what you were told.'

'That you'd run away with the food coupons.'

Hariti splutters and laughs. 'The truth would have shamed them. I guess they needed to come up with some story.'

'But tell me ... you and Robert ...'

Hariti offers Grace a triangle of bread. Her silence confirms the story.

'I can't believe it: Robert always seemed so loyal. I thought he and Kitty—'

'I don't know how to explain.'

Grace bites into the sandwich. 'We've always had the truth between us.'

'It was Smith—'

'I knew he'd be behind it.'

'Robert heard I was going to be arrested. I knew too much about …'

'I know about him and Kitty.'

'So Robert found a room for me in a block of flats.'

'I *knew* you were still alive.'

'But then Smith turned up one afternoon, sat at my kitchen table drinking tea, and when Robert came in he said I'd be arrested as a spy if Robert didn't take on some terrible mission in the East. I think it might have been Singapore. Robert agreed. To save me. He did it for love, Grace.'

'Smith has manipulated us all.' Grace can't find the words to tell her about Orlando. The shame is too great. Maybe later.

Hariti stares into her cup. 'I had to stay in that room – in that building – for the whole of the war.'

'How on earth did you manage?'

'I had an Ascot and a sink so I took in washing from all the flats. People knew there was something odd but they paid me in food and silence.'

The baby whimpers, slowly winding up like a siren. Hariti lowers the hood, picks him up, blanket and all, and holds him over her shoulder.

A tidal wave washes up from Grace's dark centre. Her body convulses, tears spilling from her.

Hariti places the baby on the blanket and kneels beside Grace, stroking up and down her back.

The tears subside. 'He's Leyland's. Did you know?'

'Yes, Grace. He found me after Robert left. I've no idea how: he must have well-informed friends. He helped me. He never abandoned you.'

'So that's how you knew which address to write to.'

'I wanted to let you know, put your mind at rest, but I had to use code that only you'd understand.'

'Smith is still a danger.'

'I knew fate would bring us together again, one day.'

'In this life or the next!'

'He told me about an envelope. Take it, Grace.'

'But what if I'm not Grace, *your* Grace?'

'Whatever the order of life and death, you'll always be my Grace.'

August 1950

KITTY HAS ENGAGED A CLEANER, a thin old woman who likes to spread dust around the house, who moans louder than the vacuum clearer, who buffs away at anything that can take Brasso, Silvo or wax polish.

A refrigerator has been installed in the kitchen and – in spite of many things still being rationed – it is well stocked with eggs, milk, cheese, vegetables. Kitty also has a cook who comes three days a week and leaves the larder shelves loaded with tarts and pies covered with tea towels.

*

Grace is still wearing black from the memorial that morning, the skirt and jacket borrowed from Kitty's wardrobe. The vicar had intoned some nonsense about reconciliation with Germany. Grace had played a tribute to Mrs Blumen: one of Bach's Cello Suites.

She stands in front of the pristine fire grate. So many times she'd knelt in front of it as if it had been an altar, rolling pages of newspaper into tight fire-starters, building a lattice of kindling to support the precious lumps of coal.

The side table is still a shrine to Robert. The pipe, the pouch of tobacco – which must surely be desiccated by now – and the box of Havana cigars.

She takes her seat in front of the piano's closed lid.

The whining vacuum cleaner drones in the hall, slowly approaching like the Luftwaffe, winding its way into the sitting room, humming from floorboards to oriental rug, back to floorboards and out into the hall.

Kitty is flustered; she waves the newspaper as she crosses to the armchair. 'Splendid playing, Grace. I was so proud.'

'Give me the key, Kitty.'

'What on earth—'

'You know.'

Orlando is standing in the doorway, his dark eyes staring. Kitty hesitates, clearly trying to compose a suitable reply. 'Why don't you go and make us all a nice cup of Camp coffee, dear. And we can listen to the afternoon concert together.'

'Kitty …'

'Not this again. We've always—'

'If you don't …', Grace gets up and crosses to the bureau, wrenches the roll top handle, '… I'll force it.'

Kitty stands up. 'How dare you? In *my* house.'

Grace's heart is pulsing in her neck, her face flushed. She marches into the hall, searches the cold silk pockets of Kitty's best coat hanging on the hall stand. The crocodile handbag is resting on a blanket in the pram. Grace grabs it, slides her fingers into the stiff leather compartments.

Kitty's hands are resting on Orlando's shoulders.

'Kitty. Give me the key or—'

'Or what, Grace? You ungrateful little girl. I've given you everything. Sacrificed—'

Grace bounds up the stairs. The wardrobe first. An old army great-coat, the gas mask box still stuffed with money and lipstick. Robert's coat and jacket. Then the dressing table angled across a corner: clothes in the drawers, jewellery in boxes on top. Downstairs, she pushes past Kitty. In the kitchen she pulls out the three drawers of the dresser. In the sitting room she checks the bookshelves and even opens the cigar box.

Her stomach is tight, her breath high in her chest. She scans the placid calm of the unchanging sitting room. All the furniture is positioned as it ever was. Even a bomb blasting the window into the fragments couldn't disturb this tight membrane of decorum. Passion and pain all swept out of sight.

Kitty hesitates in the doorway. 'I tried to protect you.'

Prickling heat of anger. Grace turns to the mantelpiece. The mirror reflects a moment of frozen time. An impasse. An old woman unable to free herself from her drowned child. A little boy created in trauma. And Grace, suspended between them.

The poker is hanging from a hook by the grate. She lifts it, feels the weight. As she advances to the bureau Kitty gasps, hand over her mouth. Grace inserts the flat end of the poker near the lock. A sharp snap. The lock breaks as the roll top surrenders. Grace yanks it up. A series of small open compartments, regimented pale blue envelopes in one, a bundle of letters in another. And in the middle, the drawer. She tugs at the handle. Locked, as she'd expected. The poker is too big to insert. She looks around. Lying on the fireplace tiles is the old hatchet. She picks it up, stands in front of the bureau.

Kitty takes a step forward. 'Grace! Please.'

Grace raises it above her head. She closes her eyes.

… sour gas … peppery brick dust … putrid river bank … damp pungent forest floor …

A scream. '*Grace!*

She slams the hatchet down.

An explosion of splintering wood.

Roaring flames. Sinking down.

Mo-ther.

Another cracking blow.

Another.

Letters scatter.

Spilt ink flows like black blood.

The drawer is free. And there it is, as she knew it would be.

Robert's handwriting on an envelope: *Grace?*

NINE

Sydenham
2000

ORLANDO TURNS OVER THE yellowing newspaper cutting. Grace remembers, he'll only find advertisements: Lipton's tea, Player's cigarettes and a hair tonic.

'What the fuck, Mother.' He turns it back over, continues to read aloud:

> *When the inn was closed at half-past eleven, as was usual, those remaining consisted of a Mr. Fielding, Mrs. Fielding, Miss E. Fielding, approximately six years of age, and Mr. J. Jones, the resident barman.*
>
> *'According to the statement of Mr. Jones who had ascended to his attic lodgings, all appeared safe, the front door being locked. He was roused about an hour later by dense smoke. To descend was impossible, the flames already making their way up the staircase. In spite of injury to his left hand sustained serving his country, Mr. Jones, he claims, escaped through the skylight. This was about fifteen minutes past three, and the alarm having once been raised in the locality, the excitement became intense.'*

Bach cello, da, da, da-da … da, da, da-da. Where *is* her cello? Locked away in a hard shell, holding its breath, waiting to be reborn, to be held with love, its perfect voice coaxed into being.

> *'At 3.37 a.m. the call was received at the Fire Brigade Depot situated within one mile, and both an escape and a manual engine were at once on the way to the fire. In the meantime, a scene of the most powerful description was witnessed by the spectators. At the windows on the second*

> floor, two unfortunate adults were seen crying piteously for help. "Wait for
> the escape," was shouted by those below.'

Elgar: cello swooping, swallows at dusk.

> 'The only thing to be done was to extinguish the flames and get the place
> sufficiently cool to effect a safe entry. When that was accomplished a sickening
> spectacle awaited the firemen. Two lifeless and charred bodies were found.
> Mr. Fielding had apparently endeavoured to protect his wife by lying over
> her. The body of the young Miss Fielding has not yet been discovered.
> During the whole of yesterday the scene of the calamity was visited by a
> throng of spectators.
>
> 'As to the cause of the fire, it is believed that a spark from the
> midsummer bonfire was most likely.'

The Irish nurse comes in on a ray of sunlight, says Grace needs to sleep.

Her eyes are closed.
   Somewhere in the room, Hariti is singing.
   She's coming closer.
   Whispering.
   'I'm waiting for you.'

EPILOGUE

Five Acre Wood
April 1955

Beneath an overcast sky, white clusters of cow parsley lean out from the scrawny hedges of Arbuthnot Lane.

'Come on, Hariti, keep up, you used to walk much faster than me.'

A few paces behind, Hariti pauses to pick tiny blue flowers. 'I'm older than you, remember!'

Grace reaches into the hedge, snaps off a clump of hawthorn buds to add to the posy.

Hariti offers her flowers.

'Hariti, they're lovely. Forget-me-nots.'

'How far do you think we are from the railway crossing? You must have walked miles … and you were so little.'

'I suppose I must have known this lane.'

'No wonder you were in such a mess. Your feet were ripped to shreds.'

'I don't know what I've ever done to deserve you.'

The tree canopy is in new leaf: acid green of weeping willows, hornbeams and horse chestnuts. Above the blanket of cloud, a skylark's forlorn song.

'Grace, have you heard any more of Leyland? Or Nancy, for that matter?'

'Come on, we can't be far from the road.'

'I don't mean to pry.'

'England is too dangerous for Leyland: Smith will never give up. And Nancy is still in America. I haven't heard anything. It was just a phase for her.'

'Are you sure you're up to this, Grace?'

The crossroads.

Grace slowly turns a full circle. 'There's the inn sign, but where is the inn?'

'Over here, Grace.' Hariti kicks the ground. 'These must be the foundations.'

'Can this be all that's left?' Patches of moss define where a building once stood. A simple rectangle. 'It feels weirdly familiar, but then it might just be wishful thinking.'

A cool movement of air dusting her cheeks and rustling the leaves. The sign squeaks and Grace shivers. She crosses to the stump of a tree.

Hariti follows. 'Was this here when you were little? Do you remember?'

'There was a story … something about people being hanged; I don't know if I've imagined it. Maybe it was somewhere else.'

Hariti runs her fingers out from the tree's rotten centre. 'No way of counting the rings, it must have been cut down a long time ago.'

Grace takes the posy of wildflowers and crosses over to the old inn sign. The paintwork has peeled and the letters have faded, but the ghostly image of a bell – in blue – is still discernible. She lays the flowers at the foot of the post. A momentary catch in her throat.

'I think that's the way, Hariti. Over that iron fence.'

The entire woodland is covered with a mass of dark green leaves, and spiking out of them fluffy white flowers on tall stems.

Their steps crush the leaves, releasing a pungent earthy, perfume. Grace puts her arm through Hariti's. 'This can't be it, I'd have remembered the wild garlic.'

'But it was summer … the equinox, remember? All this would probably have died back by then.'

Grace tries to imprint her dark nightmares onto this cool, calm wood. The newspaper's report of a fire *could* fit the puzzle, but she isn't sure.

They reach a fence. Ahead, a field sloping down. A carpet of green shoots.

She follows Hariti over the fence, walks down the slope into the middle of the field.

'Was I drowned or did I escape a fire?'

'Both. Neither. Does it matter?'

'I need to know who I am.'

Colours shift.

Green shoots have turnd to gold.

The grey sky to intense blue.

And floating high above … a dark shape, a thing with feathers.

C for Crow.

She's in the bird's eye, looking down … on a girl in a grubby white nightdress. Running for her life.

Hariti takes her hand. 'You are here, now.'

End

Sources

There is, of course, a wealth of material available – in book form and online – for anyone researching the periods before and during the Second World War.

I feel I've only skimmed the surface but I hope it's been enough to evoke the times my characters lived through. I did find three institutions particularly informative: the Imperial War Museums (iwm.org.uk), The National Archives (nationalarchives.gov.uk), and London Transport Museum (ltmuseum.co.uk).

*

BBC History (bbc.co.uk/history/ww2peopleswar) inspired the scene in which a bomb bursts through a window. From *Rye's Own Magazine* (ryesown.co.uk), I gleaned details of the Bofors guns near Tillingham Bridge. I also embellished the stories of a returning soldier, and four German spies caught by the Home Guard.

*

In Oxford's Ashmolean Museum (ashmolean.org), I came across a statuette of the goddess Hariti, protector of children. This gave me the perfect name for one of my principal characters. Apologies for taking liberties over the date the statuette was acquired (commons.wikimedia.org/wiki/File:The_goddess_Hariti_-_Ashmolean_EA1971-36.jpeg).

Acknowledgements

My first thanks must go to the writer and artist Carol Burns, who in the 1970s first instilled in me the belief that I could be a writer.

Among the many friends who, over the years, have been press-ganged into reading drafts of this novel are: Marianne Ryan, Tahmina Sorabji, Kate Sachs, Jo Hamilton and Suzy Howlett. They all offered insightful comments and pertinent challenges.

I'm indebted to Alex Lay who gave wide-ranging feedback and much fine nit-picking.

Since settling in Frome, I've discovered a wonderful community of writers. In particular, my thanks go to Frances Liardet for encouraging me to join The Write Place, Frome Writers Collective, and the Summer Bootcamp.

I could not have had a more astute editor than Barbara Mellor who has been wonderfully supportive and suggested many improvements.

My most profound thanks have to go to my creative writing mentor, Kylie Fitzpatrick. With endurance (she's had to read *many* drafts), wisdom, great skill and typical Aussie directness, she has taught me many vital lessons and sustained my belief in the whole endeavour of storytelling.

Finally, I thank my children, for waiting so long to see what all the fuss has been about.

Michael Tasker Phillips

After running a graphic design consultancy and raising a family in London, Michael moved to Frome in Somerset. *Grace* is his first novel.

He can be contacted through Archetype Books:
info@archetypebooks.net

michaeltaskerphillips.uk

Author photo: Martha Leung